THE
CORN BANDITS

WE SAW WHAT YOU DID, AND YOU'LL BE SORRY

JOHN D. RUTHERFORD

This book is a work of fiction. Any references to historical events, real people, or real places are used fictitiously. Other names, characters, places, and events are products of the author's imagination, and any resemblance to actual events or places or persons, living or dead, is entirely coincidental.

For my wife, Mary Lou, without whose love, support, and encouragement this book would have never been possible. I also want to thank her for creating the artwork that graces the cover.

I'd also like to acknowledge Yvonne J. Medley, a dear friend, coach, and founder of Life Journeys Writers Guild.

Wherever a man commits a crime, God finds a witness.
Every secret crime has its reporter.
~Ralph Waldo Emerson

CONTENTS

CHAPTER 1

Saturday, February 18, 1984

At exactly 11:00 p.m. 2,300 volts of electricity slammed into Tommy Cleaves like a runaway freight train.

Along with nine other witnesses, in the basement of the Richmond, Virginia, State Penitentiary, Mitch Armstrong watched Tommy's body contort against the wide leather straps that restrained him. Mitch felt himself shudder with each of the four electrical shocks that exploded in Tommy's body. Tommy's calf muscles and forearms spasmed into rock-hard balls. His fists clenched so tightly that his fingernails punctured the fleshy part of his palms. Through the slits cut into Tommy's leather death mask, Mitch could see that the eyes, which a few seconds ago had been looking at him, were now tightly closed causing Tommy's cheeks and eyebrows to blend together into one undefinable mass. The acrid smell of burning flesh seeped into everyone's nostrils.

Tommy twisted. He jerked. He groaned. He died.

For almost everyone in the witness room this meant that the long ordeal was finally over. Mitch was the lone exception. He had no sense of closure, no feeling of relief. A sickness now gnawed at his stomach, a sickness born of the knowledge that a horrific and inescapable truth had, only seconds ago, unfolded in front of him. He, alone, knew they had just witnessed the execution of an innocent man.

Friday, August 21, 1959

This was going to be their biggest heist ever. A cloud of tan-colored dust billowed behind the two-tone green 1955 Chevy Bel Air as it sped down the dirt road between the towering fields of corn. A tiny rivulet of sweat ran down the middle of Mitch Armstrong's back. The sensation felt refreshingly cool amid the noonday heat and humidity. Not a word was spoken. Frankie Biondo was sitting next to Mitch in the back seat of the car. Frankie wiped off his glasses and peered out through his window. Mitch, likewise, scanned the cornfields on the opposite side of the road. The two twelve-year-old boys were summertime friends and usually never saw each other very much during the other nine months of the year. But they were great pals and felt as close as brothers.

"How about here?" Frankie finally asked.

"Not yet," shot back the driver. "I'll tell you when."

Gladys Biondo, the boys called her Nana, hardly looked the part of a getaway driver. She was Frankie's grandmother, in her late seventies, and feisty. She clutched the worn steering wheel in the ten and two o'clock position, and could barely see over it. Her gray hair was pulled back into a tight bun and sunglasses covered her eyes. Whenever Nana concentrated hard, like now, her lips parted slightly and revealed a yellowish and broken front tooth. A lot of people didn't think she was very friendly, but Mitch liked her, and Nana, in turn, liked him.

Nana's head swiveled back and forth as she looked for just the right spot. Mitch knew it was almost time. Suddenly, she hit the brakes and the Chevy skidded to a stop.

"Now, boys!" she commanded.

Frankie pushed the back of the front passenger seat forward, grabbed the handle next to the front seat, and opened the door. The two boys, with brown paper shopping bags in hand, burst out of the car, and dashed into the cornfield. Mitch counted rows as he ducked and weaved between the stalks of corn. According to Nana you had to go at least ten rows deep into a field because farmers always planted horse corn on the edges to discourage would-be thieves.

"That's ten!" Mitch yelled.

The two boys stopped and began to work the current row. They moved in opposite directions. Each of the two thieves could spy an ear of corn, examine it, twist it off, and drop it into a bag in just a matter of seconds. In no time at all Mitch's first bag was full. He set it on the ground and kept moving forward as he worked on filling the next one. They had never done a double-bagger before. Another couple of minutes, another dozen ears, and—*BEEEEEEEEP—BEEEEEEEEP*—Nana was blowing the horn. That was the signal. No matter what, they had to head back when they heard the horn. Mitch turned and ran to where he had dropped his first bag. He saw Frankie coming back down the row from the other direction.

Side by side, each carrying two full shopping bags, the two boys thrashed their way through the rows of corn to the dirt road. They said nothing. Only hard breathing, pounding footsteps, and the swishing resistance of cornstalks and leaves could be heard. Stopping just inside the first row, they peeked out to make sure that the coast was clear. Satisfied that everything was okay, Mitch said, "Let's go."

Like mice, running from a cat, the two young thieves scurried to the car. Nana had already unlocked the trunk. After tossing their bags in and slamming it shut, the two boys scrambled into the back seat. Nana pulled the transmission lever into first gear, popped the clutch, and the heist was history. Spraying a plume of gravel, the Chevy fish-tailed down the road. To the boys' delight, Nana spun the wheels going into second gear, and once more when she hit third.

The boys whooped and hollered.

"The Corn Bandits strike again!" they shouted in unison.

Nana joined the celebration and added her color to the story by telling how nervous she was when a car turned onto the road while the boys were in the cornfield. "He stopped and asked if I was okay. I told him I was just resting and enjoying the moment."

"I think he was trying to pick you up, Nana. Wanna go back?" Frankie teased.

"He couldn't handle me," she laughed with a little mischief in her voice.

The boys just whooped again.

Frankie held out his open palm toward Mitch and rubbed his thumb back and forth across the other fingers. It was the signal for money. They had stolen a lot of corn that summer and what they didn't eat Nana would preserve as corn relish, canned corn, or something similar. She would then sell it at the Bohman's Point weekly farmer's market. She'd always give the boys a little cut of the profits.

Mitch whispered, "Corn Bandits, Frankie. We're just like brothers."

The sun had already passed overhead by the time the trio stopped at a roadside vegetable stand to buy a watermelon and some tomatoes. When the man working at the stand asked if they needed any corn, Mitch and

Frankie got the giggles and nearly peed their pants. Back on the road again, they started planning their evening. It was a quick drive back to Bohman's Point where Nana lived and Mitch's parents owned a small summer cottage. Mitch was going to stay for dinner. They'd do hamburgers and hot dogs on the grill, and of course have plenty of corn on the cob.

Bohman's Point was a sleepy little community on the banks of the Old Mill River, a small, often overlooked, tributary on the western shore of the Chesapeake Bay in Middlesex County, Virginia.

Mitch didn't know why Bohman's was called a point. He thought that on the map it looked more like a big head, on the end of a skinny neck, glued to a larger body of land. Some of the locals say it once was an island, others argue that it never was. But erosion, some predicted, was going to surely separate it from the mainland and cause it to become an island someday. Whatever the case, the topic was often good conversational fodder during a late night card game.

Mitch and his mother vacationed there each summer. Mitch's dad would show up for the weekends. Every summer Frankie's parents sent him to stay with Nana, who lived there all year.

Only a handful of folks were permanent year-round residents. But from June to September, Bohman's Point came alive with an influx of what the permanent residents called—the summer people. Most of the summer people came from Virginia and Maryland, with a few from as far away as Pennsylvania. They owned or rented little clapboard cottages, and spent a lot of time at the beginning of each summer sprucing up the community. They cleaned the commons, painted fences, and hauled in truckloads of clean sand for the swimming beach.

They also planned 4th of July activities, and conducted many other social events. Summer evenings often smelled of backyard barbecue grills cooking a tasty variety of meats.

The little enclave was served by one general store, had no street lights, and, with a few exceptions, the summer people enjoyed no telephones and no TV. Most of the roads in Bohman's Point were asphalt, but some were still dirt and gravel. A truck came through and occasionally sprayed them with an oil and tar mixture. It helped the roads, but didn't do much for feet, shoes, or floors.

The community had a small firehouse with a single pumper. Most times when the fire siren sounded it was a signal for nosey residents to jump into their cars and follow the truck to see what happened. That was Bohman's Point adventure entertainment at its finest.

Nearly everyone, however, had a small wooden boat of some sort. And for three summer months every year, Bohman's Point was as good as it gets, at least for two twelve-year-old boys.

The boys were famished and thought that dinner smelled good and tasted better. They agreed there's something special about charcoal-grilled burgers and dogs on a warm summer evening.

"I love hot, buttered corn on the cob," said Mitch as he started chomping on another ear.

"Yeah, hot in more ways than one," giggled Frankie.

Nana, Frankie, and Mitch all enjoyed ice-cold watermelon for dessert. The boys also knew it was a great weapon. Frankie grabbed a handful of watermelon pulp and hid it behind his back. When Mitch wasn't looking—splat—Frankie hit him with a hunk of watermelon right between the shoulder blades. The two boys yelped, laughed, and chased each other around the yard, throwing chunks of watermelon and spitting seeds at each other.

"You boys need to quiet down and go clean up," Nana finally ordered.

The boys knew it was her code for them to go for a swim.

Nana's house was at the end of a narrow lane and on top of a small rise overlooking the river. The boys called it a cliff. From the front of her house a narrow trail wound down and around the cliff to a small sandy opening surrounded by cattails and other tall aquatic plants. Mitch and Frankie named it Little Beach. It was used by very few people because of the difficulty getting to it. However, if the tide wasn't too high, adventurous folks could walk west from Little Beach along the river's edge about a quarter mile to the main swimming beach of Bohman's Point, or go east a little farther than that to a tiny half-moon cove that was hidden from general view. The cove was sometimes the site of small bonfire parties or an occasional young lovers' tryst.

Frankie and Mitch raced down the trail to Little Beach and straight into the water—jumping, diving, and splashing. Once thoroughly clean of watermelon residue and sufficiently bored with their latest diversion, rock skipping, Mitch said that he probably needed to go home and check in with his mother.

"Ask if you can spend the night. We'll sneak out after Nana's asleep," Frankie said.

Mitch's eyes lit up.

"Think Nana'll let me stay?"

"No problem. I'll clear it with her then come over to your house to get ya."

"See ya!" Mitch yelled as he ran out of the water and sprinted along the shore toward home.

That night at 11:30 p.m., the two boys were side by side in daybeds on the screened-in front porch. That was where they usually slept when Mitch spent the night. In hushed whispers they made plans to sneak out.

Frankie got up to pee. When he came back, he said, "Let's go. She's asleep."

They carefully opened the squeaky front screen door and slipped out. They scrambled down the trail to Little Beach. The boys stopped next to an old wooden rowboat that rested, upside down, on four cinder blocks next to the tall reeds at the top of the beach. It had been there for two years and nobody seemed to know who owned it.

Earlier that summer, when Mitch's uncle was visiting, Mitch stole a pack of Chesterfield cigarettes from his uncle's fishing tackle box. He hid them, along with some matches, inside the old boat. This treasure was one of the boys' most closely guarded secrets. After a ritualistic lighting of two cigarettes, they sat on the beach, puffed smoke, and listened to the water's rising tide lapping at the shore. A full moon reflected off the river and highlighted the little boats anchored close by.

"Let's go down to the cove," Mitch said.

He was up and walking before Frankie could reply. The moonlit night made it easy to navigate their way around the several driftwood logs and big rocks that had lain on the shore for as long as either boy could remember.

Once they reached the entrance to the cove, Mitch stopped and grabbed Frankie's arm.

"Somebody's there."

Across the still water of the cove the boys saw a small campfire on the shore.

"Looks like they're over close to Beck's pier," Frankie answered.

CHAPTER 2

"Let's take the back way to the big tree and see if we can sneak up close enough to Beck's pier to hear 'em." Mitch's eyes were gleaming.

Cyrus Beck's house burnt down five years prior and was never rebuilt, but the little fishing pier at the bottom of the earthen bank, a dirt cliff in front of Beck's house, was still there. An occasional early morning fisherman would use it, but that was about all the traffic it ever saw. Whoever was there right now came down the steps that were cut into the bank above the pier, and then walked a short distance along the shoreline where they gathered some driftwood and built a little fire.

"Are you crazy?" Frankie answered. "What if they catch us?"

Mitch prodded Frankie. "C'mon, don't be a chicken. We can outrun anybody."

And with that, the two boys were off into the marsh that ringed the cove, and eventually into the little stand of hardwoods that separated the marshy area from the beach alongside Beck's pier.

Years of erosion had exposed a huge tangle of roots at the base of several giant tulip poplar trees at the water's edge of the hardwoods. Local children, who knew of it, called it the big tree. The roots created a maze of tunnels that Frankie and Mitch crawled through to get to the beach near Beck's pier. Peeking out through the roots of the tree they could see the glow of the firelight just beyond a big driftwood log that hid the amorous couple sitting on the beach from their view.

Frankie was the first to crawl over to the log and try to spy on the beach people. Mitch watched as Frankie maneuvered himself to the end of the log and then carefully stuck his head around the end of it to see what he could see. He seemed to lie there for an eternity. Finally, he slowly wiggled backward away from the log and back to the big tree.

"Who is it? What did you see?" Mitch whispered.

"You're not going to believe this. It's a girl and a guy. I don't know who the guy is, but the girl is Betty, and she's almost naked!"

"Naked! What are they doing?"

"Stuff we've never done before."

Betty was Frankie and Mitch's fantasy heartthrob. She, as close as they could guess, was seventeen or eighteen years old. Betty wasn't even her real name. They didn't know what her name was. All they knew was that she was a renter. That is, her parents had rented a cottage at Bohman's Point and brought Betty and her girlfriend there for a vacation. The boys gave her the nickname, Betty, because of her blond hair and how she reminded them of Betty from the *Archie* comic books. Likewise, they called her girlfriend, with the jet-black hair, Veronica, the same as Betty's friend in the *Archie* series. If nothing else, they knew these two girls had given them reason to look forward to growing up. And as much as the two boys fantasized about Betty and Veronica, they also fantasized about being one of the many teenage boys, with the really cool cars, who seemed to appear out of nowhere once the word spread that two really great-looking girls were staying in a cottage at Bohman's Point.

Mitch took his turn crawling through the sand to the big log. Peering around the edge of it, he could see a guy and a girl sitting on a beach towel about fifty feet away from him. The small fire they built was between them and him. They were side by side and, turned, facing each other. The guy's back was toward Mitch, and the girl was facing Mitch's direction. There was no doubt. He knew it was Betty. She was wearing a man's long sleeve shirt with the sleeves rolled up. The shirt was totally unbuttoned and partially exposing her bare breasts. The two lovers were nuzzling each other, kissing lightly, and the guy was beginning to touch Betty's breasts. They were talking softly. Mitch could hear the voices but couldn't discern the words. Mitch's eyes bulged out of their sockets, his heart pounded, and his mouth grew moist. *Oh man, someday I'll be that Lover Boy.* He was transfixed and losing all concept of time or his surroundings.

As Mitch watched, Betty put her hand behind Lover Boy's head, pulled him closer, and whispered something in his ear. Lover Boy pulled back a little and started talking. His voice rose and was accompanied by hand gestures. Suddenly, Betty jumped up, closed her shirt, and started shouting, "No! No way!"

"You're not being fair. We've got to talk," Lover Boy shot back.

"What is wrong with you? I said no way."

Lover Boy stood up, stomped around, kicked some sand, took a couple of steps in Mitch's direction, and picked up a big chunk of driftwood. Mitch felt for sure he had been discovered. Just as he was about to leap to his feet and run, Lover Boy turned and looked at Betty again.

"You don't understand!" he yelled at her. "I'm halfway through college! There are things I want to do! This will ruin everything!" He kept walking around, kicking the sand, and doing more growling and grunting than talking. In the midst of his frustration, he spun around and threw the piece of driftwood in the direction of the log that Mitch was crouched behind. Betty and Lover Boy didn't pay any attention to the dull thud of the wood striking Mitch's head.

It happened so fast that Mitch lost all sense of what was going on around him. His head throbbed, he felt nauseous, and he was terrified. At first he thought he was discovered and was hit on purpose; then he heard voices still yelling at each other. He felt groggy and his vision was a little blurred, but he could see the couple, both of them now standing. He fought the impulse to get up and run, and was doing his best to force himself to remain perfectly still despite the aching in his head. What he saw next made his stomach turn.

The guy grabbed Betty by the shirt, spun her around, and then slammed her to the ground so hard it must have knocked the wind out of her. She began gasping. All the while Lover Boy was shouting, "No, don't you understand, I said, no!"

The guy then picked Betty up, slung her over his shoulder and walked off. She was crying and Lover Boy was still barking at her. Finally, Mitch's world went dark and he heard nothing.

Was I knocked out? He asked himself. *How long has it been? Frankie, where's Frankie?*

"Mitch, you okay?" Frankie was kneeling beside him.

"I guess so. What happened?"

"Man, he beaned you hard with that piece of wood. I thought you were dead. You didn't move or nothing."

Mitch wiped his hands on his bathing suit and tried to clean out his eyes, which were watering profusely. Finally able to see a little through the tears, he could tell that the fire was out and the couple was gone.

"Where are they?" Mitch asked.

"Don't know. I froze and didn't move. I saw him throw her down. Then he picked her up, kicked some sand on the fire, and walked off. I heard them start arguing again, real loud. Then I heard them splashing around in the water. I don't know what happened next, but they finally stopped yelling. A little while later I heard a car leave from the road up by Beck's old house."

Frankie helped Mitch to his feet. Mitch was dizzy and felt like he was going to throw up.

"Are you sure they're gone? I got sand all in my hair and all over my face. I'm gonna wash off and then let's get outta here."

Mitch waded into the cool, dark river up to his waist, dipped his head into the water, and then splashed water all over his face and chest. He was actually starting to feel a little bit better.

Frankie paced on the beach. "C'mon already," he yelled.

Mitch started back toward the shoreline and was only ten feet from dry sand when he tripped over something. He tried to regain his balance, but stepped on it again. It was slick and didn't feel like anything that should be there. He hopped on one foot, tripped again, and this time he fell. He landed face down on top of the submerged object. He straightened his arms and as he opened his eyes to see what was underneath him, Mitch found himself looking into a human face, barely under the water and illuminated by the moonlight. It was Betty.

"Oh shit!" Mitch yelled as he ran onto the beach. "It's Betty!"

Frankie went and looked then came back onto the beach. The two boys paced back and forth, cursed, cried out, and generally didn't know what to do.

"She's dead. I know she's dead," Mitch repeated over and over.

Finally, Frankie said, "We gotta go. We can't stay here."

"Who are we going to tell?" Mitch asked.

"Nobody."

"What? We gotta tell somebody."

"Think about it. If we do, we're in big trouble. We'll be part of it. We didn't do nothing. Somebody'll find her tomorrow."

Mitch's head was once more throbbing, and his stomach started to feel bad again. He gave in to Frankie's wishes. They snuck back into Nana's house. Frankie gave Mitch a dry bathing suit. The two boys laid in their daybeds on the front porch—sleepless and wordless. It was the longest night of Mitch's life. Shortly after sunrise, he got up, said nothing, walked out, and went home.

About two hours later the siren, mounted on a pole next to the firehouse, started to wail. Mitch's mother said, "Something must be happening. It's been dry. Probably a barn fire."

Another hour passed and then Frankie knocked on the front door. Mitch went out and the two boys walked down toward the main beach.

"They found her," Frankie said. "Some man went fishing this morning on Beck's pier and saw her."

"We gotta tell somebody what we saw." Mitch was growing frantic.

"We can't tell anybody anything. We didn't see nothing. We don't know nothing. We'll only get in trouble." Frankie was adamant.

Mitch couldn't believe his ears. He looked at Frankie, curled his lip, then turned, and walked away. For the rest of the summer he simply counted the days until school started again. That's when his family would leave Bohman's Point until next season.

Unfortunately, the following summer came faster than Mitch wanted. It was, once again, June, school was out, Mitch and his family had just arrived for the summer, and Bohman's Point was abuzz with the news. Betty's real name turned out to be Kathleen Spencer. An investigation and autopsy had concluded that Kathleen's death was probably a murder. Detective Ken Farmer, on loan from the Richmond Police Department, led the investigation. Ultimately, Tommy Cleaves, a local twenty-one-year-old, one of the permanent residents, was arrested, stood trial, and was convicted.

Tommy was a white-trash, troublemaker who had never finished high school. He and his four sisters were reared in a house hardly big enough for a family half that size. Tommy had a pointy nose and chin, big Adam's apple, and a high-pitched, very squeaky voice. Mitch and Frankie had nicknamed him Rooster Boy. They said he looked and sounded like a rooster crowing whenever he got excited and talked loud, which was most of the time. They knew whenever Tommy was part of a group of people. He could be heard long before he was seen. And almost everything that came out of his mouth was nothing but pure filth. A person only had to spend a few minutes with Tommy Cleaves to know two things—most things he said were untrue; and, more importantly, he just wasn't worth a damn.

Mitch also heard that during the winter, Nana had gotten real sick. She had a stroke and died. He didn't know what a stroke was, but figured it was bad. When he saw the adults talk about it, they'd often shake their heads and sigh.

Mitch walked down to Nana's house to see if, by any chance, Frankie was there. A big Chrysler New Yorker was parked in the gravel driveway at Nana's. It was Frankie's parents. Mitch's spirits started to lift and then crashed down again as the car, with Frankie in the back seat, started to pull slowly out of the driveway. When Frankie's dad saw

Mitch, he stopped and let Frankie out. The two boys walked to the back of the car and Frankie pointed to a *For Sale* sign sticking in the ground next to the driveway.

"We're not coming back," he said.

"What about Betty?" Mitch asked. "What are we gonna do?" Nervousness, bordering on panic, squeezed Mitch's gut.

"Nothing, we're not going to do nothing," Frankie shot back.

"What do you mean—nothing?" Mitch couldn't believe the words he was hearing. "You know, as well as I do, the guy with her that night on the beach wasn't Rooster Boy. I don't know who it was, but it wasn't Cleaves."

"You don't know shit," Frankie said. "Cleaves was arrested. He was convicted. He's in jail. That's it."

"Yeah, but he didn't do it and they said he got the death penalty."

"So what? He's just a piece of shit anyhow. Besides that, my dad says he'll die of old age before the electric chair gets him."

Frankie turned around and climbed back into the car. Mitch stood there and watched the car slowly pull away. Disbelief and disillusionment soaked into his body.

"Corn Bandits, Frankie, we're just like brothers. Yeah, sure," Mitch muttered.

After a few moments he turned away, meandered through Nana's yard, and walked down the path to Little Beach and then on to the cove—not because that's where he necessarily wanted to go, but that's where his legs and his subconscious took him. He finally arrived at the beach where he and Frankie had spied on the couple.

Mitch wandered aimlessly, kicked the sand with his bare feet, and looked at the water's edge where he discovered Kathleen Spencer. He spied the driftwood log he and Frankie had hidden behind, picked up a rock and hurled it at the log, screaming, "You did that to me you son-of-a-bitch! Then you killed her." Mitch turned and looked, again, out at the water. The words hissed out through his clenched teeth, "I don't care what Frankie says. Whoever you are, you'll be sorry. I swear. You'll be sorry."

CHAPTER 3

Saturday, February 18, 1984

The Richmond State Penitentiary was located on Spring Street adjacent to the James River. Richmond residents called it The Pen; the inmates called it The Walls; the American Civil Liberties Union called it the most shameful prison in America; and, for twenty-four years, Tommy Cleaves called it home. A home that in the winter was freezing cold, in the summer was stifling hot; and at all times it was damp, unhealthy, and noisy to an ear-damaging degree. Tommy's death row cell was located just a short walking distance from the execution chamber.

Tommy had been on death row since 1960. He almost got strapped into the chair in 1971, but his appeals attorney, at that time, got a stay of execution because of the rumblings everyone was hearing, about a possible Supreme Court action on the death penalty. Then, in 1972, as a result of Furman v. Georgia, the Supreme Court did place a moratorium on capital punishment. Tommy thought he was home-free, maybe even walk the streets again someday. However, in 1976, another case, Gregg v. Georgia, resulted in the release of the moratorium.

Tommy's next appeals attorney, Richard Krause, renewed Tommy's hope for a couple years.

"Your Honor," Krause once argued, "it should be obvious, to even the most casual observer, that Mr. Cleaves has suffered psychological damage because of the changing Supreme Court rulings. First, he was condemned to die; then his life was spared; now he is back to being a condemned man again. That is clearly emotional injury, and constitutes cruel and unusual punishment."

The judge promised to consider Krause's argument, and was willing to hear anything additional he wanted to present.

However, any hope Tommy gleaned from that appeal came to an abrupt end when Krause was shot and killed by the disgruntled spouse of one of his other clients.

Tommy was appointed yet another appeals attorney, Justin Spitzer. Tommy quickly realized that young Mr. Spitzer was no more interested in working death row appeals than he was in flying to the moon. Efforts on Tommy's behalf began to fall apart and, finally, the date was set.

On the day of Tommy's execution, Mitch Armstrong arrived at the prison shortly after 6:00 p.m. Mitch was the only person Tommy wanted to see. For almost five hours he sat with Tommy waiting for the governor to order a stay of execution.

As the appointed hour got closer, Tommy kept asking, "Hey Mitch, are you sure the governor's gonna call?"

Mitch's confident responses were always, "Yes, he will."

Governor Conrad A. Parker was halfway through his term as Virginia's chief executive. During his hard fought gubernatorial campaign, Parker often pointed to the previous administration's promises made and promises broken. Consequently, Mitch Armstrong always felt confident that Governor Parker would follow through on one of his campaign pledges, the repeal of capital punishment in the state of Virginia. For some reason, however, the initiative appeared to be stalled.

Over the past six months Mitch Armstrong visited the governor's office at least three times, seeking information on the death penalty repeal. Despite being treated like a pawn in the bureaucratic game of *shuffle and hand-off*, Mitch was finally convinced, by one of the governor's aides, the real problem was with the stubbornness of the state legislature, not the governor. However, the aide went on to assure Mitch that he was confidant Governor Parker would stay Tommy's execution. "The governor," he told Mitch, with a raised eyebrow and a syrupy smile, "still needs to place an exclamation point on that campaign promise."

But as the clock ticked onward, Mitch began to fear this was going the way of many political promises. His fears were confirmed. The phone never rang.

Finally, at 10:40 p.m., with the rattle of keys and the ominous squeal of a rusty hinge, the door to Tommy's cell opened, and a sober-faced guard reported, "Sorry, Tommy, it's time."

"Mitch?" Tommy's squeaky voice and tear-filled eyes pleaded with his only confidant, Mitch.

"What? This is bullshit!" Mitch was on his feet and moving between the guard and Tommy. He raised his hands in front of himself with fingers spread in a *stop, don't come any closer*, manner.

"Back off, Mitch," warned one of the other guards, "don't make this any harder."

Mitch's countenance would often give pause to anyone he confronted. His face bore the permanent scars of a violent encounter from years prior. That, coupled with his large, muscular frame was often reason enough for others to back down from him. There wasn't a single corrections officer in the prison, not even a team of two, capable of taking Mitch down. But Mitch was an ex-cop. He knew the rules of the game. More importantly, and sometimes sadly, he knew when the game was over. He shook his head, then backed off.

Tommy was taken toward the rear entrance of the execution chamber and Mitch was escorted to the witness room. It was actually called the witness box and was co-located inside the execution chamber. Ten gray, metal folding chairs were set up in a small area within the chamber. It was partitioned off by a single waist-high wall, on top of which were large glass windows. The witness box felt close and sweaty, and barely allowed enough space for the witnesses to remain a respectable distance from the condemned. Mitch sat down on the one remaining empty seat. Slightly to his left and no more than fifteen feet in front of him was the chair that Tommy would soon occupy. It was made of oak, with a well-worn look, and brownish patina. Leather straps, for securing the condemned prisoner, were attached to it, and it was mounted on top of a four inch thick concrete slab. Mitch thought it looked like a throwback to some less civilized time when citizens were put in stocks to be laughed at and tormented; or witches were tied into place then dunked and drowned in a pool of water as punishment for their sorcery. Shortly after Mitch sat down, a guard stepped into the room and closed the large heavy curtain that separated the witnesses from the prisoner.

Behind the curtain, Tommy was led to the chair where he was seated and securely strapped. A brine-soaked sponge was set on top of Tommy's freshly shaved head. The leather skull cap, lined with a thin metal plate, was then buckled into place. Tiny streams of water from the sponge, now tightly pressed against his skull, ran down the sides of Tommy's face. A member of the execution team attached wires to the skull cap and to the metal clamp that had been placed around Tommy's right calf. Once everything was attached and all adjustments made, another guard opened the viewing curtain. Warden James Bollen made one final call to the governor's office to confirm it was okay to proceed, and then asked Tommy if he had any final words.

Tommy was scared. His breathing came in short, jerky spurts that were punctuated with little whimpering sounds. His nostrils flared with each pulsating exhale. His eyes darted around the room like a trapped animal looking for an escape. He briefly made eye contact with Mitch and then with one of the women in the witness room. Tommy finally mumbled something that sounded vaguely like, "I'm real sorry that girl died, but I didn't do it."

Warden Bollen stepped back and allowed the prison chaplain to approach Tommy to offer some words of comfort. When the chaplain finished, a guard placed the death mask over Tommy's face and fastened the straps behind his head. Warden Bollen read the death warrant. He then nodded to the executioner, who was standing ready with his hand above the switch. The executioner gave Tommy four jolts of electricity, each lasting twenty seconds, and spaced twenty seconds apart.

After waiting a few minutes for Tommy's skin to cool, Dr. Walter Landis, the staff physician, stubbed out his cigarette and walked over to Tommy's motionless body. He opened the top two buttons of Tommy's shirt, positioned his stethoscope in several places on Tommy's chest, looked at the clock on the wall and announced, "Time of death, 11:07 p.m."

A guard stepped in front of Tommy's body, blocking it from the witnesses, and closed the viewing curtain. Silence hung over the witness box like a thick, gray fog, uncomfortable, yet strangely protective. Thirty seconds, that seemed like an eternity, went by before anyone moved. Then, one by one, everyone, except Mitch, slowly rose to their feet and began the short journey to the exit. There were no sounds other than the soft shuffling of leather soles across the tile floor.

Mitch Armstrong sat motionless. With both elbows resting on his knees and his hands clasped together with interlaced fingers, he stared at the floor. Through his periphery he could see feet and legs slowly filing out of the witness room, and he tried to imagine what possible reasons could have induced these other people to be here.

Three of the men and one woman were considered official witnesses of record, a legal requirement of the state. Mitch couldn't begin to fathom why anyone would want to participate in such a gruesome task.

The three men looked like unwilling volunteers to Mitch. He guessed they were all in their thirties and sensed that they knew each other. Their dour expressions and drooped heads made it obvious to Mitch they were not the least bit comfortable with what they were doing. He assumed they were city or state employees who had been drafted to serve as witnesses.

The woman, however, appeared much older. She wore a plain, floral print housedress, a pair of well-worn black oxford shoes, and had haphazardly folded her dark, wool overcoat in her lap. Her hair, a gun-metal gray, was neither untidy nor stylish. She, obviously, just didn't pay much attention to it. Mitch thought of the words frumpy and rumpled when he first saw her. She had a casualness that indicated she had possibly done this before. She even brought her knitting bag with her, just in case things got delayed.

Two other witnesses were Bill and Margaret Spencer. They were searching for retribution and, hopefully, to experience some sort of closure to the nightmare that began twenty-five years ago when their only child, their beautiful daughter, Kathleen, was brutally murdered. Margaret was a petite woman, and very attractive with short, gray, well-coiffed hair. She had a gentle countenance. Under any other circumstances, she would probably be described as charming. Bill Spencer, on the other hand, looked much older than his sixty-six years. He appeared tired and haggard. Kathleen's death created an emotional storm within him and Bill hadn't weathered it very well. Friends say he had never been able to let her go.

It's been over two decades since Tommy Cleaves was on trial for Kathleen's murder, but those who were in the courtroom in 1960 will never forget Bill Spencer's statement from the witness stand. Bill was the prosecution's final witness in what had been a meticulously presented case. The timeline and the trail of evidence laid out by the state, mostly provided by the lead detective, Ken Farmer, led straight to Tommy Cleaves. Talk among those who were following the trial was no longer about whether or not Tommy Cleaves would be convicted, but whether or not he would get the death penalty. Bill's testimony was very emotional, causing Judge Claude Anderson to interrupt on several occasions to allow Bill to compose himself.

After answering what the prosecutor said was the final question for Bill, regarding his daughter's activities on the day of the murder, Bill

Spencer added, "I do not want the state to convict Mr. Cleaves or cause him to spend so much as one more day in jail."

Judge Anderson and the rest of the courtroom were aghast. Murmurs rippled up and down the seated rows of spectators as many of them asked each other if Bill actually said what they thought he said.

Judge Anderson tapped his gavel three times and announced, "Order." Then, with a soothing touch added to his rich baritone voice, he said, "Mr. Spencer, please confine your answers only to the questions asked. I truly understand how very difficult this must be for you and Mrs. Spencer. I admire the fact that you are trying to be compassionate and forgiving."

"No, I'm not, Your Honor," Bill interrupted, his voice starting to crack. "It's just that if Tommy Cleaves spends the rest of his life behind bars, I'll never have the opportunity to put a gun to his head and blow his son-of-a-bitchin' brains out."

Observers would later recall how the courtroom erupted. Attorneys from both sides leaped to their feet shouting various objections. Members of the Cleaves family, along with their friends, were standing and screaming for a mistrial. Most everyone else in the courtroom catapulted to their feet to see what was going on or, in some cases, add their own exclamations to the hysteria. Bill Spencer became so emotionally distraught that he needed help back to his seat; and Judge Anderson pounded his gavel with such force that the handle broke and the head of it went skittering across the judge's bench and onto the floor. The court needed a two hour recess to totally restore its sense of decorum to the proceedings. Bill Spencer was not cross-examined. And he never appeared in the courtroom again.

Today, nothing could have stopped him from witnessing Tommy's execution.

Tommy's sister, Peggy Brittman, and her husband, Steve, were also witnesses. They created a little bit of noise as they began to navigate their ample bodies down the narrow row between the metal folding chairs, sliding some of them out of their way. The Brittmans claimed they were at the execution to offer a show of sympathy and remorse for the Spencer family. However, given Peggy's lacquered-in-place beehive hair and overly-done makeup, Mitch thought the more likely reason was to exploit one more opportunity to get their names in the paper, and their images on the nightly news.

Since none of Tommy's other sisters or relatives had ever visited him, the Brittmans, because of their one and only visitation with Tommy, became mini-celebrities during the final weeks leading up to Tommy's execution. They even appeared on the local TV show, *Good Morning Richmond*, offering their dissertation, spoon-fed to them by a producer, on the heartache that the death penalty imposes on the families of the condemned. Their little secret, however, painted a different picture. The only reason they ever visited Tommy was because Tommy's parents had both recently died, leaving a small insurance policy, as well as their little house to be equally divided between Tommy and his four sisters. Taking advantage of Tommy's state of affairs, Peggy showed up at the penitentiary with a legal document that gave Tommy's share to her. Tommy signed it.

Finally, among the witnesses, there was Detective Ken Farmer, whom Mitch regarded as a pompous ass. Mitch always thought that

Farmer looked like he had just stepped out of a Dashiell Hammett novel. He still wore the same style brown suit and shoes, and sported the same haircut and pencil-thin mustache that he was wearing over thirty years ago. These days, however, the hair and mustache were touched up a little bit through the use of some drugstore color.

Ken Farmer chose to witness the execution so he could mark this occasion as the capstone event of his thirty-five year career, which included the investigation, arrest, and conviction of Tommy Cleaves.

Farmer became the first to break the silence. Mitch always wondered if Farmer slept all the way through the night. Mitch didn't think the man was capable of going eight straight hours without hearing himself speak. Farmer started talking to one of the state witnesses as soon as they got outside of the box and just before the group began its ascent up the metal stairs.

"I just retired," Farmer said. "Thirty-five years on the force. Met with the governor yesterday morning."

Farmer then pushed pass the two men in front of him and scaled the first few steps. He stopped and turned around to address the group. The other witnesses looked at each other with confused expressions on their faces.

"Who in the hell is this guy?" another one of the state witnesses whispered to Steve Brittman.

Steve just shrugged his shoulders.

Farmer leaned up against the stair rail and blocked the path up the stairs for the rest of the group. He continued to spout off as if everyone really wanted to hear him speak. "The governor gave me a real nice plaque honoring my years of public service. Gonna send me a picture too. Not too many people get to have a picture of the governor shaking their hand on retirement day. Of course, not too many people get to bring a cold-blooded killer to justice either. Governor Parker told me how grateful he was that I had done that. That's why I'm here tonight. I told the governor I felt I owed it to the community to come be a witness. Looks like my next job is going to be working with his security detail for a while. The governor asked me to. He thinks I could give them some pointers."

Go ahead, Kenny boy, throw your skinny shoulders back and puff out your chest. You make me sick. Mitch could taste the contempt he had for Ken Farmer.

Twenty-five years ago, as a twelve-year-old boy, Mitch was too frightened to tell Farmer what he knew. Seventeen years ago, as a freshly minted sheriff's deputy, he had been cautioned to leave well enough alone.

"Tommy Cleaves is Ken Farmer's case," Mitch's immediate supervisor advised him one day when Mitch brought it up again. "Mess with Farmer and you'll lose your job."

Ken Farmer was untouchable, and that's what everyone through the ranks said, but nobody knew exactly why.

Ever since the Cleaves case, Farmer acted aloof. He often drew assignments that appeared shrouded in mystery. Farmer never offered explanations, and the rest of the detectives and beat officers never asked for any. It wasn't just mystery, they kept feeling *there's something wrong here.* Most people were content to let it go and just leave Farmer alone rather than risk the downside of something that wasn't their business.

Mitch, however, had no qualms about approaching Farmer. He tried several times, during his years on the police force, to broach the issue of Tommy's guilt with Farmer, but Farmer always shut him down.

One day, after hearing that Mitch had, again, queried one of the senior detectives about the Cleaves case, Farmer approached Mitch's desk. Mitch was up to his elbows in paperwork and didn't see Farmer coming.

"Armstrong, you've got a lot to learn," Farmer bellowed as he spread his legs, leaned over, and planted both outstretched arms onto Mitch's desk. Papers scattered onto the floor.

"A lot to learn about what?" Mitch fired back.

"About being a homicide detective," Farmer sneered.

"Maybe I do," Mitch said through gritted teeth. "But you, on the other hand, don't have much at all to learn about being an asshole." It was Mitch's final response—final, because it cost him his job.

Others would have kept silent for the sake of their careers and the responsibilities of a family. Mitch just couldn't do that. Kowtowing to bureaucratic stuffed shirts like Farmer wasn't in his genetic makeup.

After leaving the police force, Mitch eventually started working as a self-employed security consultant. In other words, he became a private investigator.

Mitch remained in his chair as he listened to Farmer finish his speech out in the stairwell. Mitch placed his hands on his forehead and leaned back as far as he could. His eyes were open, but he wasn't looking at the dirty ceiling, he was looking well beyond that. Guilt? Remorse? He wasn't sure what he was feeling. Mitch drifted back to that warm summer day many years ago. He sat there asking himself the same question he's asked so many times before. *God help me. The guy I saw on the beach that night wasn't Tommy. Why couldn't I do a better job of convincing somebody?*

CHAPTER 4

"Excuse me, Mitch, I'm supposed to be shutting down, but I can give you a few more minutes." A death row guard, Willie Baker, was straightening chairs and snapping off light switches in the witness room.

"No Thanks, Willie, I'm leaving now." Mitch stood and began his own slow retreat from the darkened room.

"Gonna miss seein' ya, Mitch," Willie said as he stooped down to pick up a piece of knitting thread, dropped by the frumpy woman. "You visited him a lot over the years. You know, except for his one sister and his worthless lawyers, you're about the only visitor he ever had."

"Yeah, he told me that." Mitch's eyes followed Willie's movements around the room.

"You're a good man, Mitch."

"I wish I was, Willie. I wish I had been good enough to stop it. I've got strong reason to believe that Tommy was an innocent man."

"Don't beat yourself up, Mitch. Just ask any of the inmates. Everyone in here is an innocent man."

"I know what you're saying. But in this case, it's more than just bullshit words. Tommy didn't do it. I know he didn't do it. And now it's too late."

"Like I said, Mitch, don't beat yourself up. You tried a lot on his behalf. Everybody knows that. This is just the way it was meant to be. Sometimes there are things we can't control."

"Thanks for the kind words, Willie," Mitch sighed. "It's gonna take me a couple days to get beyond this. But it'll be okay."

Mitch walked to the door that exited to the basement cell block and metal stairway that went up to the main floor.

As he was about to step through the doorway Willie shouted to him, "Hey, Mitch."

Armstrong stopped, turned, and looked at Willie.

"There's something I need to tell you. It always kind of bothered me in a way." Willie grabbed the back of his neck with his right hand, shook his head slowly from side to side, then looked upward as if reflecting on something. "There was somebody else. Tommy had one other visitor, just once. It was a long time ago, I'd say at least four or five years. Can't remember the guy's name, but Tommy was real agitated after that guy left. He started screamin' for his lawyer. We finally got the suit in here and they had a big blow up. Tommy eventually calmed down, but I never did find out what it was all about."

"I've got no idea either," said Mitch. "If you ever get a chance, see if you can find the old visitor's log and let me know. I'd be curious."

"Sure thing, Mitch, don't know if we still have it, but I'll check and see."

Guards were waiting upstairs on the main level to escort the witnesses across the street to the visitors' parking lot. Mitch found himself walking next to the frumpy lady. Her name was Muriel, he found out, and she turned out to be a little more talkative than Mitch had imagined she would be. Even without Mitch asking her, she confirmed that she's been a witness to other executions. Time didn't permit a discussion with her about why she did it, but she did offer up some food for thought.

"A man's eyes are the window to his soul," Muriel said. "I looked into the eyes of each and every one of the men I've seen sitting in that chair. They might've been sorry for what they did, but they knew they deserved what they were gonna get. I saw it real clear in their eyes. Even my Edward."

"Edward?"

Muriel wiped a little tear from her cheek and continued, "This man, Tommy, was different. I didn't see that acceptance in his eyes. I almost felt as bad for him as I did for Edward. And to tell you the truth, I think Edward was right. I don't believe Mr. Cleaves did it."

"Who's Edward?" Mitch asked again. "I've been trying to convince people for years that Tommy was innocent. Who's Edward?"

She did not respond.

They were already outside and had passed through the main gate. Guards were leading the group to the big gravel parking lot where a crowd of sign-waving, candle-holding protestors had gathered. For the most part, the demonstrators were peaceful. The messages on the signs and placards tilted heavily toward the biblical admonition, *thou shalt not kill*. There were also two death penalty supporters carrying a banner that read, *eye for an eye, the debt is paid.*

As soon as they were across the street one of the guards announced, "End of the line, folks. The Department of Corrections thanks you."

Muriel extended her hand to Mitch. He accepted with a gentle shake.

"Thank you, it's been nice talking to you, Mr. Armstrong."

Mitch hesitated for a moment with a quizzical look on his face. *How did she know my name?* He couldn't recall introducing himself. *I really need some rest.*

As Muriel stepped away, she glanced back over her shoulder and once more expressed her belief. "He didn't do it," she said. Muriel was immediately intercepted by a reporter, notebook in hand, who started asking her questions.

News reporters were working the crowd, looking for anyone's opinion on the death penalty, and whether or not justice had been served. Peggy and Steve Brittman were happy to oblige, as was Ken Farmer.

"So tell us," a reporter faked a comforting tone while talking to Peggy Brittman, "this must be devastating for your family." He slowly shook his head while trying to put a sorrowful look on his face.

"Oh yes," Peggy responded. She tightly clutched her husband's arm with one hand and pretended to wipe a tear from her eye with the other. "Tommy was always in trouble as a teenager. But our whole family was horrified when we learned about the Spencer girl's murder." Peggy paused, and acted like she needed to regain her composure. Then, she continued. "We just hope that the Spencers can find it in their hearts to forgive us." Peggy ended the interview by wrapping both arms around Steve and sobbing dramatically.

Ken Farmer, on the other hand, under the floodlight of another camera crew, was extolling the virtues of good police work. "You have no idea how proud I am to have led a team that brought such a callous and remorseless murderer to justice."

Farmer was enjoying his moment in the limelight, but knew he had to place a phone call. "Sorry folks, gotta run. If you have any more questions for me, just call the governor's office and ask for Ken Farmer in Security. I'll be happy to talk to you."

Farmer exited the visitors' parking lot and drove to a gas station on Spring Street. The station was closed, but Farmer was familiar with the phone booth tucked away on the side of the building. He slid into the booth and closed the glass, bi-fold door. Under the dim light of a small, bug-encrusted fluorescent tube, Farmer dropped two dimes into the slot on top of the payphone and dialed a number he had long ago committed to memory.

The phone only rang once. A gentleman, known to his associates as the Old Man, answered the call. His voice was raspy with age, but he spoke with authority. "Give me the news," was all he said.

"It's done," replied Farmer. "They announced the time of death as 11:07."

"Good. I assume there are no issues that I need to know about."

"Not really. Cleaves made a half-hearted denial. But everybody expected that. The only thing that bothered me was Mitch Armstrong. He was there. In fact, he was with Cleaves until just prior to the execution."

"He's a problem," said the Old Man. "You're going to have to fix it. I don't have a good feeling about him. He could screw this whole thing up."

"I understand," replied Farmer. He used to ask me about this case all the time when he was on the Force. Of course I'd shut him down. But he kept pursuing a stay of execution with the governor's office. He even called them two days ago."

"That's my point." Exasperation had crept into the Old Man's tone. "He's a problem and I want you to fix it."

"I'll have my people watching him," Farmer said. "But I know this guy. Now that Cleaves is dead, I'm pretty sure that Armstrong will just fade away. There's nothing left for him to fight for."

"Don't let me down, Ken."

"Oh, you can be sure I won't. In fact, I'm gonna …" His words were interrupted by a dial tone. The Old Man had hung up.

Farmer got back into his car and continued his drive home. In his mind, the future held nothing but blue skies.

Back at the visitors' parking lot, Muriel and the three other state's witnesses of record answered a couple of questions and made a few brief, but not very newsworthy, remarks to the reporters.

Bill and Margaret Spencer, wanting to share their emotions only with each other, managed to avoid the vultures, and slipped away un-noticed.

They would soon be in their car and heading back to Pennsylvania. Bill didn't care if it took all night. He was going home.

Mitch Armstrong was, likewise, able to leave the crowd behind him. The night was a moonless gray, and the parking lot offered only minimal help from the few randomly placed and dimly lit lamp posts. Mitch snaked his way through the parking lot and eventually located his car. As he normally did, Mitch parked his car as far away from other vehicles as possible. His ride, a baby blue 1957 Chevy, was in pristine condition and he took lots of precautions to keep it that way.

As Mitch approached his car, he saw the pulsing glow of a ciga-rette long before he made out the features of a man leaning against the passenger door. The shadowy figure heard the gravel crunching under Mitch's feet. He straightened up his tall, skinny frame and flicked the cigarette away, causing it to bounce off the rear fender, bursting into a miniature shower of sparks. He then removed his glasses, placed them in his jacket pocket, and wiped one hand back through his thick, jet black hair.

Mitch was furious, but training and experience interceded. Even though he was no longer a cop, he still carried handcuffs, sometime necessary in his new line of work. Mitch barked an order, "Police! Turn around and put your hands behind your head!"

The man standing next to Mitch's car slowly raised his hands above his head, turned to face the car, and then, as directed, placed his hands behind his head. Armstrong moved in close to the stranger and with a well-conditioned deftness grabbed one wrist and then the other, snapping a cuff around each.

"You're really good at this, Mitch," the man finally said.

"Who in the hell are you? How do you know my name, and what are you doing at my car?" With his left hand, Mitch grabbed the man's right shoulder and slowly turned him around.

"It's me, Mitch. Frankie."

"Frankie? Oh this is just great. What in the hell are you doing here? I kind of hoped you were dead by now."

"I'm here 'cause I knew you'd be here. And as soon as I saw this Chevy, I knew it had to be yours. For a long time I felt like I needed to talk to you."

"Are you kidding me? Is this a guilt trip or something? What did you do, have some big awakening after all these years?"

"Mitch, I just wanted to talk to you. I wanted to say ..."

"Shut up asshole. I don't give a damn what you want to say. You had plenty of chances to say something when it mattered. I've been fighting this demon for twenty-five years, and you simply walked away from it." Mitch jerked Frankie around and unlocked the handcuffs. "Get outta here. Get outta my sight you worthless prick."

"I didn't just walk away Mitch. We were just kids, I want to …"

"Get outta here!" Mitch interrupted again. He turned his back on Frankie and spewed a glob of spit to the ground. "Son of a bitch, son of a bitch!"

Mitch leaned his arms on the car roof and pressed his forehead against them. After mustering enough composure to face Frankie, he turned around, but Frankie was gone. After scanning as much of the parking lot as he could see from where he was standing, Mitch got into his car, powered up the engine, and sat motionless for a couple minutes, absorbing the soothing sound of the deep, soft, rumble coming from the Chevy's twin exhausts. But the longer he sat there the tighter he gripped the steering wheel. *Why'd that asshole have to show up? As if this nightmare couldn't have gotten worse.*

It made no sense to Mitch that Frankie would make an appearance tonight. They hadn't seen or spoken to each other since the summer after Kathleen Spencer was killed when Mitch saw Frankie and his parents leaving Nana's house for the final time. Their last conversation lasted only a couple minutes.

Over the ensuing years, Mitch could never quite wrap his arms around a reason, if there was one, that caused Frankie to totally ignore what they had seen and heard that night on the beach. Facts were facts, Tommy didn't do it.

Twenty-five years ago, when he had learned Tommy was in jail, Mitch tried to discuss Kathleen's murder with his mother, Gloria Armstrong. But nothing came of it. As she did with most things, Gloria deferred the matter to Mitchs' dad, Buster. Gloria was a Christian woman with a good sense of right and wrong, but she lived in fear of Buster, and stood always in his shadow. Mitch's full first name, Mitchell, was Gloria's maiden name. That was the only marital concession Buster had ever made.

As a young boy Mitch had to pretend that he even liked his father. As Mitch got older he quit trying to hide his disdain.

Buster Armstrong was a former high school football star, who delighted in blaming Mitch for ruining his life. Mitch had been conceived out of wedlock and Buster frequently reminded him, "If it wasn't for you, I could've played for Notre Dame."

Whether he could have or not really didn't matter. What mattered most for Mitch was that Buster had a tendency to mete out justice with the buckle end of his belt. A lounge chair and an icy tub full of *Carling Black Label* were the only things that Buster spent any time with during the summer weekends. The more Buster drank, the more likely it was that Mitch would get a whipping, usually for some minor infraction of what Mitch thought were Buster's senseless rules of behavior.

Mitch did attempt to tell his dad about being on the beach when Kathleen was killed, but Buster wanted to hear nothing of it. He cut Mitch off and snapped at him, "Don't waste my time with your stupid, made-up stories."

Mitch tried again several weeks later. As a result of that second encounter, he found himself sprawled on the ground with a throbbing knot on the side of his forehead, compliments of a backhanded swat and Buster's cherished high school ring.

Buster warned Mitch, "Boys who tell lies get put into reform school."

Mitch never brought up the subject again.

Those memories tasted bitter. Both of Mitch's parents were now dead. Gloria died in an automobile accident while Mitch was in Vietnam. Buster was driving and, although it was never proven, Mitch always suspected that Buster was drunk at the time. Buster continued his hard drinking ways for several years after the accident and eventually died of alcohol poisoning.

Mitch remembered that he felt no remorse when he learned of his father's death. He and Buster hadn't spoken much since Mitch's sixteenth birthday. That was the day the beatings with the belt stopped—not because Buster had mellowed—but because that was the day Mitch ripped the belt out of Buster's hand and turned the attack around. Buster wound up with a bloody face and a chipped tooth.

Mitch didn't attend his father's funeral. He didn't even know where Buster was buried. He told the funeral director that Buster wasn't welcome in the family plot and that he didn't care what they did with the body.

"Just send me the bill, and as far as I'm concerned, you can put the son-of-a-bitch out with the trash," were Mitch's exact words.

Mitch sat in his idling car and stared, blankly, through the windshield. Finally, he shook his head back and forth a couple times and attempted to drain those recollections out of his conscious mind. He eventually reached down, grabbed the floor-mounted shifter, pushed it up into first gear, let out the clutch, and exited the parking lot.

From inside another darkened car, parked nearby, Frankie watched as the small red taillights of Mitch's '57 Chevy got dimmer and finally vanished. He smacked the steering wheel with both hands. "Dammit, this was a bad idea! Son-of-a-bitch, I knew this was a bad idea."

CHAPTER 5

Mitch left Spring Street in Richmond shortly after midnight. He hopped onto US 301 and soon the grit and grime of downtown was in his rearview mirror. The dark, almost desolate, ride through the rolling landscape of Northern Virginia wasn't a complete salve for what he was feeling, but it helped.

He stopped once at an all-night diner. Mitch sat at the counter with a cup of black coffee and a blueberry muffin. He was still rehashing the night's events when his attention was captured by one of the booths holding three teenage boys talking loud, talking trash, and playing grab-ass. They were trying to impress the thirty-something waitress as she moved quickly about taking care of her patrons. She wore a nametag that said, *Margie*, moved with a self-assurance that comes with experience, and was handling herself well, but the boys were undoubtedly making life hard for her.

They got up to leave at the same time as Mitch. One of the boys, thinking nobody was watching, casually scooped up and put into his pocket a three dollar tip from the table of an adjacent booth.

When they got outside Mitch noted where they were parked, quickly got into his car, and backed the Chevy into place, blocking the boys' exit from their parking space. Then he just sat there, idling. The teen driver beeped his horn a couple times. When it became apparent that wasn't working, the boy sitting in the front passenger's seat got out and approached Mitch's car.

"Hey, buddy, get outta the way."

Mitch opened the door and climbed out of his car. The boy stopped dead in his tracks as soon as he recognized Mitch as the man from inside the diner. The years had packed 215 pounds of muscle and attitude onto Mitch's six feet, two inch frame. He was thick and burly. His face owned a leathery look with some pock marks and scars that most people believed were the result of an aggressive case of acne from his youth. The real cause of his unattractive complexion was a bit more shocking. Overall, most people found him intimidating, both his appearance and his demeanor.

Mitch motioned to the boy to come closer. The young man reluctantly obliged.

"I've had a long day and I'm real tired," Mitch said, "so your options are going to be very limited. Go tell your friend in the Redskins sweatshirt to go back inside the diner and return the waitress's tip to her, in person. Her name's Margie. If he doesn't do it, I'm going to arrest all three of you."

"What?"

"You heard me," Mitch said as he flashed a badge in front of the boy's face. Mitch had no more authority than the man in the moon to arrest anybody. But the teenager didn't know that, and he just assumed that Mitch's badge was legitimate. "Now get movin', go tell him. I'm gonna sit here and watch, and it would be a real big mistake to screw with me. I'll knock your asses into next week if I have to."

Shortly after the boy returned to his car, one of the back doors opened and the tip thief in the Redskins sweatshirt hustled out and went back into the diner. From his vantage point Mitch could see the boy approach Margie, and hand something to her. He immediately turned, came back out, and cut a quivered glance in Mitch's direction.

Mitch pulled forward to let the teens go free. They turned into the north-bound lane of Route 301, the same direction Mitch was headed. He decided to wait a few minutes to allow them to get some distance up the road. He didn't need to think about them anymore. *Let the little farts go, I did my duty.*

Mitch, lost in thought and watching a few lonely vehicles pass by the diner, didn't notice the solitary figure that approached his car. A light tap on the driver's side window got his attention. He turned and saw Margie standing there. Her arms were folded across her chest as she held onto the lapels of the coat she had thrown over her shoulders. Mitch rolled the window halfway down. "Hello?"

"Hi," she said, her breath fogging the cold February air. "I saw what you did for me, and I just wanted to come out and say, thank you. You have no idea how much I depend on every dollar I earn."

"Ah, you're quite welcome," Mitch said. Then, with a slight shoul-der shrug, he added, "You know, I really don't think those boys are all that bad. They just need some guidance, a push in the right direction. Maybe I gave it to 'em."

"I'm sure you did. Thanks again." Margie started to turn away, but hesitated. Reaching over to where Mitch's left hand was resting on top of the car window, she tapped his wedding band with her index finger and said, "Your wife is a lucky woman." Margie spun around and scam-pered up the concrete walkway and back into the diner.

Mitch watched her go back to work, wiping off tables. Then he whispered to himself, "Thanks, but you're wrong, Margie. I'm actually the lucky one."

In less than an hour after Mitch left the diner he was at the top of the Governor Harry Nice Bridge that connected Virginia's Northern Neck to Charles County in Southern Maryland.

Charles County is a feel-good place and rich in history. It is blessed with miles of shoreline on the Potomac River and several of the river's tributaries. The county is home to Mallows Bay, the largest and most varied collection of shipwrecks in the western hemisphere; St. Ignatius, one of the oldest Catholic churches in America; the Dr. Mudd house, where Dr. Mudd set the broken leg of John Wilkes Booth; many Freedom Trail historic sites; and, of course, Charles County was once known as Little Vegas, a gambling mecca with bigger revenues than the real Las Vegas in Nevada. To the chagrin of many locals, the days of Little Vegas ended around 1968. However the rich farmlands and rural communities are still beckoning many to settle there.

The lights of the Morgantown Generating Station were in front of Mitch. The Potomac River laid below like a giant piece of dark, gray slate in the moonless night. The shoreline was dotted with a few lights from waterfront crab houses and private docks. To the north, an eerie glow on the distant nighttime horizon marked the nation's capital, another city that never sleeps. All of it was comforting. He was only a few miles from home, and Louise.

Dr. Louise Armstrong is on staff at Physicians Memorial Hospital in La Plata, Maryland. She and Mitch share a life, and an old farmhouse they are renovating in Newburg, about fifteen miles south of La Plata. They met when she was an intern at Johns Hopkins.

Twelve years ago, a routine traffic stop went terribly bad. Mitch was shot with a sawed-off shotgun. Luckily, if one could call it that, the shotgun was loaded with double ought buckshot and only a single one of the large balls grazed his head, causing a small laceration and minor concussion. But the muzzle flash and accompanying bits of smaller debris from the shotgun blast resulted in burns and multiple fragment wounds to his face and eyes.

He was rushed to Johns Hopkins Hospital, where eight hours of surgery left him with the hope that he would regain his vision. Dr. Louise Sherwood, a brand new intern at that time, was on his floor during recovery. Mitch had no family and rarely did anyone from the police force in Virginia drive up to Baltimore to visit. Consequently, Louise spent a lot of time, on and off the clock, checking on Mitch. He liked the feeling.

During the time that Mitch's eyes were covered with bandages, his other senses seemed to sharpen. He knew whenever Louise walked into his room.

"Hi Dr. Sherwood," he said one day, before she ever spoke a word.

"How did you know it was me?"

"Your perfume. I often wonder if you look as good as you smell."

"Someday you'll see for yourself," she replied.

He liked the assurances she always gave him.

Mitch asked that Louise be in the room on the day they took the bandages off his eyes for the first big test of how well, if at all, his vision had recovered. Her fragrance and gentle touch on his ankle let him know exactly where she was standing.

The room's lighting was adjusted. After the bandages were removed, and his eyes were cleaned, one of the doctors instructed, "Try to focus on something in the room. Anything."

It seemed to everyone that an eternity of seconds elapsed, during which time Mitch moved his head from side to side, tried to adjust to the glare, fought through the haze, and finally settled on Louise.

She was a tall woman with long dark hair. Not even her white hospital coat could hide her slim, but shapely, figure. Most people agreed that Louise had a gentle face and pleasing smile.

Mitch squinted, looked at her, and asked, "Am I dead and you're an angel, or are you really that pretty?" Laughter and high fives filled the room.

Louise continued checking on Mitch, even more frequently than before. They talked and laughed. Something more was budding in their relationship, and they both knew it. Shortly after he was discharged from the hospital, they went on their first official date. It began with a drive through the country of Northern Virginia and included dinner at a waterfront restaurant. Louise had to do the driving, since Mitch's eyes were still healing. Mitch played the role of tour guide. He loved this area.

After dinner they strolled, hand-in-hand, to the end of one of the boat docks adjacent to the restaurant. They enjoyed the late summer evening as they watched the setting sun reflect off the still water. Mitch and Louise faced each other and embraced. For the rest of their lives they would recall how during that moment they were enveloped in the warmth, light, and electricity of what they both referred to as divine intervention.

"Holy crap, did you feel that?" Louise asked, at the time.

"Uh, yeah. I didn't know if it was just me or what."

The die had been cast. Neither one of them could turn back now. They were married six months later.

CHAPTER 6

"**I**'m home, Weezie," Mitch said, then quietly closed the bedroom door and walked back to the kitchen.

Louise raised herself on one elbow, turned on the lamp that was sitting on the nightstand adjacent to the bed, and looked at the alarm clock. She lingered in that position long enough for her eyes and her mind to clear. Her long, dark, chestnut hair, normally pulled sharply back into a ponytail, now fell in loose, gentle cascades across her shoulder. Finally, she stood, and wrapped herself in the afghan that had been folded at the foot of the bed. Louise padded, barefoot, down the hallway that connected their bedroom to the rest of the house, passed through the living room, stopped in the kitchen doorway, and tried her best to growl.

"You really needed to announce your arrival at 2:30 in the morning?" she asked with mock anger. "And don't ever call me Weezie again. If you do, I swear I'll divorce you."

"Yeah, I know. I'll try to remember," Mitch said, forcing the smirk that's supposed to go along with their private joke.

Louise watched for a few quiet moments as Mitch measured coffee and added water for a ten-cup brew. He was planning to stay up for a while. She wasn't surprised. Louise was one of the very few who knew the inner Mitch and how much this whole Tommy Cleaves thing had been eating at him over the years. Not too many people would believe there was a gentle side to Mitch Armstrong. The secret endeared her to him even more.

"I stayed up and watched the news," she said. "They announced it."

Mitch turned on Mr. Coffee, then walked over to Louise, who was leaning against the doorframe, and pulled her close to him. He wrapped his arms around her slim body, and whispered, "Why in the hell am I doing this?"

They clung to each other in silence.

"I can't even ask you how it went," Louise finally said. Tears were starting to well up in her eyes. "What kind of stupid-ass question would that be? You just watched a man get killed. An innocent man."

"It's not stupid, Louise. But I can't describe it. The visual was bad enough. The emotional part is gut-wrenching."

"Did you get to talk to him at all?"

"Yeah, I was in the cell with him until about fifteen minutes prior. I really thought we were going to get a stay."

Mitch stepped away from Louise and sat down in one of the straight back kitchen chairs. He rested his forearms on his knees and stared briefly at the floor, then looked into Louise's moist eyes.

"I've been giving that man hope for years. And I gave him an extra dose of it tonight. But it all turned out to be false."

"I know you, Mitch, and I know that what you gave that man was a little bit of comfort and compassion during his last hours on Earth. Don't beat yourself up for that." Louise moved over to him, sat on his lap, wrapped her arms around his neck, and rested her cheek against his head.

Mitch relaxed into her softness, her fragrance, the touch of her hand in his hair. "God, I love you," he said.

"And I'll always love you, Mr. Armstrong. Always."

They sat, not moving, for several minutes.

"I hate to ask this," Louise finally said, "but I know it was weighing on you. Was Farmer there?"

"Yeah, the prick was there." The cozy moment was over. Now the mood was clinical. "But let's forget about him for a minute, I've gotta tell you about a couple other things that happened."

Mr. Coffee beeped and Louise stood up. She poured a cup for Mitch and then sat down on the adjoining chair.

"What? What else happened?"

"There was a woman there, one of the official witnesses, she seems to know something about Tommy, and for some reason she, too, seems to think he was innocent."

"Is she a relative or something?" Louise asked.

"No, she was one of the state's witnesses of record. People volunteer for that."

Mitch saw Louise scrunch up her face. He continued, "Trust me, I don't get it either, there's just all kinds of people in this world. Maybe they think they're seeing justice done or something. I don't know."

"That's creepy. So, were any of his relatives there?" she asked again.

"Yeah, but they're another story altogether. I'll fill you in later. Let's just say that they were a couple of knuckle-draggers, dressed up to go to the ball."

Mitch held his coffee mug with two hands, comforted by its warmth. He sipped slowly.

"But this woman I'm talking about, there was just something about her. From what she said, it sounds like she had a family member, somebody named Edward, who knew Tommy. Thing is, I think that this

Edward person had also been on death row and got executed, probably a while ago."

"Do you know anything more, like her name? Can you go see her? Oh shit, I don't know what I'm saying, Mitch. I mean what good will it do now?"

"Oh, I'm gonna find her and talk to her again. I'm sorry sweetie, but I just can't let this go. It eats at me like a disease."

"I know, Mitch. I know."

"Look, I'm keeping you up. Don't you have rounds today?" Mitch asked.

"Yeah. But I was going to get up at five, anyhow."

"Go back to bed if you can. I'll wake you at five. I've gotta stay up for now. Demons, you know."

"Honey, I really don't know if I can go back to sleep," Louise protested. "Besides, you said there were a couple of other things that happened. What were they?"

"No, please, go back to bed. We'll talk some more later."

Louise stood up, looked down into Mitch's eyes, touched his cheek, and kissed him softly on the lips.

"I'll crash later," Mitch said, "I'm okay right now."

"We need a day off," Louise said, as she started to walk back to the bedroom. "A mental health day. Not you, not me, but we."

"Love you, Weezie."

"Watch it, buddy," she turned her head and threw the words over her shoulder. "I'm not kidding this time. Divorce papers on the way."

Mitch smiled. He watched her disappear into the nighttime shadows of their house.

"Yeah, I know. I'll try to remember," he said. Then in a whisper she couldn't hear, he added, "You're not gonna believe it when I tell you I saw Frankie tonight. I want you real awake for that one."

As promised, Mitch woke Louise up at five o'clock and then promptly crawled into the bed and melted into a deep slumber until almost noon. When Louise arrived home in mid-afternoon, she found him in the dining room of their old farmhouse cutting and fitting crown molding into place.

"Glad to see you're up and earning your keep," she said.

"Hi, sweetie. I really needed that sleep."

He climbed down from the step ladder, walked over to Louise, and gave her a big hug and a kiss.

"That felt good," she said. "How are you doing, now that you've got some rest?"

"A lot better."

They walked into the kitchen.

"A lot better is the good news. The bad news is that I'm thinking more clearly than ever about how much I want to make this thing right."

"I know," she said. "Last night you told me there was more you wanted to say."

"You're gonna have to sit for this one."

Louise got two cups of coffee from the never ending supply that Mitch kept brewing. Mitch pulled out two chairs from the kitchen table. They sat down.

"Okay, tell me," Louise said.

"I saw Frankie last night."

Louise was a little confused at first. The name, Frankie, wasn't ringing a bell. She started running through her mental rolodex of all their acquaintances. Then her eyes widened and her jaw dropped.

"Are you talking about your friend, Frankie, from when you were a kid? The one who was with you the night that girl got killed? You're not talking about him?"

"The one and only."

"Holy crap, Mitch. Where did you see him? Was he at the prison? Did you talk to him?"

"He was waiting by my car out in the parking lot. I didn't give him much of a chance to speak. I damn near lost it. I felt like I wanted to beat the shit out of him. He gave me some bullshit about needing to talk. I told him he was a day late and a dollar short, and to get out of my sight." Mitch glanced down at his coffee. Then he looked directly into Louise's eyes. "That's really about it."

"What happened then?"

"I kind of turned my back on him, gave him a few minutes, and when I turned around, he was gone."

"Mitch, it was late at night, you had just witnessed something emotionally devastating. Is there any chance it wasn't Frankie? Somebody else? Maybe even a hallucination? That can happen."

"Thank you, Doctor Armstrong, but it was as real as real gets. It was Frankie."

"Are you going to try to find him?"

"It's crazy, as kids we were like brothers, called ourselves the Corn Bandits."

Louise smiled. "Yeah, I know. I think I've heard all the stories. Maybe, even more than once. So, like I said, are you going to try to find him?"

"Why, so I can kill him?"

"I'm serious, Mitch. For whatever reason, he was reaching out. You're sitting there telling me you can't let this thing go. Maybe he can help."

"Let me think on that for a while. In the meantime I do want to go see the lady, Muriel."

"And when do you think you'll do that?"

"Tomorrow."

"Tomorrow?"

"Yeah I called Willie and got her number. He owed me. I got him those pictures of his girlfriend cheating on him."

Louise interrupted. "I remember the story, Mitch. But does it have to be tomorrow? Give yourself a break. We need some time off."

"Let me have tomorrow. Then I'm all yours."

Louise raised her coffee cup and looked at him over the top of it as she drank.

"You're very good at keeping your promises, Mitch. I'm definitely holding you to this one."

CHAPTER 7

Farmer slapped at the alarm clock on Monday morning following the execution. It was 5:00 a.m. and he was anxious to get up and get going. He thought his new job, Chief of Security at the State House, would be an opportunity to showcase his management skills, the talents that he alone ascribed to himself. He eased his feet into some old leather slippers, shuffled across the floor, and turned on the switch for the overhead light. He immediately looked at the retirement plaque sitting on his dresser and smiled. *Thirty-five years on the Force, twenty-five of it jumping through hoops for the Old Man, and now this Tommy Cleaves shit is finally over with. All I have to do now is make sure Armstrong is done.* He took a deep breath and could feel the relief washing over him. His glance then shifted slightly to the right, to the picture of his wife, Melissa.

Two years ago Melissa was one of the seventy-four casualties on the ill-fated Air Florida Flight 90 that crashed into D.C.'s 14th Street Bridge. She was on her way to spend some time with a new grandchild, but the trip ended all too quickly on a frigid January afternoon. Over the years of their marriage, Melissa always thought that Farmer spent too much time taking care of business for the Old Man. She never knew exactly who the Old Man was, or what kind of business Farmer was taking care of. He offered very little information to her.

"Some things are best left unsaid," is all that he ever told her.

Despite that, she'd often lament that it would be nice if Farmer could spend more time with the family.

Staring at her picture, Farmer whispered "It's okay, Missy. Things'll be better now."

After he showered and shaved, Farmer wrapped a robe around himself, walked out through the front door, picked up his copy of the morning paper, and went back into the house. The execution of Tommy Cleaves made the front page. Farmer scanned the articles accompanying Tommy's picture, looking for references to himself. He could only find one mention of his own name. His lips barely moved as he read the words to himself, *It was a good bust according to Detective Ken Farmer who was involved in the case twenty-five years ago.*

"A good bust! Involved in the case!" Farmer was livid, and circling his kitchen table shouting to no one but himself. "Didn't those asshole reporters listen to a word I said. Involved in the case? I was the case! And not a one of those jerks will ever know just who it was that got me involved."

Thursday, August 27, 1959

At the time of Kathleen Spencer's murder, Farmer had already been a patrolman for six years and a homicide detective for almost four years with the Richmond Police Department. The sheriff of Middlesex County, where Bohman's Point is located, had some contacts in the city, so he called on Richmond for assistance. They sent Farmer.

Farmer got a motel room not far from Bohman's Point, and then poked around the community and nearby places for several days, but didn't come up with any leads. His heart really wasn't in it he knew, and when he returned to the motel on the afternoon of his third day there, he was ready to call it quits. But a stranger intercepted him just as he was stepping out of his car.

"Detective Farmer, can I have a word with you?"

"Depends. Who are you?"

"That doesn't matter. What matters is that I have a client who wants to speak to you about the case you're working on."

"You're a lawyer?"

"Again, it's not me that matters."

"Your client, or whatever he is, wants to talk to me? What's he want to do, confess, make a deal, what?" There was a half-laugh and a bit of contempt in Farmer's voice.

"Nothing like that. But it will be worth your while to meet with him. He's …" The stranger hesitated, searching for just the right words, "not this accommodating with everyone—seven o'clock at the Montague Mill. It's a restaurant about five miles from here. Tell the maître d' that two gentlemen are expecting you."

The stranger turned around and walked away. Staring at the stranger's back and wanting to know more, Farmer took a step after him, but stopped, realizing that it would probably be useless.

Once inside his room, Farmer stretched out on the too hard, too lumpy motel bed, cursing the Richmond Police Department for making him stay in such a cheapskate place. He didn't nap, but did manage to rest a little while. At the same time he ran some possibilities through his head about this odd meeting he was going to. He thought there was a good chance it would be a total waste of time. He briefly toyed with the idea of not going, but then decided, *What the hell. Even if it's nothing more than some crooked-ass politician who wants to make sure he gets a piece of the credit for solving this thing. I got nothin' better to do.* He continued to shift, and roll, and mutter to himself about the uncomfortableness of the bed.

The Montague Mill was old and popular. The parking lot was full by the time Farmer arrived. He stepped out of his car and inhaled deeply, enjoying the rich aromas wafting through the air. Inside the restaurant, he told the maître d' that he was supposed to meet two men. He was immediately led to a dark mahogany booth where the stranger from earlier and another man were sitting. The second man was older and rather distinguished looking, with a thick head of silver-white hair, and wearing, what appeared to be, a very expensive tailored suit. Farmer was pretty sure he had seen him before. He just couldn't remember where. Maybe he'd been on the TV news or in a picture in the paper. No matter what it was, the man looked familiar. No formal introductions were offered. Farmer was simply invited to sit down.

The white-haired man, after waving off a waiter who was attempting to place a water glass in front of Farmer, was the first to speak. "Thank you for coming, Detective Farmer. I know this was very short notice, and I appreciate you taking the time to speak with me." The Old Man had already been served a small salad and a glass of Cabernet. There was neither food nor drink in front of the stranger from earlier, and after an awkward moment of realization, Farmer figured out that he was not joining them to dine, but only to talk.

"I understand you have some interest in a case I'm working on," Farmer finally said.

The Old Man nibbled at his salad a little, and took a small sip of wine. "My children were all born fairly late in my life. At least late for having children," he replied. "But it's allowed me to share with them some of the finer things that life has to offer."

Farmer tried not to look as confused as he felt.

"I'm sixty-three now," the Old Man continued, "and no longer have the same luxury of time that I once enjoyed. My son is getting ready to start his junior year at Princeton, and I want to see him eventually go to Harvard Law."

Farmer scrunched his face slightly and said, "He sounds like he's a very bright young man. But what does this have to do with me or this case I'm ..."

The Old Man interrupted, "He is very bright and very capable." He stopped picking at his salad, wiped the corner of his mouth with a white linen napkin, and leaned back to better assess Farmer, who was sitting directly across from him. The Old Man cocked his head to the side, ever so slightly, and looked at Farmer as if he was appraising a piece of art. Farmer felt the need to squirm, but didn't want to show that he was at all uncomfortable being scrutinized in such a manner. Seemingly satisfied with what he saw, the Old Man finally said, "And that's why somebody other than my son—or any of his close acquaintances—needs to be held accountable for that Spencer girl's murder."

The words came like a punch to Farmer's solar plexus. "What do you mean other than your son or his acquaintances? Do you have knowledge of who was involved in this thing?"

The Old Man took another sip of wine, placed the goblet back on the table, and let his fingers slowly slide down its stem. He looked at

Farmer with what Farmer would always recall as the definition of an icy stare.

"You will learn, Detective, that in conversations with me, I will always make things perfectly clear. And you, unless I give you the opening, will never need to question anything that I say. My acquaintance here, whom you've already met, will give you all the information about my son you'll need to know."

Farmer's question went unanswered. Over the ensuing years, Farmer would often speculate about the answer, but only to himself. He was at least smart enough to know that if you were, in any way, close to the Old Man, you didn't talk about the Old Man. Farmer knew there was a hidden truth to Kathleen Spencer's murder. He just never knew exactly what it was. He suspected, but never knew, for sure, that the Old Man's son, or one of his son's friends, had something to do with the death of Kathleen Spencer.

No, Ken Farmer never knew any of that. What he did know was that he had been given an opportunity, along with a short list of names that could never again be mentioned. So, Farmer did what his conscience allowed. He agreed to do whatever the Old Man wanted. And enjoyed a big payday for doing it.

Farmer left the restaurant that night contemplating the possibilities and the problem that had been presented to him. The possibilities were many, and of the type that money and influence could buy. The problem was singular—find somebody, upon whom he could hang the Spencer girl's murder.

Bright and early the following morning, Farmer was back on Bohman's Point, knocking on doors he had previously skipped. One of those doors belonged to Frankie's grandmother, Nana. After speaking to her, he got the tip of the day from young Frankie, who was hiding behind Farmer's car when he came back out of the house. Frankie told him that he had seen a car parked at the top of the steps next to Beck's pier on the night of the murder. He said it belonged to a local guy named Tommy Cleaves.

Farmer started questioning people about Tommy and it couldn't have gone better. If Farmer was a religious man, he probably would have claimed that the tip he got from the kid was a gift from God. He had a plausible suspect, and everything he learned about Tommy seemed to make it a natural fit. Nobody liked Tommy Cleaves, especially the guy's own sisters. Farmer didn't know what went on behind closed doors in Tommy's house, but based on things Tommy's sisters told him, he had an idea, and it wasn't a pretty picture.

Most people said Tommy was obsessed with talking about sex, especially rough sex. Farmer followed him to a bar one night. He sat on a stool next to Tommy, shared only his first name and nothing about why he was visiting the area. After buying him a couple boilermakers, he got Tommy talking about all his sexual exploits. Farmer eventually managed to bring the recent murder of Kathleen Spencer into the conversation.

With an overly exaggerated grin on his face, Tommy said, "Her? Yeah, I did her a couple times too. She was good; liked getting bounced around. Too bad she's dead now. I'd like to pound that one again." Then, giggling to the point that he was snorting beer out of his nose, Tommy said, "Yeah, that's it. Maybe it was me. Maybe I'm the one. I probably just screwed her to death."

Farmer listened to Tommy's bullshit all night, knowing, for certain, that's all it was—bullshit. But he also knew that if he ever had the opportunity, he would have no second thoughts about presenting Tommy's words as evidence against him.

However, the real coup de grace came when Farmer finally got a warrant, and searched Tommy's car. He found a charm bracelet, identified by Kathleen's parents as belonging to her. Despite the absence of fingerprints on the bracelet, Farmer started to think that maybe he really had solved this case. *Who cares what anybody else says*, he thought in the moment. *This is gonna make me look good.*

Tommy was arrested, booked, and incarcerated in the Middlesex County jail. He seemed to enjoy the notoriety of being a prominent name in the news. Tommy would smirk, giggle, and trade quips with reporters and photographers as he was marched in and out of the courtroom for various pre-trial motions. As a result of his own stupidity, he lived under the self-inflicted delusion that he would simply wake up one morning, be told that everything was taken care of, and that he could go home.

Tommy's court-appointed attorney tried to argue that Tommy did not have the mental capacity to understand what was going on. Judge Claude Anderson rejected the argument. Tommy was, unfortunately, the victim of bad timing. A competency standard that could have declared Tommy incompetent to stand trial was decided by the Supreme Court only a month later in the case of Milton Dusky v. United States. Tommy, instead, was tried, convicted, and twenty-five years later, executed.

From Farmer's perspective, maybe Tommy was a major player in the murder, maybe he wasn't; maybe the Old Man's son was as deeply involved as he suspected, maybe he wasn't. It really didn't matter to Farmer. He did what the Old Man told him to do, got paid well for doing it, and continued answering the call for whatever the Old Man requested. Farmer never saw anything wrong with it. He would consistently preach that justice had been served.

"Involved in the case … Am I reading this right? You run the whole damn thing and all you are is—involved? Are you kidding me?" Farmer balled up the newspaper and threw it across the kitchen, watching as it scattered apart in mid-flight. With fists clenched and pressed against his hips, he tried to regain some composure by taking a couple deep breaths. "Screw it," he barked at the empty room. Then, with the slightest hint of resignation in his voice, "I can't get upset about a bunch of shit-for-brains reporters."

Walking over to the coffee maker, he thought about his conversation with the Old Man on Saturday night, right after Tommy's execution. "I need to find a way to get rid of Armstrong," he muttered, "he's gonna be a real pain in the ass."

CHAPTER 8

"**A**nd just how did you get my phone number?"

Muriel's demeanor was a lot less friendly on the phone than it had been, Saturday night, at the prison. Feeling like he may have totally misread her, Mitch thought it best to be totally upfront and honest.

"I called in a marker with a friend at the prison," said Mitch. "He gave me your number."

The conversation eventually went well enough for Mitch to persuade Muriel to meet with him. She invited him to her home in Richmond.

Two hours later Mitch was parked in front of Muriel's house. As was his custom while visiting any new location, Mitch now sat in his car with the motor running while he soaked in his surroundings. Muriel lived in a well-kept, attractive, two-story house on the corner of Holly Avenue in an old suburban Richmond neighborhood. It had a pleasant feel to it.

What didn't feel pleasant to Mitch was the black sedan. It was nowhere in sight, but Mitch has been tailed enough times to trust his gut when he thinks he is being followed. That is one of the reasons he usually drives what he calls his work car, a gray 1982 Ford Escort, whenever he's out on business. The Chevy would just draw too much

attention. Mitch was fairly certain that a black sedan had been following him ever since he crossed the Harry Nice Bridge into Northern
Virginia. Now that it was no longer in sight gave him a little relief, but
he was still being cautious.

He finally turned off the ignition and exited the car, looked around,
briefly closed his eyes, and took a deep breath. In his mind he could
hear the sounds of a time gone by – the laughter and chatter of children playing stickball in the street, the backyard conversations over a
neighborly fence, the jingle of the ice-cream truck that sent the kids
scurrying for a dime. *Yeah, I'll bet this was a great place to grow up.*

Two concrete steps connected the sidewalk to a short private walkway to five more steps and the front porch. At eye-level in the middle
of the white, sun-bleached door was a tarnished, but attractive, brass
door-knocker.

Mitch rapped the knocker three times. Shortly thereafter the door
opened and Muriel Cathcart greeted him with a slightly skeptical smile.

"Mr. Armstrong, looks like you found the place okay," Muriel said.

"Your directions were real good, Mrs. Cathcart," Mitch replied.

"Oh, please call me Muriel," she interjected.

"And you can call me Mitch."

"C'mon in," she said.

Mitch glanced, once more, up and down the street, but saw nothing. He stepped through the doorway and into the living room. He
slowly, almost imperceptibly, turned his head from side to side while
his eyes darted quickly around the room. It felt comfortable. He was
again thinking about how totally different Muriel and her surroundings seemed to be from the way he first imagined. The house and fur-
nishings were old, but spotless. The steam radiators, located under two

different windowsills in the living room, produced a warmth that was especially pleasing. There was a small bookcase in the living room and Mitch noted the books of poetry, a couple of classics, some Reader's Digest condensed books, and what appeared to be a photo album.

"Let me take your coat, Mitch," Muriel offered and Mitch obliged.

"Thank you," he said, "you have a very nice home, Muriel."

"That's nice of you to say," she replied, "my husband, Malcolm, and my son were always real good at cleaning up after themselves and keeping things fixed. I do my best, now that they're both gone."

Muriel took Mitch's jacket and hung it in a coat closet, then beckoned him to follow her. They walked through a small dining room furnished with a highly polished dark cherry table and matching chairs. A china cabinet against one wall highlighted some old dishes, family heirlooms handed down through several generations. They came to a stop in an adjoining room that was filled with sunlight and had a tile floor. She invited him to sit down at a small Formica-top table.

"We call this the breakfast room. Ate most of our meals here. Can I get you a cup of coffee? It's fresh."

"Yes, please," Mitch responded, "just black."

Muriel stepped into her small kitchen, poured two cups of coffee and returned to the table.

"Mitch, I'm sure I came across as a bit unwelcoming on the phone. But your call caught me off guard and I was already afraid that I had said more than I should have the other night. I've got some opinions, but that's about all. So, how can I help you?"

Mitch sat up, straight-backed, "Muriel, I'm gonna be totally upfront with you. You mentioned somebody named Edward during our little conversation at the prison Saturday night. So, I did some quick research and learned that a young man named Edward Cathcart was one of the first to be executed after the death penalty moratorium was lifted. Since the last name is the same as yours, I assume that's the Edward you were talking about."

"Yes, he was my son."

"And you were there at his execution?"

"Yes."

"I can't even begin to imagine how you were able to deal with something like that. I've tried and can't even come close to getting my arms around it."

"It was the hardest thing I've ever done and I still have to ask God, every day, to help me with it," Muriel said. "Edward was so frightened. He was so afraid of dying. During our final visit he kept saying, 'Momma, I'm scared, please pray for me that I'll get into heaven.' I promised him that I would and I promised him that I'd be there and that he should look at me the whole time if he could, that I'd be praying for him."

Mitch listened intently, careful not to move a muscle, so as not to break her stride.

Muriel continued, "He said I didn't have to be there, that he didn't want to hurt me, but I told him that I would, that his soul needed me to be there more than I needed to be anyplace else. I told him that Mary was at the cross with Jesus. I said, 'I'm your mother. I have to be there, and nothing can stop me.' "

Mitch could see the tears beginning to well up in Muriel's eyes. "Please," he said, "if this is too hard …"

Muriel put up her hand and stopped him in mid-sentence.

"I'm okay. This can actually be a little cathartic."

Muriel sat still for a short while to regain her composure. Mitch took a sip of his coffee and silently cursed himself for making a slurping sound. It just didn't seem appropriate for the moment.

Then Muriel said, "I truly believe I gave him some comfort. That's why I've witnessed some other executions. I didn't know any of those men or their families, but I'd read about them in the paper. Sometimes I'd come across something they said or did or something about their families that caught my attention. Then I'd pray on it, and if I felt like I was being called to be there I'd volunteer."

"You're quite a person, Muriel," Mitch said. "Is that why you were a witness to Tommy Cleaves's execution?"

"Pretty much so," she replied. "I'll tell you about that, but first, I've got to let you know a little more about Edward. I don't want you thinking he was an evil person. I'm sure, in your research, you learned that a young woman, with two small children, is the one who died at Edward's hands. And I'm sure you'd expect to hear this from any mother. But Edward was a good man. I know he didn't intend to kill her. I'm also well aware that doesn't excuse the fact that if he hadn't been doing something wrong that young lady would be alive today." A tinge of emotion was again entering into her voice and dialogue.

"I learned that it was a burglary gone bad," said Mitch. "Do you have any idea why he was doing it?"

"He was a gambler, Mr. Armstrong."

"Please, just Mitch," he said.

"Of course."

Muriel took a small crumpled up lace hankie from the pocket of her housedress, dabbed away a tear, and continued. "Edward was a gambler. We, that is, his father and I, didn't know it. At least we didn't know how much of a gambler he was or how deeply in debt he had gotten. We just thought he played a little penny ante poker with a few of his friends every once in a while. It was a lot worse than that. He gambled on everything. Then he lost big, and he owed some people, some bad people, a whole lot of money." She looked beyond Mitch and said, "He didn't know what to do."

Muriel stopped talking, took a sip of her coffee, and just kind of stared blankly straight ahead for a few seconds.

Then she continued, "He told me later that it was a lot more money than he could ever ask us for, which is why he never came to us for help. He was scared, and I think he wasn't just scared for himself, but for his father and me too."

"I understand," said Mitch, "that can be a real tough crowd. Not the kind of people you want to cross."

Muriel spoke, but her gaze still appeared to be staring into another world. "Edward knew of a couple that lived a few blocks over from us. Their last name was Sumter. What he remembered most was that every year they got a new car. To him, that meant they must've had a lot of money. I really don't know if they did or didn't, but Edward convinced himself that they were rich and had nice things."

"I'm assuming that's the house he burglarized," Mitch interjected.

"Yes it is. He evidently stopped going to work. Edward had a job at Miller's Fabrication. They do a lot of sheet metal work. Anyway, he stopped showing up for work. At least, that's what he told me, and I really didn't have any reason not to believe him. He was so upset with how this was all affecting me."

"I'm sure he was."

"You're cup's empty. Can, I freshen it up for you?"

"Please don't go to any extra trouble for me."

"It's not all for you, Mitch. Doing little routine tasks, like filling a coffee cup, can help a person put their mind at ease."

While Muriel went to refill Mitch's coffee cup, he looked around the room absorbing details and creating mental scenarios of what their life must have been like. There were numerous pictures of two men. Mitch assumed the younger one was Edward and the older man must have been Muriel's husband, Malcolm. There were also pictures of Edward at various stages of his youth. Randomly placed among the pictures were some seashells with inscriptions as well as a few other cheap souvenirs from family vacations.

"Uh-oh," Mitch softly muttered. He walked over to the window and looked outside. Something caught his attention. The black sedan slowly crept down the street. *Damn, I don't like this,* he thought as he heard Muriel re-enter the room.

CHAPTER 9

"There it is, parked in front of that house on the corner," said the driver, "get the address."

The black sedan had been cruising the neighborhood looking for Mitch's car.

"Got it. Let's call Farmer."

They drove several blocks away and parked along the street. The driver made a quick call to Ken Farmer from the car phone and gave him the address.

Fifteen minutes later Farmer returned the call and said, "Muriel Cathcart lives there. She was one of the witnesses at the Cleaves execution. Find out what Armstrong wants from her. She lives alone."

Muriel returned with a fresh cup of coffee for Mitch.

"Here you go. I've got plenty if you want more."

"Thank you."

"Now, where was I?" Muriel asked.

"You said Edward stopped going to work," Mitch replied.

"Yes, and he started spying, I guess you would call it spying, on the Sumters. He learned that every day Mrs. Sumter would walk her two twins, a boy and a girl—cute little things—to school. Kindergarten, I suppose. She wouldn't be gone very long, but twice a week, every Tuesday and Thursday, a friend of hers, another woman, would stop by and they'd go off somewhere in the friend's car. They'd be gone for usually two hours or more. Probably shopping or out to lunch. I'm sure it was just friends being friends." Muriel paused, then said, "Of course, that doesn't matter."

"So, he picked one of those days when he knew she'd be gone to break into the house," Mitch said.

"Exactly. The problem is that on the day Edward chose to break into her house, Mrs. Sumter had forgotten to take her lipstick with her so her girlfriend brought her back and waited outside in the car while she ran in the house to get it. A lot of this information came out in court. Mrs. Sumter's friend was a witness for the prosecution."

Mitch nodded his head in agreement.

"Edward told me what happened next," Muriel said, "and I believe it happened the way he said. Doesn't change anything, but at least makes me think that he didn't mean this lady any harm. He was rooting through some drawers in their dining room cabinet looking for good silver or anything else of value when she walked in and saw him. She screamed, 'What are you doing?' or 'Who are you?' Something like that. He couldn't remember exactly what it was she yelled. He panicked and all he wanted to do was to get out of the house."

Mitch reached over and laid his hand on top of hers.

"I'm all right. Just haven't talked about this in quite a while. Anyway, Edward started for the back door. That's where he had entered the house. Wherever Mrs. Sumter was standing she must've been blocking his way out. He said when he got right up to her, he pushed her out of his way. He wasn't tryin' to hurt her but he said he was so scared and pumped up with adrenalin that he must've pushed her a lot harder than he intended to. He saw her falling backward trying to get her balance, but he kept on going and left the house. During the trial the lead detective kept saying that Edward could have used a different escape route and avoided her altogether, but that he went after her on purpose to silence her. I know he didn't."

"Was the lead detective, by any chance, Ken Farmer?"

Muriel nodded and wiped a few more tears off her cheeks.

"And that's why you agreed to meet with me."

She nodded again. "I saw a non-verbal exchange you two gave each other Saturday night. I figured your feelings about him were similar to mine."

"It's a long story, but you're pretty much on target."

She continued, "Well, according to the police and the ambulance crew, it appeared that Mrs. Sumter fell onto the floor and hit the back of her head real hard on the corner of a raised brick fireplace hearth. She was still alive by the time they got her to the hospital, but she went into a coma and died several days later."

"How'd they wind up suspecting Edward?" Mitch asked. Then he quickly added, "If you don't want to go on I understand. I truly don't mean to cause you any pain."

"I'm okay," said Muriel, "just give me a second.

"Edward went out the back door of their house, then made his way over some fences and through a couple of other people's backyards. He had parked his own car about halfway down the block, so he got to the car and left in a hurry. He said he was feeling real panicky, so he probably drove it real fast. The problem is that his car was real pretty. It was a blue Pontiac convertible. He kept it real clean and shiny looking. He was always outside washing and waxing it. Everybody knew his car, even the police. He drove right past the woman who was parked out front waiting for Mrs. Sumter. So, when she was asked what all she saw while she was out there she did mention seeing a car go speeding by. Soon as she described it, they had a good idea whose car it was."

Muriel stopped for a little while and just stared down at the table, holding her coffee cup with two hands. Then she said, "It didn't take the police long to come looking for him to ask some questions. It didn't take too much. He was just too nervous and too scared, and nothing he was telling them made any sense. So he got arrested. The facts of the trial are pretty straight forward after that. He admitted to just about everything. Of course, the state used the fact that the woman had two children to play to the jurors' sense of justice and retribution."

"I'm truly sorry, Muriel."

"I believe you are. Thank you. This is so hard for me, for a mother. But by the same token, what Edward did was so wrong. It was so, so wrong."

She sighed ever so faintly, sat silent for a few seconds, then looked directly at Mitch Armstrong. "So, tell me Mitch, why are you here?"

"I'm just tryin' to put some facts together for another case," Mitch replied, "and I thought there might be some things here that could help. When you spoke to me Saturday night you said or implied that Edward got to know Tommy Cleaves a little bit, and that Edward didn't think that Tommy killed the Spencer girl. Can you tell me a little more about that?"

"If that's the other case you're talking about," Muriel responded, "why bother? Tommy was executed. Everyone seems to be satisfied. Don't you think you should move on?"

"I would if I could," Mitch said. "But there's more to it."

Muriel cocked her head to the side and raised an eyebrow. "More to it?"

Mitch took a deep breath and exhaled. Then he looked directly into Muriel's eyes and said, "I am as certain as anyone could be that Tommy Cleaves did not kill that girl."

Mitch hesitated for a moment, hoping to get a response. He could read Muriel's expression. It said, "I told you so."

Mitch went on, "And it has nothing to do with any evidence, or any testimony during the trial, or anything that anybody said. Let me just put it this way. It's personal and I know. I know that Tommy didn't do it, but I don't know who did."

"And, now," Muriel interjected, "whoever did it is responsible for two deaths, Kathleen Spencer's and Tommy's."

"Exactly. I've tried to let it go. But it's hard. In my mind, the scales of justice are way out of balance. Maybe I'll never be able to fix it."

"Maybe it can't be fixed," Muriel said. She stood and walked over toward Mitch.

"But if I don't try to do something. If I don't try to find the bastard—excuse me, sorry about the language."

"Don't worry about your language, Mitch," Muriel said. "You've been real polite. And trust me, if what you say is true, he is a bastard."

"We'll agree on that," Mitch said. "And if I don't try to follow every lead or look under every stone to find that guy, it'll haunt me for the rest of my life."

They both heard the faint ding of a timer. Muriel stood up and walked into the kitchen.

"I've got some cinnamon rolls coming out of the oven," she said. "I can't let you leave without feeding you something."

While Muriel tended to the baked goods in the kitchen, Mitch stood up, walked over to the window, and watched some young boys have a bicycle race out on the street. They were, no doubt, establishing bragging rights, at least for a day.

He commented, "This really looks like a pleasant neighborhood."

"It is," she said. Then she added, "Feel free to look around. The bathroom's upstairs if you need it."

"Thanks," he said, "but I'm okay right now."

Muriel brought the tray of cinnamon rolls to the table along with two small dessert plates, knives, and butter.

They picked at their cinnamon rolls and enjoyed a little idle chit-chat about the house, the neighborhood, the weather, and any other somewhat mindless topic they could bring up.

Finally, Muriel said, "Back to business, I guess. Who knows, maybe I can help."

"Earlier you told me there was a little more to your reason for being a witness to Tommy's execution. Can you fill me in on what that means?"

"Edward felt sorry for Tommy," Muriel said, "and asked me, specifically, to pray for Tommy's soul. That's why I went to the execution. I think I gave Edward some comfort, and I was hoping to do the same for Tommy. But there were also some other things that Edward said about Tommy Cleaves."

All of Mitch's senses became re-engaged as he listened to Muriel. She had that faraway look in her eyes, but was speaking in a clear tone.

She said, "Edward told me that on death row the inmates don't get to interact much. They were able to communicate a bit from cell to cell. Tommy Cleaves was directly across the hall from Edward. They talked. I visited Edward a lot and he started telling me about this Tommy Cleaves person. Edward said that most inmates on death row will say that they're innocent, but for some reason he believed Tommy. He said he got real certain about it right after Tommy came back to the cell one time from seeing a visitor. Edward said Tommy hardly had any visitors at all, and this one was real strange because Tommy didn't recognize the name. He said Tommy joked about it while he was getting cuffed to be taken to the visitor's window. Tommy said that maybe it was a writer tryin' to get some inside scoop on prison life and that maybe Tommy was going to become famous."

"I might have heard about this," Mitch said. "Did Edward say that Tommy was real upset after that visit?"

"Exactly. He said Tommy came back to the cell struggling with the guards and screamin' that they should go stop that man from leaving. He was sayin' that his visitor had something that could clear him. Then he started yelling and screaming that he needed to see his lawyer. From what I remember, Edward said that a couple days later Tommy's appeals lawyer did come to visit. And Tommy was real unhappy with how that went."

"That still doesn't explain much," said Mitch.

"Not yet," said Muriel, "but here's where it gets real interesting." She pushed her coffee cup aside and leaned forward. "Time passed and Tommy got back to normal, whatever normal could possibly be in there. He and Edward were talking one day and Edward asked him about that visitor. Edward didn't want to set him off again, but he was real curious. Tommy told him that he had given up, that his lawyer said that even if what the guy said was true, that he had probably used a fictitious name and ID when he came to visit Tommy and that they'd never be able to locate him."

"So what was it the guy told him?" Mitch asked.

"That man told Tommy that he knew Tommy was innocent. He proved it to Tommy by telling him that he planted the Spencer girl's charm bracelet in Tommy's car. That was a key piece of evidence in Tommy's trial."

"Yes, I know. But anybody could have told him that," said Mitch.

"Perhaps, but this guy was able to tell Tommy, in very precise detail, exactly where the bracelet was found in the car. The exact location of the bracelet was something that never came up in the trial. There was testimony about finding the bracelet in Tommy's car, just never about it being on the rear floor of the passenger's side of the car. This guy also told Tommy that the bracelet had a missing charm and that he could prove it. That was something else that didn't come up in the trial. Then he went on and told Tommy that he was looking forward to the day when Tommy finally goes to the chair."

Mitch could feel the blood veins in his neck start to pulse and hoped that Muriel didn't notice. "This guy sounds like a real piece of work," Mitch commented.

"I'm sure he was," said Muriel. "Edward also told me that he got the feeling there was more to the whole story than what Tommy was telling him, but that didn't stop him from believing the things that Tommy did tell him."

"Did you ever bring this to anyone else's attention?" asked Mitch.

"Sure," said Muriel. "I made an appointment to go see Tommy's appeals lawyer. He gave me the standard line that everybody on death row says that they're innocent. That somebody else did it.

"So that wound up being a dead end for you," said Mitch. "You didn't talk to him, the lawyer, anymore?"

"No, I didn't. But there is something else, and this is really interesting." Muriel looked off to the side and shook her head up and down. "This man, this unknown visitor, even told Tommy that he had been on the beach the night the girl was killed."

Mitch's chest expanded as he started to take deeper breaths.

Muriel continued, "The visitor told Tommy that he knew, without a doubt, that Tommy didn't do it. He even told him that somebody else knew it too."

Mitch tightened up. His eyes ballooned wide, his nostrils flared, and his jaws stiffened. Some nasty thoughts raced through his head. *Frankie, you son of a bitch.*

"Mitch, you're scaring me," said Muriel, not feigning her alarm.

"I'm sorry," said Mitch, doing his best to bring his emotions under strict control. "It's just that I've got a pretty good idea who it is."

"Was it one of the other witnesses?"

"No."

"I saw you talking to another man in the parking lot Saturday night. You didn't seem to be too happy about it. What about him?"

Her observation made Mitch chuckle. "Don't miss much do you, Muriel?"

She smiled, sensing the conversation probably wasn't going to go much further. They stayed in the breakfast room for several more minutes sipping coffee and chatting amicably about news, weather, and how the neighborhood is changing. Mitch thanked her profusely for sharing with him, and promised to let her know if anything of interest developed from the information she gave him. She stood on the front porch and waved goodbye.

Mitch eased the Ford slowly down the street. He was seething.

You're dead meat, Frankie. You've put me through this all these years. You're dead meat.

Not long after Mitch left, Muriel heard a knock on the door and opened it while at the same time saying, "Mr. Armstrong, did you forget something?"

However, it wasn't Mitch Armstrong. A hand shot out and caught Muriel by the throat. Dolf Richter, one of Ken Farmer's hired guns, pushed through the front door and drove Muriel backwards, slamming her into the living room wall with a force that knocked a framed picture off its hook.

An hour later he called Farmer again and reported, "Armstrong is digging deeper and it sounds like he's got a lead."

"Let me think about this, but keep tabs on him," said Farmer. "What about the Cathcart woman?"

"She's finished talking—to anybody."

"Fine. Get your asses out of that area. I'll be in touch."

As soon as he hung up from talking to Dolf, Farmer called the Old Man. "We're on it, but I just wanted you to know that Armstrong has a lead. He paid a visit today to a woman named, Muriel."

"Muriel Cathcart," the Old Man interjected, "I know who she is. So what happened?"

"Evidently, she gave him some information about a visitor Cleaves once had. Somebody who claimed to have some sort of proof that Cleaves didn't do it."

"Don't make me tell you again, Ken, how important it is that Armstrong gets shut down. You've already misjudged him. Now do something about it."

"You can be sure I will. I'm going to have Dolf …" Once more, Ken found himself speaking to a dial tone.

CHAPTER 10

"So, how'd it go?" Louise asked.

She had just returned from her shift at the hospital and walked the fifty plus yards from the house to the barn, which also served as Mitch's workshop. He called it a workshop. She called it his *therapy room*.

Mitch looked up and smiled. He was buffing a scar out of the paint on the tail fin of his Chevy, a scar put there by Frankie's tossed-away cigarette butt.

"I'm doing pretty good," he said, "by the time I'm done, you won't see a thing."

"Quit trying to be funny, you're not good at it. You know what I'm talking about. How was your visit with Muriel?"

"Let's just say, I learned a lot."

"Like what?"

"Like now I know I have to find Frankie and talk to the asshole."

"That is so sad."

"What, that I have to talk to him?"

"No, that you used to be best friends and now he's 'the asshole'."

"He is. He could've helped save a man's life, but he chose to let him die."

"Mitch, there's got to be a reason. Besides, you were just kids."

"Well, we're not kids anymore, and if there is a reason it sure as hell escapes me."

"Like I said, it's sad. Anyhow, let's go up to the house. I brought home some carryout that's probably getting cold. Oh, and there's a message on our answering machine. That thing is so cool. I still can't believe that people can leave us messages. Anyway, it's that guy, Willie, from down at the prison."

"Did he say what he wanted?"

"No, but the message was weird. He said don't try calling him, but he would call later, probably sometime between eight and nine."

Back at the house, Mitch listened to Willie's message and agreed that it sounded a little strange or perhaps stressed.

After a meal of chicken and biscuits that Louise brought home, Mitch got busy calling some of his contacts up in Pennsylvania. It didn't take long to learn that there was a sandwich shop in Philadelphia called Biondo's Deli. Mitch knew that at one time Frankie's parents owned a small diner in Philly, so this seemed like a good lead. Maybe Frankie was in the same business. He called the phone number that he was given for the deli and asked to speak to Frank Biondo.

"Let me check if he's still here," responded the gruff and impatient employee who answered the call.

Mitch hung up before anyone got back on the phone. He'd already heard enough. It had to be Frankie's place.

Shortly before nine, Willie called.

"Got some news for you, Mitch. I was able to locate some of the old visitors' logs and got the name of the guy who visited Tommy that time I told you about."

"That's great Willie, thanks. Who is it?"

"Harry Burke. Ring any bells with you?"

"Not a one. But that doesn't mean anything, it could be an alias. Anyway, I just thought I'd take a shot." Mitch didn't think it was necessary to let Willie know that he was already pretty sure who the visitor was. "But I really appreciate you checking on that for me."

"Not a problem." Then Willie hesitated.

"You still there, Willie?"

"Yeah, sorry. It's just that I think I need to tell you something else."

"What?"

"This is why I said to wait for me to call. I wanted to make sure I could control what phone I was on, and that I'd be alone when I talked to you. Ken Farmer, that new security chief from the executive building, has been here. He's been asking about you?"

"What was he asking?"

"Mainly stuff about how many times you had been to visit Cleaves. If we ever heard what you and Cleaves talked about. He also asked about the lady, Muriel Cathcart, who was one of the witnesses. Wanted to know if we had seen her talking to you. And, if we had, did we hear anything the two of you might have been saying."

"So, what did you tell him?"

"Nothing. Told him that we don't eavesdrop on inmates' visitors, and that he'd have to check the visitors' logs himself to find out how many times you've been here. And, don't worry about that, Mitch. He's not going to find the logs he's looking for."

"Thanks, Willie. Farmer's an asshole. I don't know what he's up to. I used to know him when I was on the force. It didn't end real well."

"Yeah, I figured out the asshole part real quick. He had some other guy with him. I overheard them talking. All I can say is, watch your back, Mitch. If they're not following you, they're trying to keep tabs on you somehow."

"Thanks, Willie. I'll keep an eye out for them." Then Mitch hung up the phone.

"You've got that look," said Louise.

"What look?"

"The how-do-I-keep-this-from-Louise look."

"It's Farmer." Mitch let his shoulders fall a little. "He's making it obvious that he wants me to butt out."

"That's no surprise. Based on what you've told me, he actually believes he solved the case, and that Cleaves was guilty. And now, he doesn't want anything to besmirch his reputation."

"I think there's more to it. I'm pretty sure I was followed today. I can't think of anybody else who would be doing that."

"You do remember, don't you, that you're a private investigator, and that you've got some clients with some really nasty people in their lives."

"I'm comfortable with my cases and who I'm working for or against. This isn't one of them. This is definitely something else, and Farmer's different. He's a blowhard and doesn't have the brains or the guts to be doing something like this on his own. He's already got the job he wants, and Cleaves is dead. He doesn't need to be keeping an eye on me. Somebody else is pulling the strings. Somebody else wants to keep me away from the truth. I'm even a little concerned about Muriel. I hope I didn't drag her into something she doesn't need to be part of."

"Now you're starting to scare me."

Mitch feigned Louise's voice when he said, "And that was my reason for the how-do-I-keep-this-from-Louise look, as you put it."

"I'm a big girl, Mitch. I'd rather know what we are dealing with than have to wonder."

"You're right. I'm not going to hide anything from you. And, I do want you to be real observant and real careful."

"So, what's next?"

"I've gotta see Frankie. I'm pretty sure he screwed with Tommy Cleaves five or six years ago. Why Tommy never told me is something I'll never know. But I'm gonna make sure I get some answers from Frankie."

"So, when are you planning to see him?"

"I'm gonna have to wait awhile and decompress. If I go to see him now I can assure you it wouldn't end well."

"Mitch, I've gotta ask, maybe one last time. Are you sure you want to continue with this?"

"More than ever."

Megan Fields, the self-appointed child and pet caretaker for Holly Avenue, walked up onto Muriel Cathcart's front porch. She was conducting a door-knocking campaign to help locate the Baxters' missing cocker spaniel.

Megan rapped the door knocker several times, but got no response.

"I know she's home," Megan said aloud, "her car is in the driveway." Megan also thought it was her duty to keep tabs on everybody's comings and goings.

Not being the type to just give up and leave, Megan wandered down the porch. She wanted to look through one of the front windows. Megan did know that Muriel and the Baxters never got along very well. *So, who knows?* Megan thought, *maybe she's hiding the dog.* Megan stopped at the first window, pressed her nose up against the glass, and peered inside. What she saw would cause her to let out a screech that was heard for blocks.

When the police arrived, they confirmed Megan's worse fear. The twisted, contorted, and bloody body draped over the end of the living room couch was, indeed, Muriel.

CHAPTER 11

The smell of fried onions drifted onto the street. Biondo's Deli was a popular place to buy hoagies and cheesesteaks on Germantown Avenue in the northwest section of Philadelphia. Hoagies, some parts of the country called them grinders or subs, were a staple of most Philadelphia delicatessens. Most delis also had a large griddle where thinly sliced beef and onions were chopped and fried to make steak sandwiches. Put a few slices of cheese on the pile of simmering meat and onions and it becomes a cheesesteak. To all of this add some fast talking, fast working, rudely impatient counter help, along with a crowd of similarly impatient lunchtime patrons and you've got the quintessential Philadelphia hoagie shop. Biondo's was definitely the place to go to buy lunch or a take-home dinner.

Mitch walked through the front door to a cacophony of sandwich orders being placed and delivered. Mitch had once, on TV, seen the hectic trading floor of the New York Stock Exchange. *This has to be worse*, he thought. Oddly enough, everyone on both sides of the counter seemed to know exactly what was going on and who was being served next.

Mitch finally made eye contact with a counter server who shouted at him, "C'mon, c'mon, c'mon whadda you want?"

"I need to see Frankie, I mean Frank, Frank Biondo," Mitch answered.

"Not here," the man shouted back, then looked at another customer and blurted out, "You, what's it gonna be?"

"Where is he?" Mitch yelled to the server.

"I said he's not in. You deaf?"

Mitch muscled his way to the front of the crowd. He stared directly into the deli worker's eyes, slapped his open wallet and badge on the countertop and repeated, "Where is he?"

"He said he'd be in by four."

"Thanks," Mitch said.

Mitch turned abruptly around and pushed his way back through the crowd of patrons. As he exited the door he heard the counter attendant spit out, "Asshole." Mitch was tempted to stop and go back, but knew it wouldn't be worth it. He'd gotten what he wanted. All he had to do now was wait.

After several trips around the block, Mitch discovered a small gravel parking lot adjacent to the alley behind the deli. From the side street where he was now parked, Mitch had a clear view of the little parking lot. He could also see what he thought was the rear door of Biondo's Deli. His reconnaissance was confirmed when he saw one of the counter help guys, he saw earlier, slip into one of the cars parked in the little lot, and leave. Shortly afterward, at 3:55 p.m., Mitch saw an old yellow Chevy Malibu inch its way down the alley and into the parking lot. A few seconds later Frankie Biondo climbed out of the car, flicked his cigarette away, crossed the alley, and entered the deli through the rear alley door.

Mitch never cared much for stakeouts. And that's what this was pretty much going to be. He didn't want to confront Frankie inside the deli. He wanted to make sure that he had him all alone. So, he slid down a little in his seat, kept the motor running and the heat on, and waited. He really didn't care how long it was going to take.

Mitch's waiting paid off. Four hours later he climbed out of his car as he watched Frankie scamper across the alley. Frankie had pulled his jacket closed and lowered his head in defense of the winds and chilly night air. He was intent on just getting to his car as quickly as possible. He didn't notice the figure walking toward him.

"What's your hurry, Frankie?" Mitch growled.

"What? Mitch, is that you?"

"Surprised, Frankie? Or should I say Harry, as in Harry Burke? Wasn't that the name you used when you visited Tommy in prison?"

A tone of apprehension was evident in Frankie's voice. "What are you doing here?"

"I'll bet some wild thoughts are spinning through your head right now. Aren't they, Frankie boy? Must be asking yourself, what can of worms did I open?"

"C'mon Mitch, I tried talking to you down in Richmond, but you wouldn't listen. I never held nothin' against you."

Mitch couldn't believe his ears. "Never held nothin' against me? What in the hell are you talking about? A man just died for something he didn't do, and we should have been able to stop it. What got into your head all this time? Didn't you ever care?" Mitch grabbed both sides of Frankie's jacket, whirled him around, and slammed him up against the side of his car. "Son of a bitch! What the hell is wrong with you?"

Frankie couldn't stand up to Mitch and he knew it. But he had things he needed to say. With his voice rising an octave, Frankie blurted out, "Am I sorry that worthless piece of shit spent over twenty years in prison for something he didn't do? No. Am I sorry he got the chair for a crime he didn't commit? Not even close. I framed him, Mitch. I framed the no good son of a bitch, and then I visited him in prison and told him what I did."

Mitch dropped his hands, started to turn, then backhanded Frankie across the mouth. He followed up by driving a rock-hard fist into Frankie's gut. Frankie is tall and skinny. Not much of a fighter. The punch doubled him over and sent him sprawling to the ground. Blood dribbled from his mouth and ran down the side of his chin. Mitch jerked Frankie off the ground and, once again, locked him against the side of the car.

"My only regret," Frankie said, as he was gasping for breath, "is that I wasn't in that room to watch him fry."

"Holy shit! I'm not believin' this. What is going on? What's wrong with you?" Mitch's grip tightened as he pressed Frankie harder and harder against the car. Frankie grimaced and turned his head to the side, expecting to get hit again. Then, Mitch dropped his hands from Frankie's jacket. "Oh shit, what's the sense? I don't know what you turned into. I just gotta somehow make myself not care."

"Mitch, I had things I wanted to say to you down at that prison." Frankie pulled a dingy handkerchief from his pocket, padded his cut lip, felt his front teeth, and wiped his mouth clean. "I knew, or at least I was pretty damn sure, you'd be there. Please, man, can we talk?"

Mitch looked at Frankie with a combination of anger and vile disgust.

"Come with me," he said, "but don't make me regret it." They walked over to Mitch's car and he motioned for Frankie to get in the passenger side. "We're not going anywhere," Mitch said. "I just don't want to sit in that piece of shit you're driving." Once inside the car, Mitch turned to Frankie. "Make it good."

Both men sat motionless, with no words spoken for at least thirty seconds.

"Mind if I smoke?" Frankie asked, as much to break the silence as to feed his craving.

"Yeah, I do," Mitch said. "Unlike you, I take care of things."

More silence, much more silence. Then in a barely audible tone, Frankie said, "When I visited Tommy in prison, I had to remind him who I was. That shithead could barely remember something that I'll never forget. Life just ain't fair."

"What are you talking about?"

"He raped me, Mitch. I was twelve years old and he raped me."

"What?"

"Oh, man." Frankie rocked his head back and stared at the car ceiling. "I never told this to another soul."

"If you're making this shit up, I'll kill you. I swear I'll kill you," Mitch said.

"Screw you, Mitch. Just screw you," Frankie screamed. "You have no idea what I went through."

Another pause, another long silence.

"All right, I'm listening." Mitch's tone wasn't sympathetic, nor conciliatory. It was controlled. And it really did mean that he would listen. Then Mitch added, "Roll the window down so you can blow the smoke out. But don't you dare drop an ash inside."

Frankie rolled the window down, reached into his shirt pocket, and pulled out a pack of Marlboros. He shook a cigarette up into the ready position, grabbed it with his lips, and lit it. The familiar metallic snap of a Zippo lighter being closed resonated with Mitch. It brought back pleasant memories and almost made him wish he still smoked. Frankie hung his arm outside, turned his face toward the open window, took a long drag, then exhaled the smoke into the frigid darkness.

"I'll be careful," he said.

Then, Frankie's expression changed, and showed that his mind had drifted back in time. He spoke slowly. "It was two days after they found the girl's body. I hadn't seen you in a couple days, I hoped you weren't mad, and I wanted to find out if you said anything to your parents. So, I came over to your house. When I got there your Mom said you had gone to the rope swing with Terry and Donnie."

"Yeah, I kinda remember that. I was probably real pissed at you if I went and hung out with Terry and Donnie. They were nerds," Mitch said. He kind of laughed.

Frankie continued, "So, I headed over to the hollow where the rope swing was. I took the little path between the Cleaves and the Garwoods. When I was right in between the two houses I saw Tommy Cleaves in their backyard. When he saw me he yelled, 'Hey you, get your ass over here.' I asked if he meant me and he said somethin' like who else would he mean, nobody else is here."

"You didn't run?" Mitch asked.

"I really didn't think I needed to," Frankie said. "Then Cleaves yelled again and said 'C'mon four-eyes, I need some help moving this.' He lifted up the edge of a big piece of plywood and said he needed some help moving it to the other side of their shed. Then he raised his right arm and showed me that he had a little cast around his right wrist and thumb. I figured, what the hell, so I went over and helped him."

Frankie lit a second cigarette off the still glowing stub of the first one.

"As soon as we leaned the plywood up against the other side of the shed I started to leave and he grabbed me by the arm and said he wanted to show me something he had inside the shed. He said he bet I'd never seen anything like it before. So, I asked him what it was."

"Oh shit, Frankie, I know where this is going," Mitch said as he combed his fingers back through his hair.

Frankie looked directly at him. "You don't know shit, Mitch, you don't know shit."

"We went inside the shed and he closed the door. I remember there was a window on the back side of the shed that nobody could see from any of the houses. It was hot as hell in there."

Frankie took a deep drag on his cigarette. "He told me to drop my bathing suit. I don't remember if I said anything, but I tried to leave. He pushed me real hard on the chest and shoved me toward the back of the shed. I remember I scraped my side against the wooden handle of an old push-type lawnmower. It really hurt. Then he told me again to drop my suit and hit me smack on my ear. My ear started ringin' and it hurt really bad. I said to him, 'what are you doing,' and all he said was that I'd find out. Then he smacked me again. Now my ear was screamin' like a fire alarm was going off inside it."

Frankie threw the half-smoked cigarette into the darkness and lit another one. He remained quiet for a long while. Then he said, "So I did what he told me to do and dropped my bathing suit. I thought maybe he's just goofy and wants to look at me, or maybe he's gonna take my bathin' suit and run off. But that wasn't it. He grabbed me, turned me around, pushed me down real hard, and stood there, holdin' me down with his foot on my butt. I didn't know what all he was doing while he was standing there, but it seemed like he was tryin' to unbuckle his own pants. Then he dropped down to his knees behind me with one hand pushin' real hard on the back of my neck."

Frankie drew on his cigarette, and slowly shook his head back and forth a couple times. "Then it happened, Mitch. He did it to me."

Mitch could hardly believe what he was hearing. His temples began to pulsate. He felt like he was being choked.

"I started to scream and he held my mouth shut. I don't know how long this went on, but when he was done he said to me that we weren't finished for the day and that I had some more surprises coming. Then the son of a bitch tied me up. He tied my hands together real tight and then tied the other end of the cord to one of the shed rafters. He picked up a nasty old rag off the floor, smelled like gasoline, and tied it around my mouth as a gag. Then he left."

Mitch was dumbfounded. "Frankie, I don't know what to say."

"There's nothin' you can say. None of his family was home. I was there for a couple hours. He did it all over again, plus other stuff. He made me do some things. You know what I'm talking about. I try not to remember everything he did. I've forced a lot of it out of my mind. I was so scared. I was cryin' so much. I thought he was gonna kill me. Finally he untied me and told me I could leave. But he said that if I mentioned a word of it to anybody that he knew where I lived and that he'd beat me to death and burn Nana's house to the ground with her in it. He told me that he was the one that burnt down Cyrus Beck's house 'cause the old geaser yelled at him one time and shot a BB gun at him for trespassin' on his pier. He said everybody thought a lightning strike started that fire, but it was really him. He was just able to make it look like a lightning strike. I was a kid, I believed him."

Mitch couldn't look at him. He directed his gaze at his leather covered steering wheel.

"It's gets worse," Frankie said. "I ran all the way home, and then hid in the garage. I hurt really bad. After a while I went inside and told Nana I wasn't feelin' too good and wanted to lay down. Told her I had eaten a mess of green apples. She got angry with me. I didn't care."

Frankie lit another cigarette and stared out the window with vacant eyes. Mitch felt like he had stepped into a nightmare, somebody else's nightmare, and he couldn't even begin to think of a way out or to help.

Frankie continued in a somber monotone. "After I was in my room for a little while something else hit me out of the blue. My glasses, my glasses got knocked off in the shed and that's where they still were. I had already lost a pair that summer out in the river, and got in big trouble for it. Now I panicked."

"After all you'd been through, you panicked over your glasses?" Mitch asked.

"Yeah, you gotta understand how messed up I was. My head was spinning. I hurt like crazy, I was still bleeding, this was just like a final straw or somethin'. I couldn't stand the thought of gettin' into anymore trouble. It was startin' to get dark, so I told Nana I was feelin' a little better and had left somethin' over at your house and had to go get it."

"So, you went back to the shed?"

"Yeah, and the son of a bitch caught me and did me again. I bit my tongue, hung onto my glasses, and when he started to get off me I grabbed my bathing suit, bolted, and took off running."

"It took a few days before I totally stopped bleedin' and started to feel a little better. All that time I had to act better than I felt to keep Nana from finding out about it."

"And you never told your dad or anybody?"

"No, nobody. Not until now. I was too scared and ashamed to tell my dad." Frankie took a long, hard draw on the cigarette. "In retrospect, all this Tommy shit would've been taken care of if I had told him."

"What do you mean?"

"As I've learned since then, my family, especially my extended family, has a pretty fatal philosophy, regarding retribution for grievous wrongdoings. Tommy would've met his maker a long time ago."

Mitch's head nodded slightly forward as if in deep thought. He then turned slightly and cut his eyes in Frankie's direction. "You never got any kind of professional help?" he asked.

"Oh sure, I was gonna go spill my guts to a shrink."

With each word he spoke, Frankie got more and more careless about cigarette smoke inside the car. Mitch no longer seemed to mind.

"Oh shit, yeah I thought about it. I mean my life has been so totally screwed up. I've had nightmares all these years. I've had problems with women. My relationships have all sucked."

"But you never got help, you never told anybody. Why?" Mitch asked again.

"You're asking me, why," Frankie said. "What about you, Mitch? Did you ever tell anyone that your piece of shit dad used to beat you with a belt? We all saw the welts and bruises on the backs of your legs.

Don't look so damned surprised. I came over to your cottage one night to see if you could come out. I got to the front door and heard you wailin' and saw your dad beatin' the crap outta your ass with his belt buckle. I just went away. Next day you acted like nothin' ever happened. But me and Nana could see the marks with our own eyes. You never told anybody."

"That was bad, but that was way different," Mitch responded. "I never experienced anything like you did, Frankie. And I mean it, there are people who can help with this stuff."

Frankie lit another cigarette, blew the smoke out the window and whispered barely loud enough for Mitch to hear, "Yeah, like you'd really know." Then Frankie turned to face Mitch and said, "I guess you could say I did get some help. Last month, down in Richmond, the guy in the execution chamber that threw the switch that lit Tommy up—he helped me real good. Yeah, I know you think it's real bad that Tommy died for something he didn't do. But he really was a murderer, Mitch. So what if he didn't kill that girl? He didn't kill me either, but sometimes I wish he did, because what he killed was worse, he killed my spirit."

"It doesn't have to be that way, Frankie. I'm not gonna pretend that I can appreciate what you've been through. But you can repair it, you've still got a life. And now you've got your retribution. The Spencer family doesn't know it, but they don't even have that. I've been beating myself up for years thinking I should be able to do something to find justice, real justice for that family. Kathleen Spencer is dead and her killer is walking free. What does she have?"

Frankie opened the door, got out, and walked around the car to Mitch's side. Mitch rolled down his window.

"I'll tell you what she's got, Mitch," Frankie said. "She's got peace. Maybe she doesn't have justice. But where she's at, she doesn't have to think about it anymore."

Frankie turned and walked away.

CHAPTER 12

"What do you mean you lost him?" Farmer paced back and forth in front of the sparsely populated bookcase in his office.

Dolf Richter fidgeted ever so slightly in a straight-back chair in front of Farmer's desk. Farmer had modified the legs to make the chair a slight bit wobbly. He thought that would put most visitors at a disadvantage and give him an upper hand in whatever business matter was being discussed. Dolf was uncomfortable and a little nervous, but not frightened, at least not yet. He had no fear of Ken Farmer. However, he was thinking of Farmer's boss, and that was cause for alarm. It wasn't Farmer's boss at the capitol or the governor's office who made him feel this way. It was the man who had been Farmer's real boss for the past twenty-five years. It was the Old Man who frightened him.

Dolf first met the Old Man a little over twenty years ago. The Old Man had been informed of Dolf's successful criminal activities on the streets of Richmond, such as extortion, blackmail, numbers, drugs, and a few rumored murders. He commended Dolf for his work, but made it very clear that nothing happens in Richmond without his approval. He also informed Dolf that Ken Farmer would thereafter be his point of contact.

"Do you have any idea how important this is to the Old Man?" Farmer continued. "Didn't I make that clear to you? Didn't I tell you to personally be part of the team, watching Armstrong?"

"You did and I was," Dolf spit the words back at Farmer. "It was downtown Philadelphia, we got cut off by a cab driver, and we lost him. But we went on to the address he was supposed to be going to, sat across the street and watched. To the best of our knowledge, Armstrong never showed up."

"You need to find out who he was planning to meet there."

"I know that. The tap on his house phone is up and working now. The recorder in your home office should start picking up everything. I've got one too."

"One other thing, Richter, I think we both know that Armstrong is no dummy. If he isn't already, he's gonna start being very suspicious and cautious. And he can be dangerous. I've got a guy that I'm going to hook you up with. He can be very helpful."

"I pick my own crew, Farmer. You know that."

"Not this time. His name is Turk. I've seen what he can do."

"I don't care what his name is. I said I pick my own crew."

"And I said, not this time. This is a strong recommendation from the Old Man."

Dolf let out a deep breath of exasperation and dropped his shoulders ever so slightly. "Okay. Let me get back to work."

"No more screw-ups, Richter. We've both got a lot riding on this."

Dolf bit his tongue and, inside his own head, cursed bitterly. He hated Farmer.

Mitch's return from Philadelphia was a little more pleasant. Louise was awake and waiting for him.

"So, how'd it go?" she asked, with a slight hint of apprehension.

"I wouldn't say we mended fences. We're not the best of friends again, but I understand a little more. At least, I somewhat appreciate where he's coming from."

Mitch then spilled out the details of his conversation with Frankie.

"I guess some of your questions got answered," Louise said, "but did it help you get any closer to what you're looking for?"

"Not really. Or, let me put it differently. If it did, I just don't see it yet."

"You need some rest, sweetie. Things always look better in the morning."

"Hmmm. Some things look pretty good right now."

"Then why don't you crawl into bed and I'll show you just how good those things might be."

The love-making was intense. Mitch was exhausted. His sleep fell over him like a coma. And then …

"Son of a bitch!"

Louise, deep in her sleep coma, jostled and grunted something unintelligible.

Mitch fumbled in the dark and knocked the ringing phone off the nightstand. He swung his feet out from under the covers and onto the floor, reached down and located the receiver with his right hand, then picked up the phone base with his left.

"What!" he barked.

"Mitch, is that you?"

"Of course it's me. Who in the hell are you?"

"It's me, Frankie."

Mitch turned on the nightstand lamp and looked at the alarm clock. "Do you have any idea what time it is? It's four o'clock in the friggin' morning."

"Sorry, Mitch, but I been up all night thinking, and I gotta tell you somethin'."

"Oh, this had better be good."

"Listen to me, Mitch," Frankie said, "it was a red '56 T-bird."

A puzzled look crossed Mitch's face. "What in the hell are you talking about?"

"The day the Spencer girl got killed. I saw her in a red '56 T-bird. The guy drivin' it was the same guy who was with her on the beach that night."

"Gimme a minute. I gotta wake up," Mitch said. He set the receiver down and turned off the lamp.

"Who is it?" asked Louise, now waking from a deep sleep.

"I'll take it in the kitchen. Just hang up when I've got it."

"Sure," she said. "You know? Sometimes I think your clients are real assholes."

"It's not a client. I'll fill you in later."

Mitch closed the bedroom door behind him, clicked on the hall light and walked to the kitchen. He took the glass pot from the coffee maker and poured a cup of yesterday's coffee, put it in the microwave, and picked up the phone.

"I've got it," he said.

After he heard the rattle and click of the bedroom phone being placed back onto its cradle, Mitch said, "I hope you know how you're screwing up my morning, Frankie."

"Sorry. I know you're not gonna believe it, but my conscience started bothering me. All that shit you said about justice and retribution, it started getting to me. Now, I'm just trying to help."

"So what's this about a red T-bird?"

"I don't know if you remember or not," Frankie said, "but once in a while we used to see a red '56 T-bird cruisin' the streets through Bohman's Point."

"Vaguely. I remember there was a '57 Chevy that always caught my attention. C'mon, Frankie, what's this all about?"

"Well, it doesn't really matter if you remember or not. I'm tellin' ya, Kathleen Spencer was riding in it the day she got murdered, and the guy driving it was the same guy who was with her that night on the beach."

Mitch dropped his head slightly, and squeezed the bridge of his nose. "How much more is there to this story?"

"A lot."

"Let's not do this on the phone," said Mitch. "We need to talk face to face."

"I'll spot you half the distance," said Frankie. "How about if we meet somewhere on I-95 up around Baltimore?"

Mitch took a deep breath and tried to visualize a map in his head. After a short pause he said, "That'll work. There's a little chicken and ribs place called Skipper's Barbecue, right off the exit at White Marsh. I think it's exit sixty-seven or sixty-eight. What day is good for you?"

"I'm my own boss."

"Then it's today at noon. I'll see you there."

"Okay."

"Frankie, don't make me drive there for nothin'."

"You're gonna trust me again, Mitch. I promise it."

Mitch hung up the phone and retrieved his coffee cup from the microwave.

Seventy-five miles away and only moments after it received the disconnect signal from Mitch's phone, the automatic recorder in Ken Farmer's home office shut off.

Sitting at the kitchen table Mitch started racking his brain one more time for details of that summer. This is a drill that he's done over and over again for the past twenty-five years, searching for the one elusive piece of information that he's somehow continued to miss. He thought that he kind of remembered a red T-bird, but he never attached any special significance to it. There had been lots of guys coming to Bohman's Point and lots of cars that, as a kid, he could only dream about.

Mitch picked up his coffee, opened the kitchen door, and stepped onto the back porch. It was late March and still cold at night, not suitable for his bare feet, boxers, and T-shirt, but the elements didn't seem to be touching him right now.

Mitch's thoughts were running all over the place. *I may not be a religious man, but I truly think I was meant to be on the beach that night. That poet, Emerson, was dead on. Wherever a man commits a crime, God finds a witness. There's a son of a bitchin' murderer out there, walking free, and I'm gonna nail his ass. Frankie, maybe you really are back in my life for a reason.*

"You really think I can go back to sleep?" Louise was standing in the kitchen doorway.

"It was Frankie. I guess our meeting was a little more fruitful than I thought."

"Why, what did he say?"

"It sounds like he's got a little more insight into the guy we saw on the beach than I thought he did. He wants to meet and talk about it."

"When and where?"

"I'm not giving him time to change his mind. I told him today. We're going to split the distance and meet at Skipper's up on the other side of Baltimore."

"Are you okay, sweetie? You're looking really—how should I say it? Troubled."

He responded to Louise, but he was really giving himself the third degree. "What if there *is* something to whatever Frankie's going to say? What if this leads me someplace? What good will it really do? Like everybody says, Tommy was a piece of shit, anyhow. Now, he's dead. So, why bother? The Spencers are satisfied, wrongly, but they don't know that. Is it worth all this trouble or am I just feeding some stupid, self-serving desire to right a wrong?"

"I'm concerned, Mitch. I'm not concerned that you're all of a sudden consumed by this again. It never left you. I'm just concerned about you and what this is doing to you."

"I know. I appreciate it. I'm not going to let it get the best of me. I love you."

"Love you, too. And don't you ever forget, I also want to help. Any way I can."

"Thanks, Weezie, I know you do."

"Hey, watch it buddy! You know, using that name—grounds for divorce."

"Sorry, forgot."

"Yeah, right. Anyway, no going back to sleep for me. I'm going to go shower and get ready for work," said Louise as she walked away.

"Not sure when I'll get home today," said Mitch.

"Okay. Just be safe."

"I will."

CHAPTER 13

Skipper's isn't fancy. The little restaurant began life as a small rib shack that once looked like nothing more than a poorly constructed backyard project. It was a big green wooden box with fold-down plywood shutters that were opened and closed with clothesline and pulleys to reveal two screened windows—one to place an order and the other to pick it up. That old shack is now a monument to great food and word-of-mouth advertising. The green wooden box is gone and in its place is a log cabin diner with enough seating for fifty or more people. It also has a brisk carry-out business. It's still just chicken and ribs and a few sides, but those who have eaten there say you couldn't want anything more.

"All right, Armstrong, now I'm gonna find out who this friend of yours is." Dolf had been sitting in the parking lot for an hour. He watched as Mitch exited his car and walked over to the entrance to Skipper's.

Mitch walked in, looked around, and saw Frankie sitting in one of the lacquered and well-worn wooden booths. Two bottles of National Bohemian beer sat in front of him, one on his white paper placemat and one on the placemat on the opposite side of the booth. Mitch slid onto the wooden bench seat across from his former friend.

"You clean up better than I thought you would," said Mitch. "Maybe it's because this is the first time I've seen you in daylight in decades."

"Hope you like Natty Boh. I ordered one for you," said Frankie.

"This is Baltimore. It's against the law not to like it."

Mitch stared hard at Frankie, who kept averting his gaze.

"We'll talk," said Frankie, "just quit looking at me like that."

"You're different," said Mitch. "Take off those goofy glasses and you kind of look like Sal Mineo. I didn't think that when we were kids." Frankie stared, blankly, at him, so Mitch explained. "Sal Mineo was a singer, in a movie too with James Dean."

"I know who Sal Mineo was," Frankie interrupted, "you don't need to explain it to me. And I'll take that as a compliment. But my glasses aren't goofy, they're called horn rimmed, they're stylish. It's retro-fashion. And that's more than I can say for you. Damn, Mitch, you look like an old leather shoe that was left out in the rain. You're scary as shit. Do you know that?"

"People have told me," said Mitch, "but don't blame my parents. It's not all genetic. A sawed-off twelve gauge had a lot to do with it."

"Holy shit! Man, I'm sorry."

"Things happen for a reason. If it wasn't for that shotgun, I'd have never met my wife. I've got no complaints at all."

"Married, huh? Lucky guy. How about your parents, how they doing?"

"Both gone. My mother died in a car accident. My dad died drunk, after a weekend bender with a hooker in Atlantic City."

"Sorry."

"Your parents okay?"

"Yeah, they're hanging in. Starting a retirement countdown."

"So, what is it, Frankie. What's all this about a red T-bird?"

"Let's order first," said Frankie.

He motioned to the waitress who was passing the table with a tray full of steaming plates. She returned shortly thereafter and took their order for two chicken and rib specials with coleslaw and baked beans.

"And two more Natty Bohs," Frankie added.

"Sure thing, sweetie, got you covered."

Frankie turned his attention to Mitch.

"The day it happened. When I went over to your place to get you to go out with me and Nana to get some corn, I walked past the Spencers' cottage. I saw the red T-bird parked out front. The top was off so I walked up to it and was looking at it real good when they came out of the cottage."

"Who exactly do you mean by they?"

"Kathleen and some guy. Never saw him before, at least I didn't recognize him. I figured he was her boyfriend. They were laughing and she was hanging all over him. He made some wise-ass comment to me about maybe I should stop drooling, and maybe when I grow up I can get one too. Then he said that I probably didn't know which one he was talking about, the car or the girl. She giggled at that. They both got into the car and she turned around and looked at me. God, she was beautiful, Mitch. We'd never gotten that close to her before. I could smell her. It was real fresh, real clean smelling. I'll never forget it. Of course, what she said next made me feel like a jerk. She called me a little boy and told me not to worry, that I'd grow up someday. Then they took off."

"I gave 'em the finger. He must've seen me in the mirror 'cause he hit the brakes. I took off running. Went straight to your place. Just never said anything about it."

"So you got a real good look at that guy?" asked Mitch.

"Oh, I sure did. I saw him and I heard him. He had a strong voice, not real deep but real mature. We would have called it old sounding."

Frankie paused, took a sip of his beer, and stared out the window.

After waiting several more seconds Mitch prompted him, "And …?"

"And he was definitely the same guy that was on the beach that night with Kathleen," said Frankie. "Not a doubt in my mind. He was the guy that killed her."

"Shit, this is making my life hard. Any hope I ever had of letting this go is gone."

"Sorry, Mitch, I'm actually trying to make it easier."

"Here you go boys." The waitress placed the plates of barbecued ribs and chicken on the table. "I'll be right back with your sides."

"Thanks, Paulette," said Mitch.

"Paulette? You know her?" queried Frankie.

"It's on her nametag you moron." Mitch shook his head. "You haven't changed, Frankie. You never look both ways, you just walk out into the street."

"At least I know how to charm women."

"What's that supposed to mean?"

"Before you got here, she was real chatty with me. Wanted to know where I was from and all that kind of stuff. But once you arrived she's kept her distance."

"She probably thinks you're gay and I'm your boyfriend."

"You wish. You're so full of shit."

For the next forty-five minutes they were just two men having lunch together. They picked at the ribs and chicken on their plates, licked barbecue sauce off their fingers, and drank National Bohemian beer. They talked about football and how terrible it was that the Baltimore Colts snuck out of town in the middle of the night and went to Indianapolis. They reminisced about the good old days of number nineteen, Johnny Unitas. They ordered two more beers. Time passed more quickly than either would have imagined.

Mitch changed the subject back to the reason for their meeting. "Frankie, this morning on the phone you said there was a lot more to the T-bird story. I haven't heard it yet."

"It's not so much the T-bird as it is what happened on the beach."

Mitch raised his eyebrows. "Keep going."

"I told you that night that when Kathleen and the guy were yelling at each other I couldn't make out what they were saying. That's not entirely true. While you were laid out with that knot on your head, I actually did hear some of what they said, and saw a little bit more of what was going on. More than I ever told anybody. I still don't know for sure what started the fight, but I definitely heard the guy say that he'd go find somebody, beat the shit out of him and tell everyone he did it because she had been raped. Then he'd be some kind of hero."

"So he said somebody raped her?"

"No. He just said he'd tell people that. So she says to him to go ahead, but she'll tell the truth and everyone will know what a liar he is. Then she started crying and screaming at him. I couldn't understand everything she was saying. But she did say that she hated him. She started backing away and he grabbed her by the wrist and pulled her toward him. Then she said something about look what you did now, you broke my bracelet."

"The charm bracelet?"

"Yeah. He said it was no big deal and he'd buy her a new one. She picked it up and threw it at him. The next morning before I went over to your cottage, I went back down to the beach and found it. Didn't show you, 'cause I was really scared about all this. I didn't know if we were gonna get into any kind of trouble or not. We were kids, Mitch. Dumb little kids."

"How did it end that night at the beach?"

"Pretty much like I told you back then. He said some things I couldn't hear too well. I saw him hit her. Then he picked her up, kicked some sand on the fire, and walked off, back toward Beck's pier. I heard 'em start arguing again, real loud. Then I heard 'em splashing around in the water. I don't know what happened next, but they finally stopped yelling. A little while after that I heard a car, the T-bird, I could tell by the sound of its pipes, up on top of the hill above the steps. I listened as it drove away. When I felt sure everyone was gone I went to see how you were. Man, you really did get knocked out. I was scared shitless."

"You've got no idea at all who owned that T-bird or where it came from?"

Frankie shook his head. "Not a clue. Never saw it but those couple of times that summer, and never saw it again."

"And Ken Farmer never had any reason to look for it, because he never knew about it, plus he found evidence in Tommy's car," said Mitch.

"Who's Ken Farmer?"

"He's the asshole detective who investigated this case, and eventually arrested Tommy."

"Did he question you about it?" asked Frankie.

"He talked to a lot of people at Bohman's Point. He did stop by our place, but my dad wouldn't let me talk to him. He just told Farmer that none of us knew anything. At the time, I was kind of glad he said that."

"Why'd you say that Farmer was an asshole?"

"I've got my reasons."

Frankie gave Mitch a quizzical look, then dropped his gaze when it became obvious that Mitch wasn't going to elaborate.

"I didn't remember his name, but he must have been the one that talked to me and Nana about a week after it happened," said Frankie. "Because of where Nana's house was, he wanted to know if we had seen or heard anything. I asked him, when I was all alone with him, if he would keep what I said secret, and he said yes. So I told him the only thing I had seen that day was a car parked up at the top of the steps above Beck's pier. I said it was early in the evening when I saw it. I told him that I couldn't say for sure, but that the car looked a lot like Tommy Cleaves's car."

"All of which was total bullshit," said Mitch.

"Right. But he said he'd come back the next day and have a visit with Cleaves. Called him Mr. Cleaves. And I asked him again if he'd keep it secret and not tell anybody, even Cleaves, that I'm the one who had told him all this stuff. He said he wouldn't tell."

"So that night you went and put the charm bracelet in Tommy's car."

"Yeah, I did."

"Minus one of the charms."

"You're a good detective, Mitch."

"Was a good detective, but that's another story. Do you still have the charm?"

Tommy reached into his pocket and pulled out a small, folded up brown envelope, the kind you get from the bank to put currency in. He opened it up and shook out a small silver charm, the silhouette of a girl's head wearing a graduation cap. Inscribed on one side were the initials, *KMS*, and the date, *5-16-59*. On the other side, *Love, Mom & Dad.*

"And did you show this to Tommy, the time you visited him in prison?"

"Yeah. It really set him off."

"You're not making any of this shit up are you, Frankie?"

"I'm not making up a damn thing. I've already used up all the lies I get in this lifetime. I already told you what happened to me that summer. Unlike your shotgun-in-the-face story, my nightmare never had a happy ending. Maybe there's a way now for me to get some good out of it. I don't know."

"I've got to think on this for a while," said Mitch. "I'd like to believe I can call on you again, Frankie. This case has eaten at me for years. Every road I took turned out to be a dead end. Now I'm looking down one more tunnel with one more flicker of light at the end of it. Don't snuff it out on me. Don't play games with me."

"I'm not screwing with you, Mitch. It might be hard for you to believe, but I really do want to help you. It's nothing about Cleaves or anything to change how people might think of him. Like I told you, as far as I'm concerned, he got what he deserved. But there were some things you said. It's about the Spencers, it's about you, it's about justice, I guess. You got to me Mitch. I really do want to help."

"Here you go gents." Paulette placed the credit card receipt and Frankie's credit card on the table. Frankie had given it to her when he first arrived at Skipper's.

"My treat, Mitch."

"Thanks. You didn't have to, but thanks anyway."

As they started to stand up, Mitch's eyebrows came together forming a very curious expression.

"Let me see that," said Mitch. Reaching across the table he picked up Frankie's credit card. "You gotta be shitting me. Your name's Francis?" Mitch said with mocking incredulity in his voice.

Mitch was smiling for the first time since their lunch meeting began.

"Francis," he repeated, dropping the credit card back onto the table. "Francis. I'll be damned, you learn something new every day."

"Oh, screw you, Mitch, it's just a name."

"Yeah, but Francis? All this time and you never told me. You didn't have to use it in school did you?"

"Don't be such an asshole. It's a name, a family name. Lots of people are named Francis—Francis Scott Key for example. But you probably don't even know who that is."

"Then why did your family call you Frankie? Your real name wasn't tough enough?"

"Stop being such an asshole."

"Man oh man, Francis, who would've guessed?"

"Asshole."

"But you still like me. Even after all these years. I guess I just brought out the best in you."

"It's typically women that do that, Mitch. Or are you trying to tell me something?"

"Watch it tough guy, or should I say—Francis?"

They walked out of Skipper's looking like two old friends, comfortable in the ease with which they spoke to each other. All the way across the parking lot Mitch kept repeating, "Francis," and Frankie kept shoving him on the shoulder.

"Well look at that," Dolf muttered to himself. "I think I've located Armstrong's friend."

Dolf followed Frankie back to Philadelphia. Frankie had no reason to suspect that he was being followed and went straight to the Deli. Dolf parked about two blocks away from the Deli entrance, rolled up his shirt sleeves, mussed his hair a little, and tried to look as casual as possible. Five minutes later he walked through the Deli entrance and straight to the man at the cash register. After checking out two other patrons, the cashier looked at Dolf.

"Place orders over there," the cashier said as he pointed toward the long counter where several other customers were standing.

"I'm not here to get something. I was just wondering if you had any job openings."

"Don't know. You'd have to talk to the owner and he's busy now. Try later."

"Well, if I come back later, who do I ask for?"

"The owner, didn't you hear me?"

"Doesn't the owner have a name? He'd probably like it if I could call him Mr. Smith or whatever."

"Yeah, sure. It's Biondo, Frankie Biondo."

"Thanks. I'll be back."

Dolf turned away and walked out of the Deli. He then drove back to Skipper's. He needed to speak to Paulette.

Back at Skipper's, Dolf kept his conversation with Paulette as brief as possible. She had no idea that just about everything Dolf said to her was a lie. She was under the impression that she was actually helping a police matter being run by her uncle, Ken Farmer.

"This has really turned out to be a very fortunate turn of events. When we found out that those two were meeting here, and your Uncle Ken remembered that you worked here. You can be a big help to us Paulette."

"I'll try. I'm just excited that I'm kind of involved in a police investigation like this. It was great that the first one told me he was expecting a friend. It kind of tipped me off that it was probably the two you were interested in."

"Well, these are bad men," said Dolf, "so you need to be careful." He then looked around, and feigned concern that someone might be watching them. "They're very involved in drug smuggling and anything you can remember will really be appreciated."

Paulette was giddy with excitement. "I really couldn't hear a lot of what they were saying. But they were here for a long time and did a lot of talking. From the expressions on their faces, I'd say they were discussing some pretty serious stuff."

"But you never heard anything specific. Is that right?"

"That's right, I really didn't hear anything, but I did see something. I was walking by when I saw that one of them was showing the other something that looked like a charm or a little pendant—maybe from a necklace or charm bracelet. It had really gotten their attention. Do you think it means something?"

"Could be. You're doing great, Paulette. Every little thing helps."

"Oh, I almost forgot, I got one of their names. The one who paid, I saw his credit card. His name is Francis Biondo."

"That's terrific, Paulette. I thought that was his name, but now you've confirmed it. Good job."

Paulette's face expanded with a big self-congratulatory grin. They chatted a few more minutes, with Dolf making up stories about the drug trade and how important this case was.

Dolf yawned and said, "It's getting late and I've got a bit of a drive ahead of me."

It wasn't so much the drive that he was thinking about. Dolf was just getting weary of chatting about made-up stuff with a twenty-something waitress.

"I'm not sure if they will ever be back in here. But if they ever plan to come back and we hear about it, we'll contact you and ask for more help. On the other hand, if they ever show up unexpectedly, please listen and find out anything you can and then give your uncle a call."

"Oh, I certainly will. It was really nice talking to you, Mr. Richter."

"Okay, Paulette, take care."

Dolf left and returned to Richmond, fantasizing his next move.

CHAPTER 14

"It's Biondo, B-I-O-N-D-O, Francis Biondo. But he goes by Frank or Frankie." Dolf was on the phone, reporting the details of his latest find to Ken Farmer. "Mean anything to you?"

"Sounds familiar, but I can't place it right now," responded Farmer. "I'll get back to you, so don't wander off. We've still got a lot to do."

"Sure," Dolf replied, then hung up.

"Biondo, Biondo, Biondo," Farmer kept muttering to himself, "dammit, I know that from somewhere."

Farmer pulled the Kathleen Spencer case file from its drawer and started thumbing through it. *It's gotta have something to do with this, otherwise, why would Armstrong be tracking this guy down? Damn, I need that son of a bitch off my back.*

When Mitch got home, Louise was still at the hospital. She had mentioned that she had a couple patients on the ward she needed to check on that evening. What Mitch did find was a note from Louise saying that Willie Baker had called, and that he wanted Mitch to call back, no matter what time it was. He left a couple of numbers. Mitch heated up a cup of coffee and then called Willie.

"I hope you're sitting down, Mitch," were Willie's first words.

"Why, what's up?"

"Muriel Cathcart, that lady you asked about, she was one of the witnesses."

"Yeah, I went to see her. What about her?"

"Well," then Willie hesitated, "she's dead."

"What? What happened? She seemed fine when I left her. Wasn't acting sick or complaining about anything."

"I hate to say this, Mitch, but I think the only thing wrong with her was that she got a visit from you, a visit that somebody else wasn't happy about. It looks like she's been murdered."

"What? You're shittin' me!"

"I wish I was. We're just hearing it, second hand, here. So I don't have all the details. But it's coming from a couple different sources. Not sure if they're reporting it on the news yet or not."

"This is unbelievable. Who found her?"

"Some neighbor lady. From what I hear, she really freaked out and called everybody—the local police, state police, mayor's office, and anybody else she could think of." Willie stopped and drew a deep breath. "Mitch, are they going to find your fingerprints there?"

Mitch's mind was swirling. Finally, he said, "Probably not." After another pregnant pause, he added, "I gotta go. Willie, let me know if you hear anything else."

"Sure thing. Talk to you later."

This wasn't making any sense. Why her? Then, Mitch started thinking about what Willie said about fingerprints. Mitch knew he shouldn't be concerned. He had a legitimate reason for visiting her, he felt. It's just that if Farmer got wind of it, and thought he could implicate Mitch, he would. Mitch worked to relive the visit in his head in as much detail as his mind would allow. *It was cold and I was wearing gloves when I lifted the brass door knocker. Inside, I'm certain that I didn't touch anything that could've picked up a print except for the dishes and silverware when we had the coffee and rolls. But she put all of them into a sink full of soap and water right before I left. There were big placemats on the table we sat at. I don't think they're going to find my prints anywhere.*

Biondo. There it was. Farmer found it.

That was the kid that led me to Cleaves. I talked to him and his grand-mother. He's the one that told me Cleaves's car was at the scene. Farmer suddenly jerked upright and his eyes bugged open. "Son-of-a-bitch," he said aloud. "Cleaves's car and the charm bracelet I found in it. Paulette told Dolf those two were looking at something like a charm from a charm bracelet. This Biondo guy must know something." Farmer took a deep breath, then let it out slowly. "It's definitely time to tighten the screws."

Just then Farmer's private office phone rang.

Ken answered the phone, "Farmer."

"Tell me we are getting close to shutting this down. I just heard about the Cathcart woman." The Old Man had a hint of frustration in his voice.

"We learned enough to make it worth it. I promise you the whole matter will be put to rest real soon."

"I'm not a patient man, Ken. When I say get something done, I like to know it's getting done."

"You can be sure that ..." Once again, Ken found himself talking to a dial tone.

Damn you, Armstrong. I think it's time to see about making you go away for good.

CHAPTER 15

O ver the next few months, Mitch finished some jobs for other
clients. He also spent plenty of time with Louise, just the two
of them. Then, in the waning days of summer, he scheduled
an appointment to meet with Bill Spencer.

"Are you sure about this?" Louise asked Mitch before he left the
house. "From what you've told me about this man, I doubt he'll be real
happy to see you. We're having a nice summer, don't let him ruin it for
you."

During his three and a half hour drive to see Bill Spencer, Mitch
pondered what Louise had said. He has faced burglars, thieves, mur-
derers, rapists, just about any of the cast asides that society can spew
up. He has comforted the injured. He has informed spouses and parents that a loved one has been killed or is missing. Despite the harden-
ing of the soul that seems to accompany this line of work, Mitch held
on to a compassionate side that was very real to those who knew him,
even if it was rarely seen by those who didn't. It was that other part of
Mitch that made him second-guess what he was about to do more than
anytime he could remember.

Bill Spencer is a department head and principles-of-accounting
instructor at Delaware County Community College in Media, Pennsylvania. Bill was once energetic and had a zest for life that many

people said was antithetical to the sometimes mundane nature of his work. He began his professional career working as an accountant for a very large firm of tax attorneys, married Margaret, his college sweetheart, eventually became a CPA, and started his own company. He soon tired of the entrepreneurial routine and felt the world of academia calling him. He sold his business and became Professor Spencer. The hours were better, the responsibilities fewer, and the benefits couldn't be matched. He finally settled into, what he considered, the good life with Margaret, and the joy of their lives, their daughter, Kathleen. She was their only child, and Bill doted on her. She wasn't spoiled, she was just incredibly loved.

Kathleen graduated from high school in 1959 and was accepted at West Chester State Teachers' College for the fall semester of that year. She planned to be an elementary school teacher. Bill and Margaret couldn't have been more proud of their daughter.

Unfortunately, it all came crashing down on a hot, humid, summer morning. The Spencers were spending the summer at Bohman's Point in a cottage that belonged to one of Bill Spencer's relatives. At approximately one o'clock in the morning of August 22, 1959, Bill and Margaret went to the pay phone outside of the Bohman General Store to call the state police. Their daughter, Kathleen, had not come home. She left a note on the previous day saying she would be out with friends for the rest of the afternoon and evening. That wasn't unusual. It was unusual that she was not home by midnight.

A state police trooper arrived at the Spencer's cottage within thirty minutes. He took a statement from the Spencers and tried to assure them that their concerns were probably based on nothing more than kids being kids. Nine hours later another trooper had to deliver the news that Kathleen's body had been found in the water adjacent to Beck's pier.

Bill Spencer never recovered. His demeanor soured, and his personality turned inward. As much as his wife, Margaret, tried over the ensuing years, she could never get Bill out of the depression that engulfed him. They lived. They existed. They carried on. Margaret tried her best to make something positive out of life. Bill, on the other hand, never again truly experienced joy.

Mitch now faced the self-imposed task of trying to explain to Bill Spencer why he believed that the man who was just recently executed for the murder of Bill's daughter is not the man who committed the crime.

Several days ago, with a phone number provided by Willie Baker, Mitch called Bill. The conversation didn't go real well and, much to Mitch's displeasure, he had to stretch the truth a bit.

"I hope you don't think I'm being insensitive," Mitch said during the phone call. "But I'm doing some research for a paper I'm writing on the social impact of the death penalty, and how it affects the people closest to the case that led to someone's execution."

"And you want to interview me?" Bill responded. "I think that's pretty sick."

"Please sir, I really don't want to dredge up a hurtful past. But the work we are doing might be able to help someone else who is facing a similar set of circumstances." Mitch didn't like to mask the truth, even a little bit, especially with people like Bill who were suffering a loss. He promised himself that someday he would indeed write such a paper.

"All right, I'll meet with you," Bill finally agreed. "But don't count on it being much of an interview."

Mitch was now sitting on a very uncomfortable oak bench outside an office that was marked with a two-line identification, Dr. William J. Spencer, PhD, on the first line, Department Head on the second. The department secretary, Mrs. Penny, told Mitch that Professor Spencer would be with him shortly. She then went back to her work with no offer of coffee, water, or a place to hang his jacket.

After five minutes, the door opened and Bill Spencer stepped out of his office, stared at Mitch disapprovingly, then with a curl of his index finger motioned Mitch to follow him back inside.

Bill's office was Spartan. Like the outer office, it had rustic looking oak furniture. Bill's desk was full, but tidy. There was a stand-alone coat hanger in one corner, and along the far wall was a chest high bookcase on the top of which were two pictures. Mitch recognized both of them. One was Margaret, whom Mitch saw at Tommy's execution in Richmond. The other was Kathleen. It looked like a high school senior photo, and was the same one that had been published in the local newspaper at the time of her death and then again later when Tommy was arrested and charged.

Bill motioned to an armless oak chair on the opposite side of the desk from him. They both sat down. Bill folded his arms, cocked his head to the side and continued to stare at Mitch.

"I recognize you, Mr. Armstrong," Bill said. "Part of me doesn't believe you. The other part of me asks—why would anybody with any shred of decency want to come and talk to a father about something like this?"

"I know this isn't the best way to begin a conversation," Mitch said, "but let me start by apologizing. I'm not in the process of writing a paper. Maybe someday I will, in fact I promised myself I would. I convinced myself that it would in some way make my being here seem less deceptive."

"For you, perhaps."

"Yes, you're right, less deceptive for me. But sir, I really need to talk to you, and I didn't think you'd speak with me if I told you exactly why."

"You've already told me enough. Nice meeting you, Mr. Armstrong. Goodbye."

Bill stood up, stepped around from behind his desk and opened the door. With an underhand gesture of his free arm he motioned to Mitch that he should depart. Mitch hesitated, then stepped through the doorway.

Realizing that the very reason he was here was starting to slip away, Mitch grabbed the doorjamb, twisted around, and said, "Tommy Cleaves was not the man who murdered Kathleen."

Bill was already walking toward his desk with his back toward Mitch. He stopped abruptly, but did not turn. The two men were motionless.

"Did you hear me, Bill?"

Nothing.

Mitch sensed the moment was lost. He nodded to Mrs. Penny, departed the reception area, and started the trek down the long hallway toward the exit. He heard Bill's office door close, not smoothly. It was slammed shut.

At the end of the hallway he leaned into the heavy wooden exit door that opened to the outer courtyard and campus quad.

"Mr. Armstrong. Oh, Mr. Armstrong."

It was Mrs. Penny. Mitch stopped and turned his head.

"Mr. Armstrong," she gasped as she scampered down the hallway, her short steps making a clickety-click sound on the tile floor. "Professor Spencer said he had something else he wanted to say to you."

Mitch followed Mrs. Penny back to Bill's office. The door was now standing open and she motioned to Mitch to go on in. Bill nodded toward the chair and Mitch sat down. Bill's hands were clasped together with interlocking fingers and resting on top of his desk.

"What are you possibly talking about?" Bill finally asked.

Mitch looked at the open door, and Bill rolled his chair from behind the desk and pushed it closed.

"Please hear me out and let me finish before you pass judgment," Mitch said. "I'll make this as quick as possible. On the night that your daughter was murdered, I and one of my friends …" Mitch held his hands up in an *I surrender* manner. "Now bear in mind, we were both only twelve years." Mitch lowered his hands and continued, "But we were on the beach at the time that the murder took place."

"You saw it happen?"

"Not the actual event, but we were there. We both definitely saw and heard your daughter and the boy she was with talking, then arguing. There was no doubt about who your daughter was because we had already seen her that summer. But not the boy. We didn't recognize him."

"Was there anyone else with them?"

"No. And let me get right to the point. My friend and I both knew Tommy Cleaves pretty well. At least we knew who he was and saw him a lot. He was about eight or nine years older than us. Tommy had such a distinctive voice that we even gave him a nickname that only the two of us used. We called him Rooster Boy."

Bill Spencer's hands were still clasped together. He began slowly rotating his thumbs around each other in a forward motion. His head dropped slightly and he peered at Mitch from over the top of his glasses.

"The boy that was with your daughter—"

Bill interrupted, "She has a name."

"I'm sorry. The boy that was with Kathleen was not Tommy Cleaves. We saw him and we heard him. I am as sure as I am sitting here that it was not Cleaves. Plus the fact that, from what we saw, the two of them had what appeared to be an intimate relationship. There's no way that any decent girl, such as Kathleen, would ever have a boyfriend-girlfriend relationship with somebody like Cleaves."

Mitch looked at Bill Spencer who seemed to be getting a little agitated. Bill raised his hand for Mitch to stop.

"I don't know what you're trying to do, Mr. Armstrong, but I'm finding it hard to believe that you're just now letting people know all this."

"You've got to remember that we were just kids at that time," said Mitch. "I was too young and too scared to go to the police. I tried talking to my parents about it, and they didn't want to hear it. And my friend who was with me simply clammed up about it. He had his reasons. The main thing, though, was that we were just little kids—with big fears."

"But you grew up."

"Yes. I lost total contact with my friend, and as I got older I'd even doubt myself once in a while. Memories from our youth sometimes get cloudy. I eventually became a police officer and a detective working in the same department with Ken Farmer. I tried talking to Farmer about it, but he blew me off and, for a while, I let him. I don't let too many people get away with treating me like that."

"You don't look like someone who gets ignored very often," said Bill.

"Anyhow, Farmer earned such a reputation for solving this case as quickly as he did, that many of my friends on the force told me it would be career suicide if I didn't back off. As it turns out, I didn't take their advice and it cost me my job. But I never regretted it."

"I'm still not putting the pieces together, Mr. Armstrong. You're still not making a lot of sense to me."

"I've re-established contact with my friend who was with me on the beach that night. He now confirms everything that I've said all along. I've also come across some other evidence that Tommy Cleaves was framed."

"What evidence?"

"I still have to protect some other people, but as soon as I can put all the pieces together I'll tell you everything I know."

"So you're telling me, Mr. Armstrong, that because of Kathleen's death some other poor innocent soul lost his life."

"I hesitate to call Tommy Cleaves a poor innocent soul. Tommy was an evil person who did some despicable things in his lifetime. I'd go so far as to say that he deserved what he got. It's just that he wasn't guilty of the crime that he was executed for."

Bill Spencer stood up and moved over to the window. He pushed back the heavy, ivory-colored curtains, and watched some students walking across the quad between classes.

"Kathleen would have been a good teacher," Bill said.

"I'm sure she would have, Dr. Spencer."

"So, now what, Mr. Armstrong? Now what? If I'm to believe you, what do you expect me to do? Why did you even bother to come see me?"

"I'm looking for the man who killed Kathleen. He's responsible for two deaths now. In my heart I know that I was on that beach that night for a reason. I haven't been able to let it go. And it truly troubles me to bring this to you now."

Bill returned to his desk and sat down. Mitch's eyes followed him the entire time, searching for any insights to what he would say or do.

After what seemed like an appropriate pause, Mitch asked, "Dr. Spencer, did any of Kathleen's boyfriends drive a red Thunderbird?"

"Your so-called killer had a red Thunderbird?"

"It's a lead that I'm checking out."

"I was only at the cottage on the weekends, and not every weekend. Kathleen's friends must have known that. They probably had an aversion to fathers because I rarely saw any of them, and I never saw a red Thunderbird."

"Maybe your wife?"

"I don't want you to see her, talk to her, or even try."

"Excuse me?"

"She's very sick. She had a stroke about two weeks ago, and is not recovering very well."

"I'm sorry. I saw her with you outside of the penitentiary in Richmond. She looked well at the time."

"The stroke was sudden and unexpected. But I'm sure the stress of the final weeks leading up to the execution took its toll. I didn't want her to go to the execution, but she insisted. She said she needed the closure."

"Again, sir, I'm very sorry."

"I appreciate your concern."

"May I ask you something else? Something about Kathleen's friends."

"Go ahead."

"Kathleen had a friend. A girl with black hair. She was there for a short while at the beginning of the summer, then she left, I guess. Do you know if there is any way I could get in touch with her?"

"That would have been Vonnie Woodall. Her first name is really Yvonne. She and Kathleen had been friends since grade school."

"Do you have any idea where she is, or if she's married and has a different name?"

"She married a boy named Owens, Jim Owens, if I remember correctly. Margaret and I were invited to their wedding. I seem to recall Margaret once saying they moved to Dover, Delaware."

"Anything else about her that you might remember?"

"Is she on your list of suspects, too?" Bill asked, mockingly.

"No, but any and all information helps."

"Wouldn't surprise me if she's a hairdresser. Seems like all that girl ever wanted to do was fool with Kathleen's hair. Even talked about going to school for it. But I guess that's not much to go on."

"Maybe, maybe not," said Mitch.

Bill stood up. "This changes a lot of things."

"I know," said Mitch. "I'm sure you must've felt a sense of closure when Tommy was executed."

"In something like this, Mr. Armstrong, there's no such thing as closure. The wound gets a scab or a scar, but never goes away. I'll admit that the night of Cleaves's execution, it made me feel that, for the first time in twenty-five years, the nightmare had, in some way, come to a fitting resolution. For me, it will truly never end. But when Cleaves was executed, it seemed as if everything that should happen, in fact, did happen. And now you've walked in here and ripped off the scab."

"I'm sorry, sir. I don't want to cause you or anyone else any pain. But the horrible truth is that Kathleen's murderer is still out there."

Bill's gaze had a piercing, chilling effect on Mitch. The man behind those eyes hated Mitch right now almost as much as he hated his daughter's killer. Mitch could feel it.

"That'll be all, Mr. Armstrong. I'm not totally on board with this. But for now, I'll give you a slight benefit of the doubt. If you find out anything, you'll let me know?"

"Of course."

"And if you're wrong," Bill said, then hesitated, "well, let's not even go there."

Mitch walked out of the room. Bill closed the door behind Mitch and returned to his desk. He sat down, stared blankly across the room, curled his arms in front of him on the desk, laid his head on them and sobbed. Before long his entire upper body was shaking.

CHAPTER 16

O nce inside his car, and before leaving the college campus, Mitch called Louise from the car phone.

"This was tough," Mitch said, "but I've got another lead we need to check out."

"We?"

"Thought you might like a little road trip. I need to talk to somebody who possibly lives in Dover, Delaware."

"You do know, don't you, that you can use a telephone for talking, kinda like what we're doing right now?"

"It's not the same, Weezie, you know that."

"I know that if you call me Weezie again, I won't be here when you get home."

"Sorry, but it's such a pretty name."

"I'll ignore that. Speaking of getting home, when do you think that'll be?"

"I might be a little later than I anticipated. I've got some other things I want to check out."

"I don't like this, Mitch. Be careful, don't do anything foolish."

"I'll be careful, sweetie. I'll give you a call when I have a better estimate of when I'll be home."

"Wait, Mitch, I almost forgot. Frankie called. He said he wants to talk to you when you get a chance. He said to tell you that the more he thinks about the meeting you guys had at Skipper's, the more anxious he is to try to help."

"Sounds good, I'll call him sometime tomorrow. Right now I just need to let all this stuff stew inside my head for a little bit."

"Okay, love you, see you when you get here. And I mean it, be careful."

"Love you, too."

Mitch exited the parking lot and smiled a little into his rear view mirror as he watched the dark sedan follow him out. *You aren't too damn obvious, are you?*

Mitch knew he was being followed. He guessed that it was Farmer's doings, but he still didn't know for sure if Farmer had already tapped his phone or was getting real antsy about the people that Mitch was visiting.

Mitch pulled into a convenience store not far from the campus, the same one that he stopped at earlier in the day prior to his meeting with Bill Spencer. He checked it out very well at that time because he was being followed. He thought it might come in handy later. He now parked near the end of the building, went inside, and asked to use the restroom. Mitch by-passed the restroom door and went straight to the rear exit.

He exited the building and worked his way along the outside walls until he was peering around a corner of the building and looking at the car that followed him. Mitch was pretty sure he had only seen one person in the car and that was all he saw now. Using other parked cars and a dumpster as cover, he managed to maneuver himself to a point directly behind the car. *What an amateur,* Mitch thought to himself, *the asshole's turned the engine off. Stupid.*

Mitch withdrew his .38 special and walked, from the rear of the car, up to the driver's side window. He tapped the window with the barrel of his gun. The startled driver looked up, then reached for the ignition. Before the man could turn the key Mitch smashed the driver's window with a baseball sized rock he had picked up from the dirt lot in the back of the building. The window totally disintegrated. Mitch dropped the rock, reached in with his left hand, and grabbed the driver by the front of his shirt collar, twisting it tight, causing the man to gag.

He thrust his gun hand in and pressed the barrel against the man's temple. "Who sent you?" Mitch growled and slightly loosened his grip.

"What are you talking about?" the man gasped.

"I'll count to three, and you'll talk or you'll die. Your choice."

"I … I … I'm not …"

"One …"

'Please don't," the man whimpered.

"Hurry up asshole. Two …"

"Ken Farmer," he blurted out. "But that's all I know. He didn't say why. I swear."

Mitch withdrew his gun and loosened his grip on the man's shirt collar.

"Put one arm through the steering wheel and put both of your wrists together," Mitch ordered. He then handcuffed the man's wrists. "Tell Farmer I'm looking forward to paying him a visit."

Mitch looked around and didn't see anybody observing what was going on. *Even if somebody did see me,* Mitch thought, *so what?* He got into his car and left. Shortly thereafter he, again, called Louise. "Everything's fine," Mitch reported, "I'll fill you in when I get home. Should see you in about three hours."

The following morning, Mitch called Frankie. Not wanting to discuss too much on the phone, he suggested that Frankie come down to Newburg to see Mitch and meet Louise. They set a time for the following day.

Mitch and Frankie sat at the kitchen table drinking coffee. Louise had, earlier, been called into the hospital for a patient problem and left the house before Frankie arrived.

"So that's the whole story, Frankie. I've never looked at the death penalty as a deterrent. It's supposed to be justice. But in this case there hasn't been any. I'm driven to solve this thing, and it looks like something is driving Farmer to stop me."

"Just to save his reputation? C'mon Mitch. You're being followed, and a woman has been killed, probably because she talked to you. And somebody wants to know why. I get the feeling this is a lot bigger than you think and involves somebody besides Farmer. I've actually got some experience with this kind of stuff."

Mitch was about to push Frankie a little to find out just what he meant by experience when the back door swung open and Louise walked in.

"So you're the infamous Frankie Biondo." Louise smiled, extended her hand, and followed with a brief, but warm, hug.

"That would be Francis, I do believe," Mitch interjected.

"Shut up, Armstrong. Can't you see your wife is coming on to me?

"Don't mind him, Frankie," Louise quipped. "Despite his occasional lapses in manners, he's actually quite a nice person." Her eye roll got Frankie laughing.

"I had a feeling I'd like you, Louise."

After a little friendly banter, the three of them got back to talking about Tommy Cleaves and Farmer. Mitch told Frankie that he had done some research and, in fact, located Vonnie Owens in Dover. Just as Bill Spencer had suspected, Vonnie was in the hair business and owned a beauty salon. Mitch had contacted her and was planning to make a trip there on the upcoming Saturday.

"Dover, huh," Frankie said. "I know a really great criminal lawyer in Dover. A guy named Winston."

"Why would you need a criminal lawyer in Dover?" asked Mitch.

"Actually, I first met him in Hackensack, New Jersey. He … sort of helped me."

"Oh, tell me more." Mitch leaned back in his chair, looked at Louise, with a half smile, half smirk, and said, "I think this is going to get interesting."

"It shouldn't come as any big surprise," Frankie continued, "I kind of alluded to it when we were talking in your car up in Philly. Anyhow, with a name like Biondo I had some Italian family connections. And it just so happens that my connections were the kind that …" he paused slightly, "unconnected people like to talk about."

Mitch chuckled and shook his head. "You gotta know I'm loving this. How about you, Weezie?"

"I'm intrigued," replied Louise, "and if you ever call me Weezie again—let's just say I know people." She looked at Frankie and gave him a big wink.

"I'm not so much into that anymore," said Frankie. "This was a number of years ago. I got into a little trouble with, shall we say, the way I collected overdue accounts for my uncle's business. Winston, the lawyer I mentioned, represented me and I walked."

"But there was a problem," Frankie continued. "Winston started getting threats from my uncle's—uhhh—competitors, we'll call them. I managed to put a stop to it, no details necessary. Let's just say Winston was very appreciative. He eventually relocated to Dover. He said it was because of taxes. I think he just wanted to get away from the New Jersey family infighting. Doesn't matter. The fact is he's a great lawyer. I'd use him again if I ever had the need to. Not that I expect that to ever happen."

"Really?" asked Mitch.

"Really. I'm an honest, respectable business man." Frankie looked in Louise's direction. "Louise, don't ever let him talk trash about me."

"If he ever does, I'll let you know. In fact, I'll tell your uncle too."

They all laughed, but they all knew.

"Winston. We'll try to remember the name. But I would hope we'll not be needing him," Mitch said. "For now, though, let's get back to the business at hand. Frankie, I need you to take a trip to Richmond. I'd really like you to meet Farmer or at least see him. I'd like you to do it discretely. Don't know how. But I want you to see who we're dealing with, and I don't want him to know who you are."

"I'll figure something out, Mitch. Just leave it to me. In the meantime, you guys enjoy your trip to Dover."

CHAPTER 17

"Wow, this is so beautiful. I love September. We need a sailboat."

Sunny skies and blue water dotted with white sails caused Mitch's feel-good endorphins to kick in. He and Louise were at the top of the Chesapeake Bay Bridge, halfway between Sandy Point on the west and Stevensville on Maryland's eastern shore.

"Shut up and keep your eyes on the road," said Louise.

She wasn't enjoying the view quite as much as Mitch. Her eyes were closed and her hand tightly gripped the door handle, ready to escape—just in case Mitch should lose control of the car, crash through the railing, and cause them to plummet hundreds of feet off the bridge and into the waters of the Chesapeake Bay. Her lips were moving ever so slightly as she silently mouthed the words for another decade of the Rosary.

"You know, it's a good thing that after med school, you chose to specialize in endochoreography," said Mitch.

"Endocrinology," she corrected him. "And stop trying to be funny. Your comedic timing and delivery both suck."

"Anyway, it's a good thing you did that and not psychiatry. You don't like bridges, you don't like to make left hand turns, you've gotta close all the closet doors at night so the boogeyman doesn't jump out and get you."

"Stop with the jokes. And in case you didn't hear me before, I said shut up. I just don't want you to wreck my new car."

"Man, this is beautiful."

"Stop looking at the water."

"How do you know I'm not looking at your legs?"

"Oh, that's all I need," said Louise, as she grabbed her skirt hem and gave it a little tug, "both of your heads, distracted."

Mitch smiled, enjoying the friendly banter. It was a nice, albeit brief, distraction from the thoughts that had occupied his brain almost non-stop since Tommy's execution. Now he was driving to Dover, Delaware, to interview Vonnie Owens. Mitch talked Louise into going with him. He insisted that it was to keep him company and to give him an opportunity to drive her new Mustang. She, however, was quite sure that it was because of everything that has happened since Tommy's execution: Muriel, Mitch being followed, and who knows what else. She knew Mitch didn't want her to stay home alone and, despite her protestations about the bridge, she was more than happy to be with him.

"You can relax now," he said. "We're back on terra firma."

Louise opened her eyes and looked outside, relieved that the bridge was behind them.

"Isn't there another way we can take when we go home?" she asked.

"We can always go north and come down through Baltimore. Of course we might have to go through the tunnel under the harbor." Mitch knew the tunnel wasn't mandatory, but threw it in just to check her response.

"Oh crap, never mind," Louise sighed.

They soon passed the Route 50 cutoff that heads toward Ocean City and the Atlantic beaches, drawing off most of the traffic. They were now sharing the open road with very few other vehicles and were silently enjoying the scenery. On both sides of the road were large farm fields, and clusters of forest land. They occasionally spotted deer feeding on the edges of the fields. A noisy flock of geese flew overhead and a pair of bald eagles were floating on an updraft. Add to that a clear, sunny sky and this short respite from the troubles that had been haunting him gave Mitch a brief moment of peace.

Before long they left Route 301 and took some of the back roads through Templeville and Marydel. There was even less traffic except for an occasional Amish horse and buggy.

Idle chitchat finally gave way to talking about the job at hand. "I overheard your phone conversation with this Vonnie woman," Louise said. "Why were you so evasive with her about why you wanted to see her today? You said you were an investigator, but you never did tell her exactly what you were investigating."

"I learn a lot by watching the way people physically respond to a question as much as by what they say," said Mitch. "And I get a lot more out of first reactions than I do out of rehearsed reactions."

"You don't possibly think she's implicit in this do you?"

"No, not at all. But sometimes people know things that they're not even aware of that will come out when they're not given a lot of time to think about their answers. I don't know why, I've just found that the brain works that way."

"You were pretty smooth talking to her on the phone. Maybe you're the one who should've gone into psychiatry."

"Not me. One doctor in the family is enough. I don't have the kind of smarts it takes to do that."

"Bullshit," said Louise. "Sometimes, I wish I had the smarts you do. But don't quote me on that. I'll deny I ever said it."

One and a half hours after crossing the Bay Bridge they pulled into the parking lot of a small strip mall on State Street in Dover. The little shopping center had an English village appearance. One long, low building was home to several businesses—a drug store, bakery, dry cleaners, dress boutique, and beauty salon. Each storefront had at least one very large glass window, trimmed in brown. The exterior walls were a rust colored brick. An overhanging roof with cedar shake shingles extended about ten feet over the sidewalk. Mitch and Louise found an empty space in the front row and pulled in, nose to the curb. They took a moment to absorb the details of the center, then exited their car and walked up to the entrance to Vonnie's Salon.

"Very nice," said Louise. "Now we're talking my language."

Mitch opened the door and they stepped inside.

Neither Mitch nor Louise noticed the plain, black, four-door sedan pull into the parking lot as they entered the salon. It parked as far away from the salon as possible while still allowing the passengers a view of the salon entrance.

"There they are," Dolf Richter said. He was in the driver's seat of the black sedan. Sitting next to him was a monstrous piece of human flesh named Turk. "I hate that son of a bitch."

"It's just a job," Turk said, "don't take it personally. Why do you say you hate him?"

"You probably noticed I limp a little bit. Got a bad knee. Some years ago he was a beat cop in Richmond. He busted me for something minor. I mouthed off to him and the prick shattered my kneecap with his police baton. I had a bad reputation, so he never got into any trouble for it."

"You sure there isn't more to the story?" asked Turk.

Dolf didn't know Turk very well. Farmer had paired them up. The main thing Dolf knew was that he didn't want to get into an argument with Turk.

"Go call Farmer and let him know that they're here."

Turk got out of the car and walked to the phone booth outside of the drugstore at the opposite end of the building.

"*Verdammt noch mal!*" Dolf muttered the German expletive to himself. Continuing in English, he growled, "That man is big."

He was right, Turk was huge. He hadn't just simply occupied the passenger side of the front seat, he filled that half of the car. He was well over six feet tall and somewhat north of 300 pounds. He had a big chest, thick waist, big arms, and gigantic hands. His dark hair was close cropped and the back of his head was wrinkled with deep creases that made it look like an oversized cantaloupe. Dolf never worked with Turk before, but he knew why Farmer liked to use him. Turk could, and would, do things to people, bad things. In the short time that Dolf had been with him today, Dolf quickly learned that Turk was absent of anything that even closely resembled compassion.

Turk stood outside the drugstore and used the phone from one of the wall-mounted booths. The black receiver, which was big enough for most people to use as a weapon, looked like a child's toy in Turk's hand.

The call went to Farmer's private line, accessible only from his desk. He answered with a terse, "Ken Farmer."

"They're here."

"Good. You know what to do. Keep me posted."

"Yeah, will do."

Turk returned to the car, got back in and stared at the entrance to Vonnie's.

"I'm taking a nap," said Dolf as he slid down in his seat. "Wake me in a little while. Then you can rest, too."

Turk looked at Dolf as if the man had completely forgotten they were here to do a job. He then turned his gaze back to the salon entrance, and for the next two hours remained as focused as a predator in the wild.

⌒

Once inside the salon, Mitch was even happier that Louise was with him.

"I am definitely out of my element," he said. "I've never been big on organized chaos."

The salon was busy. The whirring noise of at least six hand-held blow dryers was in direct competition with the similarly cranked up volume of non-stop feminine chatter.

"Looks like a wedding party," said Louise.

Mitch gave her a questioning look.

"I've done this before," she said.

"Hi! How can I help you? Do you have an appointment today?" Sadie, a perky, blonde, overly helpful receptionist with a big Cheshire cat grin beamed as Mitch approached the reception desk. His tough appearance didn't seem to bother her.

"I've got an appointment with Vonnie," Mitch said.

"Then, I'll bet you're Mr. Armstrong."

"Bingo."

"Vonnie'll be right back. She had to run out to the supply store."

"That's okay. I'm a little early."

"You can have a seat in our waiting area. My name is Sadie. Just let me know if I can help you with anything. How about a coffee?"

Mitch said yes to the coffee, and sat down in one of the leather high back chairs and tried his best to soak in the surroundings. The sights, the sounds, the smells were all unfamiliar territory for him and he felt, he hesitated to think, uneasy. Louise, on the other hand, seemed to be quite comfortable and enjoying herself as she walked around examining the retail shelves full of hair, skin, and nail products.

Five minutes later, the front door flew open and a five-foot-two-inch, pleasantly plump, whirling dervish with short dark hair rushed in. She had a purse slung over her shoulder and an overstuffed plastic bag clutched tightly in each hand. Lettered on each bag was *DBS, Dover Beauty Supply*. She was on a mission, and practically dropped the bags into the receptionist's lap.

"Just in time, Vonnie," Sadie said. "Georgie just took her client back. Oh, and Mr. Armstrong is here." She nodded toward the chair where Mitch was sitting.

With what Mitch thought was an amazing change of composure, Vonnie turned around and slowly, if not gently, walked over to Mitch and extended her hand.

"Mr. Armstrong? I'm Vonnie Owens."

"Hi Vonnie. I'm Mitch Armstrong, and the pretty lady over there, who is obviously shopping, is my wife, Louise." Mitch gestured in Louise's direction.

Louise joined them and also introduced herself to Vonnie. Mitch was astounded at how quickly that brief introduction morphed into a discussion about haircuts, hairstyles, and hair products. He finally had to interject and asked if there was someplace where they could talk in private.

Vonnie led them to her office. It was cluttered, but when the door closed, the noise went away and Mitch felt a little more relaxed and comfortable.

"You really got my curiosity up Mr. Armstrong. How can I help you?"

"I'll get right to the point, Vonnie. I'm a private investigator and a former police detective. I want to ask you, if I may, some questions about Kathleen Spencer."

Mitch would later recall that he never saw the color drain out of someone's face as quickly as it left Vonnie Owens. He now knew where the expression, white as a ghost, came from.

"Oh," said Vonnie. "Of all things, I surely wasn't expecting this."

"I'm sorry if I upset you."

"Mr. Armstrong. This is a very old, very hurtful memory. What can you possibly want?"

Vonnie stood up and grabbed a box of tissues from a bookshelf.

"I keep these for my staff when I'm having a heart-to-heart with one of them. It's not too often that I ever need one for myself."

"I'm sure the memories are painful, but the reason I'm here is for justice for Kathleen. She hasn't gotten it yet," said Mitch.

"What are you talking about? It's been years since they arrested the s.o.b. that killed her. He was sentenced to death."

"Yes. He was executed just this past February."

"So again, I'm asking you, Mr. Armstrong, what in the world is this all about?"

"Tommy Cleaves was arrested, tried, convicted, and executed for the murder of your friend, Kathleen Spencer. However, there's a big problem with all of that."

"There is?"

"I'm not real sure how to put this, Ms. Owens," Mitch hesitated, "but Tommy's not the man who killed her."

"What?"

"The state executed an innocent man."

Vonnie stood up and started walking around in tight little circles behind her desk.

"What are you saying? This is crazy. Who are you, really? Make me understand something."

Just then, the office door flew open and a young, horrified, wide-eyed shampoo assistant stepped in.

"Oh, we've got a problem. We've got a problem," she kept repeating.

"Calm down, sweetie. What's going on?" asked Vonnie.

"Freda just waxed off the bride's left eyebrow."

"Oh, shit. I'll be right back." Vonnie fired off some eye daggers at Mitch.

"I'll be waiting," said Mitch.

Vonnie scampered out, pulling the door closed behind her.

After a few seconds of awkward silence Louise said, "Uh, I'm not feeling real good about this."

"Thanks for the insight, Sherlock. I just hope to hell I can calm her down a little."

"It ain't looking good, Mitch Boy, and I really don't think this little emergency of hers is helping any." Louise stood, moved behind Mitch and rested her hand on his shoulder.

"I was hoping we'd have something worthwhile to talk about going home. Now I'm not so sure," said Mitch.

"She's gonna give us something. Think positive."

"Hope so, baby, hope so."

Thirty uncomfortable minutes later, Vonnie came back into the office, shaking her head. "People just wouldn't believe what goes on here."

"You've gotta fill me in. I've been in here biting my nails," said Louise. Her tone was sympathetic, understanding, and genuine.

Mitch was happy she took over. He just sat back, watched, and listened.

"Well," said Vonnie, "the bride, thanks to a full week of partying and the two bottles of wine they brought with them this morning, was actually laughing her ass off. She thought it was hysterical. Mother-of-the-bride, however, wasn't so happy. That lady was talking about suing me, suing Freda, suing the shopping center, suing the governor. If you'd have stuck your head out there, she probably would have threatened to sue you too."

"Now I'm sorry I didn't go out and watch." Louise started to lean in closer to Vonnie. Her body language was saying that it was a great story and she wanted to hear more. "So, how'd you fix it?"

"Despite what the bride's maid-of-honor wanted to do," Vonnie started giggling, "that crazy girl is drunker than the bride. Chances are she won't make it for the wedding. Anyway, she volunteered to shave off her eyebrows and glue 'em onto the bride."

Vonnie and Louise were both laughing.

"I've got a great makeup artist," Vonnie said, "one of the best I've ever seen. She took over and, I swear, that bride looks better right now than she would have before she lost the eyebrow."

"What about Mom?" asked Louise.

"Oh, she got what she wanted. I'm giving her the bride's services for free. Best her ugly daughter's ever gonna look in her life, and it won't cost Mom a cent."

"Holy crap. You're amazing. I couldn't do this." Louise was still laughing.

"All in a day's work. As I said, this is a crazy business. Now I'm the one who needs a drink."

"You deserve it," said Louise.

Vonnie sat down, spread her arms out and laid both hands on the desk, palms down. She then turned her head and looked directly at Mitch.

"Well, Mr. Armstrong, shall we start over?"

CHAPTER 18

Mitch shook his head a little, then said, "I can't compete with this, and I hate to make your day any worse, but if you're up to it, I'd still like to ask you a couple questions?"

"About Kathleen Spencer?"

"Yes."

"She was my absolute best friend, and I've never had another friend like her."

"You spent a little time with her at Bohman's Point in Virginia during the summer of '59."

"I'm really not comfortable talking about this." She lowered her head and stared at the desk top.

Silence is a powerful tool during an interview or an interrogation, Mitch had learned. People hate it and will often say something for no other reason than to break it. He let the silence marinate.

Finally, Vonnie asked, "And how do you know about me being at Bohman's Point?"

"I spoke to her dad. And I was there, too," said Mitch. "You had long black hair back then. I was twelve at the time. Adolescent hormones were just starting to kick in; and my friend, Frankie, and I thought the two of you were the most beautiful girls we'd ever seen."

"I'm flattered." Vonnie tilted her head a little to the left and looked at Mitch with an arched eyebrow. "Did you have any fantasies?"

"Can I plead the fifth?"

"I'm feeling generous today, Mitch. I won't embarrass you in front of your wife."

"Oh, please," interjected Louise, "don't let me stop you."

"Fantasies, huh?" Vonnie smiled at Louise then cut her eyes toward Mitch.

"We were young," Mitch protested. "You and Kathleen reminded us of Veronica and Betty from the old Archie comics."

"Really?"

"You were Veronica," Mitch continued. "Kind of weird, isn't it? You were Veronica, and your real name is Vonnie. Both begin with a V." Mitch chuckled, trying to make a joke, but he was definitely struggling.

Vonnie looked at Louise. "Is he always this smooth?"

"I'm surprised you're not half undressed by now," she replied.

Mitch gave Louise a quick look of disapproval. Louise just smiled with smug satisfaction. Mitch was always in such firm control of most situations that Louise got bits of enjoyment out of these rare moments when he displayed a little social awkwardness. She re-crossed her legs and shifted a little in her chair. It seemed to indicate that she was going to enjoy being present and listening.

"If I remember correctly," Mitch said, trying to regain control, "you were only there for a short while."

"That wasn't the original plan," said Vonnie. "We were supposed to spend the better part of the summer together. But I screwed up."

"How so?"

"I flunked algebra. All my other grades were good. I'm just not a numbers person. Anyway, I was one of those people at graduation who gets to dress up in a cap and gown, walk across the stage, shake hands with the principal, and have him hand you an empty diploma folder. Do you have any idea what that feels like? Pictures with the relatives, partying with your classmates, but knowing you've still got to go back to school."

"So you had to go to summer school?"

"Yup. I got about two weeks at Bohman's Point, then back to Pennsylvania for summer school. Anyway, I wound up getting a C in the class," Vonnie said with a goofy little grin.

"Did you ever see Tommy Cleaves during the two weeks you were there?"

"Oh yeah. What a creep. Talk about white trash. It just made me sick to think of what they said he did to Kathleen."

Mitch had been taking notes on a small spiral notepad. He stopped for a minute and just started tapping the pad with the point of his pen.

"So you had no reason to doubt that Tommy was the guy who did it?"

"None at all."

"Did you communicate much with Kathleen after you went back home for summer school?"

"Not a lot. There was only the payphone at the Bohman store. They didn't have a phone in the rental cottage. So we talked a few times and wrote some letters."

"Do you recall any of the phone conversations?"

"Uhhhh, not really. Like I said, we only talked a couple times."

"I know this is a long shot, but did you keep any of the letters?"

Vonnie hesitated, then said, "No, too incriminating."

"Incriminating?"

"Probably a bad choice of words," said Vonnie. "We used a lot of girlie code in our letters. We had some secrets that had to be kept from our parents. At least, back then, we thought that was the smart thing to do."

"What kind of secrets?"

"Wow, this is something that I've kept to myself for years. I guess it was my own little way of honoring her memory. I'm not too sure that I want to give it up now."

"I really don't know how I can make you believe me," said Mitch, "but I've been in police work and private investigations for almost twenty years. I've solved cases. I've investigated cases. I know when a lead is going the wrong direction. I know when it's time to give up on something. I also know that there are some cases you just can't let go. I think every cop or ex-cop has at least one of them that will stick in the back of his mind forever. This one is mine. And my reasoning is even stronger than most—I was there when it happened."

Vonnie shot him a look of shocked disbelief.

"I didn't actually see the murder committed. But Frankie and I were there, and we saw the two of them on the beach that night. We saw and heard them argue about something. I don't know what it was they were arguing about, but it got heated. I saw the guy who was with her, and Frankie saw him too. And as sure as night follows day we are certain that the guy with Kathleen was not Tommy Cleaves. And that man, whoever it was, is now responsible, not only for Kathleen's death, but Tommy's too, and, possibly, more."

Mitch stopped and looked deep into Vonnie's eyes.

"Vonnie, if there is anything you can tell me, I promise you it will be used to respect Kathleen's memory, and bring to justice the man who destroyed so many people's dreams."

Vonnie sat with her right elbow on the desk, resting her chin on her thumb, with her forefinger placed across her lips as if to say *shoosh*. Her eyes traveled up and down, left and right. Without moving her head she looked at Mitch then Louise, then back down at the desk top. Finally, she spoke.

"Kathleen was pregnant."

CHAPTER 19

"Pregnant. I wasn't expecting that," said Mitch. "You knew for sure?"

"Yeah, she was as regular as clockwork and had missed a period."

"She told you that in her letters?"

"I said we had a code. Trust me, I knew exactly what she was talking about."

"Did she tell you who the father was?"

Vonnie took a long pause, staring blankly into a place only she knew. "Not really. She never used his full name. Again, she was just trying to keep a little secrecy in case somebody else read the letters. All she ever said was that she met someone, and couldn't wait for me to meet him too. When she started having suspicions about her condition, she started saying less about him. I think it was just being kind of protective until they figured out how they were going to let everyone know. She knew that her parents, especially her dad, would be crushed by the news."

"What kinds of things did she tell you about her new boyfriend?"

"The usual. He was great looking, nice car, from a well-off, real hoity-toity family. He was already in his second or third year of college.

I think some Ivy League school like Princeton or Yale. One of those expensive places."

"Anything more specific, like height, hair color, what kind of car he drove, where he was from?"

"Hard to say, or I should say, hard to recall. Before I had to leave and go back home we had boys coming into Bohman's Point from all over the place, driving all kinds of really cool cars. I really can't match one with the other."

"Yeah, I know. You two were the talk of the town among us younger kids. We were envious of those boys not just because of you, but because of their cars too."

"Well, I'm glad I got to add some excitement to your life, but as far as Kathleen and her new boyfriend were concerned, I got the feeling their whole relationship was very secretive. Kathleen's dad wasn't real big on her having any kind of steady boyfriend. I told her that he really sounded cool and asked if he had any friends she could fix me up with, if I got a chance to visit before the summer was over. She said there was a couple other guys that hung out with him once in a while, but she really didn't like them very much."

"So, Kathleen was the only one with a boyfriend?"

"Yeah, but I didn't care."

Over the next sixty minutes, Mitch gained scant additional information. Vonnie talked about her closeness with Kathleen, and told a lot of stories about them growing up together, but little else about the summer of Kathleen's murder. Even though he did not get much more out of the conversation with Vonnie, Mitch was looking forward to being alone with Louise again to discuss Kathleen's pregnancy. Something just didn't feel right.

During their final ten minutes together Mitch and Louise chatted with Vonnie about nothing significant, just some pleasantries to finish their conversation. The salon was closing for the day, and Vonnie groaned a little bit about having to stay to catch up on some inventory work. Mitch and Louise thanked Vonnie for her time. She escorted them to the front door and they said goodbye.

~

Turk reached over and punched Dolf on the shoulder.

"Wake up, Richter. We're just about ready."

"Whoa. What's going on? How long did I sleep?"

"Too long."

They watched as Mitch and Louise waved goodbye, climbed into the Mustang, and departed.

Five minutes later Sadie walked out the front door with two other employees. She closed the door, took a large keychain out of her purse, and locked it. Vonnie was still inside.

"Perfect," said Dolf.

Sadie and the other two girls stood in front of the salon for about ten minutes, chatting and making plans for the evening. Finally, they each got into different cars and left the parking lot.

The salon was on the end of the building and adjacent to a small wooded area. Nobody would approach from the woods and it was unlikely that anyone would be coming from the other end since the salon was now closed.

Turk and Dolf got out of their car and walked up to the front door. Turk walked around the corner and out of sight, hidden from view by anyone in the salon. The door was wooden and had a thick glass window. Dolf grabbed the handle and jiggled the door a little to make some noise. Then he knocked on the door and pressed his face up against the glass trying to look in through cupped hands.

Vonnie had been in a back room shutting off lights when she came around the corner and saw Dolf at the door. She walked up to the door and shouted, "Sorry, we're closed."

"*Bitte!*" Dolf pleaded, using the German word for please. "My wife, she will be really mad."

"Sorry," Vonnie shouted again. She shrugged her shoulders, and turned her hands over into a palms up position, indicating there was nothing she could do.

"All I need is a gift certificate. My wife needs it tonight. I promised her I'd get it. She'll kill me. *Bitte*, please." He put his hands together, palm to palm, in a praying gesture.

Vonnie looked at the pleading man, then took a deep breath and said, "Cash only, and I can't make change."

"That will work. It's for twenty-five dollars. I've got two tens and a five." He placed his left palm on the glass, his right hand over his heart, and bowed his head in a "bless you" type of way.

Vonnie unlocked the door and pushed it open for Dolf. As soon as he stepped in, she started to pull the door closed, but a huge hand caught the edge of it and stopped it cold. Turk then filled the doorway.

"Excuse me, sir, we're closed."

The words were barely out of her mouth when Turk shoved her backward. She stumbled almost losing her balance. Dolf then stepped behind Turk and took care of securing the door.

"What's going on?" It wasn't fear that filled Vonnie's eyes. It was stark terror.

Turk grabbed her behind her head with his right hand, pulling so hard on her hair that the skin of her face and forehead was drawn back taut, causing her eyes to bulge out, giving her a skeletal look. He grabbed her left wrist with his left hand and, still holding her by the hair, marched her to a far corner of the salon away from the line of sight of any of the windows.

Dolf joined them and asked, "What did they want from you?"

"Who?" she said with a quivering voice.

Releasing her wrist, Turk reached over and picked up a small, damp cleaning rag that was lying in a crumpled ball on the countertop of one of the styling stations. He pulled Vonnie's head further back until her face was angled upward and stuffed the rag into her mouth. He then grabbed the four fingers of Vonnie's left hand and squeezed. He could feel her knuckles crackling and crumbling under the pressure as if he were squeezing a handful of plastic popcorn.

Her muffled scream was more of a piercing squeal.

"This is not a difficult question," said Dolf. "You had visitors today, Armstrong and his wife. What did they want?" Then he nodded at Turk, who removed the rag from Vonnie's mouth.

She was crying, breathing in deep agonizing spurts, and began pleading, "Please don't hurt me."

"Then tell me what they wanted."

"He asked me about Kathleen Spencer."

Then she looked at Dolf, hoping that was all he needed to hear to make this nightmare stop. He nodded again to Turk who placed the rag back into Vonnie's mouth. Then Turk changed the grasp of his left hand so he was just holding her thumb, and snapped it backward like it was nothing more than a wooden matchstick. Vonnie's knees buckled from the pain.

"Now listen to me," Dolf growled, "you will tell me every word that was spoken. You will not stop until you've told me everything. You will forget nothing. Every time I think you're leaving something out, every time I think you're having a memory lapse, every time I think you're making something up, my friend here will do his best to get you back on track. Now begin."

Turk pulled the cleaning rag out of Vonnie' mouth.

Thirty excruciating minutes later Dolf and Turk were satisfied that they had been told everything they needed to hear. Turk stepped in front of Vonnie. He covered her face with his left hand, while still holding the hair at the back of her head with his right. He shoved her against the wall with his knee, and gave her head a violent twist. Her neck snapped. He released his grip, and her lifeless body fell to the floor like a wet towel. Turk was sure of himself, but he felt for a carotid artery pulse just to confirm she was dead.

Dolf found Vonnie's purse sitting on the reception desk, dumped out its contents, and picked up her wallet. Turk pried open the cash register drawer. It was empty, but that didn't matter. They weren't looking for money, they were establishing motive. The two men walked out of the salon, got into their car and drove away. They turned off State Street onto Division Street and located another phone booth. Turk made the call while Dolf deposited Vonnie's wallet into a large trash can.

"We've got some news," Turk said into the phone. "She told Armstrong a lot about Kathleen Spencer's boyfriend and about Kathleen being pregnant."

"I'll be here at the office when you get back." Farmer hung up his phone and leaned back into his chair. *Armstrong, you don't know who you're screwing with. You just don't know.*

Unknown to Dolf or to Farmer, Turk placed one more call. It was answered after one ring.

"It's done, and you're correct, sir. Armstrong's going to be a big problem. I've already called Farmer."

"I'll follow up with him. Good work."

Turk expected the ensuing dial tone. He knew the Old Man didn't like to stay on the phone.

CHAPTER 20

Shortly after leaving the salon, Mitch and Louise stopped to fill the car up with gas. After pumping the gas and cleaning the windshield, Mitch climbed back in and began a careful exit from the gas station. Neither one of them had spoken much since leaving Vonnie's. Mitch looked at Louise whose gaze seemed to be transfixed somewhere out in the open, beyond the car's side window.

"So what's your take on all this?"

She brought her thoughts back inside the car. "I'm not buying it."

"Not buying what?" asked Mitch.

"She knows the name of Kathleen's boyfriend. I don't care if she said she didn't. Trust me, she does."

"What makes you think that?"

"Maybe guys don't talk, Mitch, but girls do. There's no way Kathleen's best friend didn't know the name of the biggest love of Kathleen's life. Especially if she knew that Kathleen was pregnant. There's something else, too. She didn't get rid of Kathleen's letters either. Kathleen was her best friend. Her best friend died. Vonnie still has those letters."

Mitch's grip on the steering wheel tightened a little. "So, how do we find out or get her to tell us? Any suggestions?"

"I've got some ideas, but we'll have plenty of time to talk later. Right now, my dear, I'm just really anxious to get to the mall."

Southern Maryland didn't offer much in the way of shopping, so the Dover Mall had been one of the reasons that Louise signed on for this little road trip. The mall had opened just two years prior, and Louise was anxious to check it out. It was only four miles from Vonnie's Salon. State Street to 13 North, to the mall, five more minutes and they were there.

Once inside, they slowly wandered to the food court. They planned to get a bite to eat before heading out to Boscov's, or Leggett's, or any of the little specialty stores that had captured Louise's attention. Louise ducked into the ladies' room and came out to find Mitch with a not too happy look on his face.

"What?" she asked.

"You're not going to believe this. I left my knife at Vonnie's."

"Your what?"

"My little red pocket knife," Mitch explained. "The one with the toothpick and tweezers in it. I used the toothpick and then set the knife on the edge of her desk next to where I was sitting."

"Yeah, I remember you, so politely, digging a piece of breakfast bacon or something out of your teeth."

"I've gotta go back and get it. It won't take but twenty minutes. Vonnie mentioned she was going to stay a little late tonight to catch up on some paperwork."

"Why bother? It's just a little knife. We're in a mall. I'm sure we can find a place that sells them."

"It's my lucky knife. I bought it the day I got shot."

Louise shook her head. "That makes it lucky?"

"If I hadn't stopped to buy the knife, I wouldn't have been at the intersection later on when the guy ran the light. I wouldn't have chased him; I wouldn't have pulled him over; he wouldn't have shot me."

Louise rolled her eyes. Her speech picked up a slight tone of exasperation. "You stopped to buy a knife. Doing that puts you in a time and place that causes you to get shot. How is that lucky?"

Mitch turned and looked deep into Louise's eyes. "If I hadn't been shot—I'd have never met you."

"Oh." Her voice dropped as she said it. In a matter of two seconds she went from testy to teary. "Dammit, Mitch, you can drive me crazy. Sometimes I wish I didn't love you so much."

"But you do," he said with a cheery grin.

"Go get your knife. I'll stay here, and explore a little bit more. I'll meet you back here in the food court in thirty minutes. Or, if you want, I can go with you."

"No, you stay. You'll have more fun looking at things here." Mitch gave her a quick kiss, then turned around and headed out to the parking lot.

A smile picked up the corners of Louise's mouth, and the sparkle returned to her eyes as she watched him disappear down the concourse. *God, I love that man.*

Mitch got back into the Mustang and retraced the route back to Vonnie's Salon. He felt some relief as he entered the parking lot and saw a car still parked at the far end in front of Vonnie's. He assumed it was hers.

Mitch was a little surprised to find the salon door unlocked. He pulled it open and stepped inside.

"Vonnie, are you here?" Mitch called.

No response. He stepped further into the salon. Most of the lights had been turned off. His ghost-like reflection in a multitude of mirrors was a little unsettling. There was a faint glow of light coming from the direction of Vonnie's office.

"Hello," he called again.

Still nothing. He walked up to the reception desk, and immediately saw the emptied purse as well as the open and damaged cash register. All of his senses went on high alert. He could feel his skin tighten. Listening for anything, he slowly moved his head in an attempt to absorb the entire scene. He scanned the salon for any movement, anything that looked out of place. Then he saw it. A dark shape took form on the floor in the far corner. It was a body.

"Oh, shit."

Mitch hurried over to it, knelt down, and immediately recognized the face.

"Vonnie, can you hear me?" he said. He placed two fingers on her carotid artery. Nothing.

Mitch's eyes darted about as he listened for any other noises in the salon, even though his sixth sense told him that nobody else was there. Then, a sucking, whoosh sound, accompanied by outside noise, set off his internal alarm. The front door had just opened.

Bruce Shaw, an off-duty cop and night security guard for the shopping center, was making his rounds. He noticed Vonnie's car still in the lot, after her normal hours, and found the door open. He stepped inside the salon to fuss at her a little for being careless about not locking the door.

"Vonnie, you here?" Bruce called. He walked further in, then detected movement in the corner as Mitch stood up.

Shaw's senses went into high gear. The visuals were coming in fast and he didn't know what they were, but he didn't like them. He drew his gun from the holster behind his back.

"Police," he shouted. "Put your hands over your head."

Mitch raised his hands as commanded. "I'm an ex-cop. I know the drill," he said.

"Then you know what's next. Put your hands behind your head and get on your knees."

Again, Mitch did as he was told. Shaw quickly and efficiently cuffed him and made him sit down on the floor.

"You'll need an ambulance, but I can tell you, she's gone," said Mitch.

Shaw was already fighting through the static and crackling of his hand-held radio.

Within minutes an ambulance, three city police cruisers, and at least a couple dozen curious on-lookers had filled the parking lot with lights, radios, and lots of chatter.

Mitch was Mirandized, placed in the back of a police car, and taken to the station on Queen Street. As he already said, he knew the drill. He knew he'd be better off keeping quiet until he got to the station where calmer heads would prevail.

A few minutes of window shopping should have been fun, but Louise just couldn't get her mind into it.

I should have gone with him. The thought was nagging at her. She kept thinking about the Star Wars movie. *There's a disturbance in the force.*

Thirty minutes turned into forty-five, then an hour, then an hour and a half since Mitch departed the food court to drive four miles back to Vonnie's Salon to get his pocket knife. Louise had transitioned from to irritation, to concern, to fear.

She already tried calling Vonnie's Salon, but got the answering machine. She left a message, then tried again twenty minutes later. Same result. She had to do something, but wasn't sure what. She had just decided to call a taxicab and go to the salon when she noticed a uniformed police officer walk through the entrance into the food court. He stopped just inside the doorway and appeared to be looking for someone. She walked toward him, slow and casual at first, then faster and faster. Her heels made loud clopping sounds on the marble floor.

"Are you looking for somebody?" she gasped. Emotions, more than physical exertion, caused her to be out of breath.

"Are you Doctor Armstrong?" the policeman responded.

"Yes, what happened?"

"Doctor Louise Armstrong?"

"Yes, yes. What happened, what's going on?"

"I need you to come with me, Ma'am."

"I need you to tell me what's happening." Her voice was starting to achieve a shrillness that she didn't like but couldn't stop.

"We need to go to the police station," he responded, holding the door open and motioning for her to go outside.

Louise stopped in her tracks. Images of a horrible traffic accident were taking shape in her mind. "I need to know what's going on, and I want to know where my husband is."

"Doctor Armstrong, your husband is at the police station."

"Why, what for?"

"He's being questioned about something. That's really all I know. But if you please come with me, I'm sure you'll get some answers soon."

Louise knew that she had no options, no one to turn to, and that she had to go with the policeman. But she was terrified. *What happened? What was going on?* The trip down to the Queen Street Station pretty much retraced the route they had taken from Vonnie's to the

Mall. The station was located in a clean, pleasant neighborhood. That, however, meant little to Louise. She stared out the window but didn't see a thing. She was numb.

Patrolman Vince Marker parked adjacent to the side entrance of the two story building. He asked Louise to remain seated. He walked around to her side of the vehicle and opened the door. He escorted her into the building, through a short maze of hallways to a small interrogation room. He asked her to sit down and told her that someone would be with her shortly.

"Where's my husband?"

"Ma'am, I'm sure this will all be straightened out real soon," said Patrolman Marker.

Louise was soon joined by Detective Kyle Woodburn. He was wearing a long sleeve white shirt. Nevertheless, he still looked unkempt. His tie was pulled loose and the shirt was open at the collar.

Louise stood as soon as he entered. "Where's my husband?"

"You'll see him soon. But I need to ask you a couple questions." Woodburn's manner was anything but cordial.

"No, I need to ask—you—a couple things. Where's my husband?"

"No need to get upset, Mrs. Armstrong. I'm sure we'll get this resolved in short order."

"Don't tell me not to get upset. I want to know what's going on. I demand to know. If you can't tell me then I want to call an attorney, someone who'll get some answers for me."

Woodburn's demeanor now turned to gruff and borderline rude. "Mrs. Armstrong, a couple hours ago a woman, named Yvonne Owens, was found, dead, in her place of business. Her neck was broken. She was discovered by the security guard, an off-duty police officer.

Your husband was standing next to her body. The officer placed him under arrest. He is still being questioned. Now, will you talk to me or do you still want a telephone?"

For about ten seconds, Louise traded an icy stare with Detective Woodburn. "I'll take the phone," she said. Louise was led to a room with a telephone. "I need a phonebook."

"Here you go, sweetie." The female desk clerk dropped a huge Yellow Pages directory on the desk next to the phone. "I'm sure you can find a lawyer or two in there." She popped her chewing gum as she walked away.

What did Frankie say that guy's name was? Louise kept asking herself. *Windsor, Winslow, Winters? Dammit, think! It was something like that.*

Then she saw the half page ad for Winston Legal. "Winston, that's it," she whispered aloud. The bold type proclaimed: IT'S ALWAYS A WIN WITH WINSTON – CRIMINAL LAW & PERSONAL INJURY.

That's him, gotta be, no other Winstons. But—always a win with Winston?— Oh, just gag me. Shit, what have we gotten ourselves into? I hope to hell this guy's as good as Frankie said he is.

Louise placed a call to the listed number and got the answering service. She explained the situation and added her own degree of urgency. She also made sure the service knew that Winston Legal was recommended by Frankie Biondo. She kept her fingers crossed that Frankie's recommendation would be a help and not a hindrance.

CHAPTER 21

After Louise called Winston Legal, Detective Woodburn took her back to the interrogation room. He left the door open and asked her to wait.

In fifteen minutes, the desk clerk returned. "Come with me please," she said. "There's a Mr. Biondo on the phone for you." The clerk escorted Louise to a private office and pointed toward the phone. "Just press the blinker."

"Frankie, is this you?" Louise was nearly in tears.

"Louise, what the hell is going on?" Frankie replied.

Louise gave him a quick overview of the events as she knew them and then added, "Frankie, I'm scared."

"I know this is easier said than done, but you've gotta relax Louise. I've talked to Win and he's on his way. Trust me, if anybody can straighten this out, he can. He'll keep me posted and I'll be back in touch with you guys as soon as I can."

Louise was again taken back to the interrogation room. She felt a slight sense of relief after talking to Frankie.

Almost an hour had passed when Louise heard some chatter out in the hall. She recognized Detective Woodburn's voice.

"Well, lookie here, if it isn't Winnie the Pooh. What are you doing, Winnie? Here on business, or just out for a little stroll?"

Woodburn put extra emphasis on the word 'little,' then laughed at his own joke.

Briefcase in hand, impeccably groomed, and sporting a custom tailored, three piece suit, Attorney Winston J. Winston was walking down the hall, all four feet and two inches of him. He was heading toward the room where Louise was waiting. He and Detective Woodburn had sparred repeatedly over the past several years, and never in a good-natured way. Winston was a great litigator, with a history of exonerating defendants by tearing apart the details of Woodburn's arrests and investigations. Woodburn always blamed it on a poor showing by the local State's Attorney's office. However, most observers agreed, it had more to do with Winston's knack for making Woodburn look foolish on the witness stand.

"Very funny, Woodburn. Could you be any more stupid?" Winston replied.

"Ooh, snappy comeback, Winnie."

"Look it up, numbnuts."

"Look what up?" asked Woodburn. He stood in the hallway, his outstretched arm supported him as he leaned against a wall and crossed his legs. He towered over Winston.

Winston stopped, and turned to face Woodburn. "Section 504 of the 1973 Rehabilitation Act. Make disparaging remarks about my appearance and I can sue you, clean out your bank account, and get you fired." Winston was well-aware he was stretching what the law said, but was quite certain Woodburn wouldn't know it. "And, to make matters worse, my client can sue you, too, for trying to intentionally inflict emotional distress on his lawyer. You're denying his right to unencumbered access to an attorney." Again, it really wasn't what the law said. But Woodburn was none the wiser.

"Like anybody'll believe I did that shit," said Woodburn.

"Look around," Winston twirled with his hand raised in the air, pointing at the other police officers who had gathered in the hallway. "We've got witnesses. And don't think for a minute that they're gonna help you. They might tell you they will, but trust me, they'd rather see you lose your job than run the risk of losing theirs. And if they have to face me in court, that's what'll happen. Like I said, could you be any more stupid?"

Woodburn snarled, "Screw you, Winston."

Winston started back down the hall, but hesitated. He just couldn't resist. He turned, once again, to face Woodburn. "Wait a minute, I forgot something. I think you could be more stupid. When I said, 1973 Rehabilitation Act, I'm surprised that year didn't ring a bell with you."

"Why should it?" Woodburn shot back.

"Well, according to my sources, before you got this gig, 1973 was the year you flunked out of the State Police Training Academy. Let me see, what was the reason they gave? I think they called it—lack of academic sufficiency. Just a polite way of saying—you're a dumbass." A few chuckles could be heard among the onlookers, but were quickly muffled when Woodburn snapped his head around to catch the offenders. "Aw, I'm sorry," intoned Winston, "I shouldn't have said that. Now all your buddies know."

Winston made a sharp about face and continued his march down the hall, while whistling the tune to the children's song, *Winnie the Pooh*. He smiled when he heard the door to the bullpen slam shut with a force that rattled some windows.

Winston walked into the interrogation room, closed the door, and looked at Louise. "Here I am."

Louise was pacing in tight little circles, trying to get rid of some nervous energy. Her five feet seven inches, coupled with high heel shoes, made her taller than a lot of men. Winston, with his thick curly black hair, eyebrows that almost touched each other, and four foot stature certainly wasn't what she had expected. "Hello," she said.

"Kind of surprised, aren't you?"

"Surprised? I guess you could say that."

"Let's get it over with," he said. "Yes, I'm short. And I don't like being called a dwarf, or a midget, or even a little person. I like being recognized for who and what I am, and that would be, Winston, the attorney."

"I'm Louise Armstrong," she said while extending her hand, "and I don't like someone thinking that I'm condescending before they've even met me."

Winston accepted her hand and shook it heartily. "Fair enough, Doctor Armstrong. I guess I jumped the gun."

"No problem, and, please, just call me, Louise."

"And you can call me, Winston, or Win. Doesn't matter, people call me both."

"Winston's your first name?"

"Yup."

"And your last name too?"

"Right again."

"Your name is Winston Winston?"

"You're catching on. But here's the good news, with me it's always a win-win situation. Get it?" He winked with his left eye and made two clucking sounds with his tongue. "Actually, it's just that my parents had a sense of humor."

"They didn't think you were already going to face enough challenges?"

"To tell you the truth, Louise, I don't look at them as challenges. They've been opportunities."

"Frankie said I'd like you. He was right."

Winston gestured toward the table that was bolted to the floor in the middle of the room. "Shall we sit down and get started?"

"Please, yes. The waiting is driving me crazy." Louise sat with her back to the wall and facing the door.

Winston climbed into the chair on the opposite side of the table. "I've already spent some time with your husband. And he's fine. As you know, I spoke to Frankie, too. He, also, gave me some background information. I do need to get back in with Mitch again, but first I need to ask you some questions."

"Great. Let's get this over with."

With his thumb, Win pointed over his shoulder to the mirror behind him. "See that? It's a two-way mirror, and there are a couple of goombahs on the other side watching us." He turned his head and gave a big, toothy smile to the mirror, then turned back around to face Louise. "They have assured me they are not going to eavesdrop, not going to monitor, not going to record this conversation in any manner. Guess what? They're gonna do all the above."

Winston then took a yellow legal pad from his briefcase and slid it across the table to Louise. "Lift up the first page and you'll see some questions that I've written down. I want you to read each question, to yourself, without moving your lips. I will then ask you for an answer and you will give it to me. I might ask some follow-up questions. Answer them as succinctly as possible. You will not say anything else unless I ask for it. Ready?"

"Go ahead," said Louise.

"Okay, first question, is the answer yes or no?"

As directed, Louise read to herself. *Did either you or Mitch ever meet Vonnie Owens, in person, prior to today?* ... "No," she responded.

"Second question, yes or no?"

This time she read, *Did Mitch have any alcohol, medication, or drugs before he went back to the salon?* ... "No."

"Third question, yes or no?"

Louise read, *Did you or Mitch think Vonnie was holding back some information?* ... "Yes."

"Which one of you thought that?

"Me."

"Did you share that with Mitch?"

"Yes."

"Did it seem to upset him?"

"No. It just gave him more to think about."

"Okay, Louise, back to the notepad. Fourth question, in as few words as possible."

Again, to herself, *Why did Mitch go back to the salon?* ... Louise hesitated for a brief moment, then, with a slight smile, said, "To get his little red knife."

"Really? Doesn't sound like a big enough deal to me."

"Trust me, it is," said Louise. "It has a whole lot of sentimental value. Plus, he just figured it would be a quick trip to the salon and back. Twenty minutes, max."

"Fifth question, yes or no?"

Earlier today when you met with Vonnie Owens, did either you or Mitch argue with her? ... "No."

"You look troubled, Louise. Are you?"

"Yes. I'm still not sure what you're learning or where we're going with these questions."

"Oh, you'd be surprised. It's amazing how complex even the most simple things can become if somebody's not telling the truth. Let me just say I need this for confirmation of what I think I already know. You're gonna have to trust me, Louise, I've been here before. Plus, there's an added bonus." He pointed over his shoulder again with his thumb. "These guys have no idea what we're talking about, and it's bugging them. Now, the last question, number six, yes or no?"

Louise read the last question. *In your mind, is there any possibility, whatsoever, no matter how slight, that Mitch assaulted Vonnie Owens?* "Absolutely no!" Louise's answer was accentuated with an increased volume, a narrowing of her eyes, and sharply pursed lips.

Winston, very obviously, liked the manner of her response and smiled. "Okay, I'll take the pad back now."

Louise lowered the first page and slid the pad across the table to Winston. "For what it's worth, Win. I do trust you."

"Works for me, Doctor Armstrong." Winston put the legal pad back into his briefcase and slid down off his chair. "I just need a few more minutes with your husband. The two of you should be leaving real soon."

Winston walked back down the hall and caught the attention of Detective Woodburn. Winston beckoned with his finger, "Come with me, Woodie." When they reached the door of the interrogation room where Mitch was being held, Winston stopped. "Now's your moment, Detective Woodburn, exactly what are you charging him with?"

"At the very least, unlawful entry."

"C'mon. It's a public business, it wasn't very late, and the main entrance was unlocked. That charge ain't gonna fly."

"He's still a murder suspect, Winston."

"You mean a person of interest. He told you why he was there. Her staff can verify it. Even your own people said it looked like a robbery gone bad, and nothing was found on Armstrong to indicate he had anything to do with it. You're not scoring big points here, Woodburn. We're done. You know how to reach me, and I know how to reach Armstrong. Charge him, depose him or arrest him at some point if you want to, but as for now—bye, bye."

Woodburn scowled, then turned and walked away.

As soon as he was out of sight Winston breathed a huge sigh of relief. *Thank God he is such a dumbass.* He opened the door to the interrogation room where Mitch was being held and said, "Pack your bag, Mitch, you're outta here."

"Where's Detective Woodburn?"

"Don't worry about him. He's more stupid than he looks and he's afraid of me, or at least what I'd do to him in court."

Win and Mitch walked back down the hall to the room where Louise was waiting. Win knocked once on the door, opened it and said, "Let's go, Doc, train's leaving the station."

They stopped briefly at the front desk so Mitch could retrieve his personal items, which included his little red knife. It had been picked up by the arresting officer as evidence after Mitch initially told him the reason he was in the salon.

"I can't believe they gave that back to you," quipped Win, "sometimes I think this whole station is filled with a bunch of numbnuts."

Mitch just shrugged his shoulders.

"Can I give you guys a lift somewhere?" asked Win.

"Our car is still at Vonnie's,"

"I can take you there."

On the quick ride to Vonnie's, Win mentioned that Vonnie's death was going to hit the local business community pretty hard. They also talked some more about Mitch's suspicion that this was all due to his revitalized interest in the murder of Kathleen Spencer.

A hush, however, fell over all three of them as they pulled into the parking lot at Vonnie's Salon. There were two police cars present and lots of yellow crime scene tape. It still seemed too surreal.

Winston spoke to one of the officers, he knew, and explained that they were there to pick up the Armstrongs' car.

Shortly afterward they said their goodbyes. Winston said he'd take care of everything as long as no surprises came up. Mitch said he couldn't think of anything that could possibly surface. Winston then told them to go home, try to relax, and that he'd be in touch. Mitch and Louise thanked him profusely.

"You're welcome," Winston said. "Say hi to Frankie Biondo for me. He's a great friend. I owe him, big time. I'd do anything to help him. Plus, I like screwing with the locals whenever I can. Keeps 'em on their toes. You guys take care. I'll talk to you soon."

CHAPTER 22

"I knew I shouldn't have let you go without me." Frankie was shaking his head as Mitch recalled the events of the trip to Dover.

"Like you could have done anything to stop it. It's Farmer, Frankie. It's gotta be Farmer. It's no coincidence that Vonnie and Muriel are both dead, shortly after I talked to each one. I might not know what the completed puzzle picture is supposed to look like, but nevertheless I've got to start putting the pieces together."

It was mid-morning and the two were sitting, once again, in Mitch's kitchen. Mitch and Louise had, just the night before, returned from Dover. Frankie seemed to be taking a sabbatical from his business in Philly. He had just spent a couple of days in Richmond.

"Enough of that. So, tell me, Frankie, did you get to see our boy?"

"Yeah, I saw him, I met him, I talked to him, and I concur, he's a pompous ass. I also spent some time renewing some old acquaintances. They confirmed something for me. Farmer is tied in with someone. They don't know who, but they're certain he could have never landed the job that he's got unless he's tight with somebody that carries a real big stick. And it's not somebody on the Force or in the capital."

"I agree, but let's take it from the top. How'd you get to meet Farmer?"

"Oh, you're gonna love this. I rented a car, then rammed it into Farmer's car in the capitol building parking lot."

"You did what?"

"You heard me. Look, I wanted to see this guy under stress. Get a better feel for what he is. So, I used a fake ID."

"Harry Burke?"

"No, somebody else. I've got several. Besides, if something went wrong, I wouldn't have done that to you."

"Sorry, should have known better."

"Anyway, I've got a fake ID, it's a fake driver's license. So I used it to rent a car. Then, I got into the employee parking lot. Oh, that was a trick too, had to call in a marker for that one."

"Wait a minute. Just, who are you, Frankie? You've got mob connections in New Jersey, lawyers in Delaware, people who obviously 'owe you' in Virginia. Who the hell are you?"

"Just me, Mitch. Your friend, Frankie. I told you, lots of things have happened over the past twenty-five years."

Mitch wiped his hands back through his hair, and gripped the back of his own neck, "Wow, you seem to be full of surprises. Okay, so continue."

"Okay, so I cruise the parking lot a little while, then found his car. It was in a space that had a sign with his name on it. I stopped, backed up, took aim, stomped on the gas; and, voila, he's gonna need a new right rear fender."

"Oh, I'm lovin' this," Mitch said, "keep going."

"So then, security comes over and when they see whose car I smashed they go into a real tizzy. Tell me not to move or even think about leaving. They get on the radio and evidently call into the building to Farmer's office. About ten minutes later this guy with ratty look-ing, drugstore hair, an old brown suit, and an angry look on his face comes walking toward me. As he starts getting closer and can see me, he picks up his pace and puts on this horrible scowl. Guess he was trying to scare me."

"Sounds like Farmer."

"Oh, it was. And boy was he pissed. He walks all around, looking at his car, then at mine, then me, then back to his car. The whole time he's harping about how expensive his car is, how careless I was, how much this is going to cost, how I better have insurance. Never once giving me a chance to say anything."

"As I said, sounds like Farmer."

"Finally, I get to go into my scared as shit routine, and tell him that I've got to call my insurance company, that I've got some issues that might be a problem, et cetera, et cetera."

"So, let me guess, he takes you to his office."

"You got it."

"You're good, Frankie. And I'm assuming that all the while he's got no idea that you're the kid who, so to speak, helped him solve the Kathleen Spencer case."

"Yeah, I know. Isn't that great? So, we get to his office, and he huffs and puffs all over me. He takes my fake driver's license and makes a copy of it. So, I act like I'm scared shitless, and then a stroke of luck hits. He gets called out of the office to take care of something. I'm left in his pri-vate office alone. Of course he snarls at me and he shouts, 'Sit still, don't touch anything, and you better start thinking about how you're gonna make this right.' Then he leaves, and as soon as he walks out the door I start looking around. I'll tell you what I found in a minute."

"This is getting better all the time," said Mitch.

"About five minutes later he comes back, and threatens me some more. Finally, I get to call my insurance company. Of course, before I left Philly, I'd already told my deli manager that I'd be calling sometime that day on our 'special' business line. Told him that he was supposed to be my insurance agent in case somebody else wants to talk to him. When I get off the phone, I tell Farmer that because of some problems I've had in the past, they're not going to pay anything. He has a meltdown and, tells me that I'll have to pay out of my own pocket. I say I don't have any extra cash and can't afford it. He goes crazy. You kind of getting the picture?"

"Yeah, and loving every bit of it."

"Finally, he says he wants to see my vehicle registration, and I told him it was in my car. I also said that all this is making me sick to my stomach and that I need a restroom. He directs me to one down the hall from his office. Tells me to hurry up and get feeling better, and that I better not forget to go get the car registration."

"So, what did you do?"

Frankie started to laugh. "I left the building and never looked back. He was too stupid to go with me. I guess he figured I was so scared of him that I'd come right back without anybody checking on me. He had even called the guard station so they would know what I was doing and to let me back in after I went and got the registration. I walked right out of the building; walked right out of the parking lot; got a couple blocks away as fast as I could; took a cab to the downtown lot where I left my own car." Frankie relaxed back in his chair like he had just finished a good meal. "I had a nice leisurely drive through Virginia; stopped and ate dinner; spent the night at a comfortable motel; and, here I am."

"Unbelievable." Mitch sat there shaking his head with a smirk on his face that just wouldn't go away. "So, did you learn anything?"

"I confirmed that Farmer's an asshole who probably isn't smart enough to be orchestrating this whole shooting match by himself. Somebody else has got to be involved in this."

"Yeah, we agree on that. You said you found something in his office. What was it?"

"Gotta save the best for last. I don't know if it will give us any answers right now, but I'm not a big believer in coincidences, and I just got a feeling this is going to be important at some point in time." Frankie reached into a side pocket of the blue blazer he was wearing and pulled out a 6x8 color photograph and placed it on the table in front of Mitch. "I had a small pocket camera with me and took this picture when Farmer was out of the office. Got it developed at a 'while you wait' photo store on the way home. It's actually a picture of a picture. Farmer has the real picture in a frame sitting on one of the book shelves in his office. Take a good look, Mitch."

Mitch stared at the photo. It showed an 8x10 frame that had two pictures in it, one above the other. One picture was the side view of a car and driver, the other caught the tail end of the car as they passed by the photographer. There was another passenger in the small convertible, but he was sitting on top of the back of the passenger seat and was turned away from the camera. Mitch stared intently, then looked up at Frankie. "That's Farmer behind the wheel. Looks like he's in some kind of parade or something."

"Yeah. And what's he driving?"

Mitch looked at the picture again, closed his eyes, dropped his head, and slowly shook it back and forth before dragging out the words, "Holy shit, a red '56 T-bird."

"Mitch, this might *not* be the one from Bohman's Point. But like I said, I don't believe in coincidences. We've got something here. We need to pursue it."

"Oh, we will, Frankie. We will. I've still got some contacts on the Force. They never liked Farmer and never will. I'm sure I'll be able to find out what the picture is all about. If he thought it was worth putting in his office, I'm sure, that at some point in time, he must have had it on his desk at the precinct. And knowing Farmer, I'm sure that everybody heard about how important the parade or whatever he was doing had to be. I'll find out."

"I guess we're not so different now, after all, Mitch. This thing is really getting to me. I want to see somebody pay."

Later that day, after Frankie left to head back to Philly, Mitch placed a call to the precinct station in Richmond, where he had once been assigned.

"First Precinct, Sergeant Patterson, how can I help you?"

"Mike, great hearing your voice. It's Mitch Armstrong."

"Mitch! Well, I'll be dammed. It's been a few years. How the hell are you?"

"Yeah, it's been a while, Mike. I'm glad I got through to someone I know."

"What's up Mitch? I doubt you called just to chit-chat."

"Yeah, you're right. But I got a little favor to ask. I hate doing this out of the blue. You know, I haven't spoken to anyone there for a while, and now I'm calling to ask for help with something."

"Hey, that's okay, Mitch. What are friends for? So, what can I do for you?"

"Well, it has to do with my favorite homicide detective."

"You mean everybody's favorite, don't you?" Patterson's voice dripped with friendly sarcasm. "You do know, don't you, that he retired earlier this year? Took a job with the Capital Security."

"Yeah, I'm aware of all that. But here's the question, and it's kind of a crazy one. Do you remember, or could you check around and see if anybody remembers, him ever having a picture on his desk or around the office somewhere that showed him driving a '56 T-bird?"

"Oh, I don't have to check around. I know that picture well. All you had to do was glance at it when Farmer was in the office, and he'd stop you and give you the whole lowdown on it. That prick loved letting everybody know how important he was."

"So there's a story associated with the picture." Mitch went from laying back in a big easy chair to sitting up straight.

"Oh there's a story. Here's the quick and dirty version. The T-bird belongs to Governor Parker. It was in a Fourth of July parade, the year he was campaigning for election. Farmer drove, and Parker sat on the seatback and waved to the crowd. To hear Farmer tell the story, you'd think he was the governor's campaign manager or something. The reality is, Farmer never makes it real clear, and nobody really knows why Farmer was driving. Best guess is that the campaign needed a driver, wanted a police officer, and Farmer's name got drawn from a hat. So, tell me, Mitch, what's the interest in the picture?"

"Mike, there's really not a lot I can say right now. Somebody has recently seen it in Farmer's office, knew that I worked with him at one time, and wondered if I knew what the significance of the picture was. If it gets any more interesting than that, I'll let you know."

"Good enough, Mitch. Fine, don't tell me. But you've got me curious."

Mitch chuckled. He and Mike Patterson chatted for a few more minutes, just friendly banter and catching up.

CHAPTER 23

Ten days had passed since the murder of Vonnie Owens. It turned out that Win Winston was every bit as good an attorney as Frankie Biondo promised he would be. In some respects even better than they expected. At the present moment, Mitch was completely off the hook, and the local police were pursuing what is, according to Winston, some pretty solid evidence. So solid, but leading in such an unexpected direction, that the locals were in contact with the FBI. Win said he was anxious to talk to Mitch about it. They would have that opportunity today.

Vonnie Owens was a well-known and well-respected pillar of the community. She had been a business owner for fifteen years, a current and very active member of the local Chamber of Commerce. She was the kind of person who would attend most civic events, and had a way of making folks feel good that they had chosen to attend also. It was, therefore, not surprising that her memorial service at the Presbyterian Church of Dover was filled to capacity.

Win Winston was seated in the last pew next to a very attractive blonde. They arrived together. They shared a comfortable closeness, and it was easy to sense that they were more than just acquaintances. Win had been watching the door as people filed in, and when he saw

Mitch and Louise he motioned for them to join him and his companion in the space he was saving in the pew.

Louise was in awe as she took in the magnificent vaulted ceiling. The rich but soft melody of the Skinner pipe organ, as the organist played from a selection of well-known hymns, caused a comforting warmth to settle over her. "This place is over two hundred and fifty years old," she whispered to Mitch. "It's beautiful." He nodded in agreement.

The organist finished *How Great Thou Art* and followed with *The Old Rugged Cross*. Then as the final strains of *Abide With Me* gently faded away, Vonnie's casket, draped in a pall, was brought down the center aisle and situated in front of the altar.

Vonnie's minister, Reverend Charles Gray, stood up and began to speak. He first gave recognition to Vonnie's family members, who were seated at the front of the church. Reverend Gray followed with a series of prayers and scriptures, the commendation, the blessing and, finally, the procession to end the service. Everyone was encouraged to attend the interment prayers, which would be held right outside of the church.

It was a short walk to the church cemetery, long enough, however, for Win to introduce his fiancé, Grace, and to let Mitch know that he and Mitch really, really had to talk. It was a sunny day with little humidity, seasoned with the smell of freshly cut grass. It all felt appropriately pleasant. Respectful silence seemed to be the order of the day as the crowd slowly emptied out of the church and filled the area surrounding Vonnie's grave. The graveside remarks were short, but heartfelt. Vonnie's husband and several other family members each placed a single rose on top of Vonnie's casket.

Reverend Gray concluded, "We all know that Vonnie was always a gracious hostess. So, would you please join us back in the social hall for some refreshments and fellowship? I'm sure she would enjoy that."

Before going into the hall, Win tugged on Mitch's jacket, indicating he wanted a private moment. "Would you ladies please excuse us for a minute," Win said as they walked away from the crowd and left Louise and Grace to themselves. Once they were sufficiently separated from everyone else, Win began, "I didn't tell you this before, but Vonnie and I were friends for quite a few years. I was a client of hers at the salon for a very long time. If I had ever suspected that you actually did have anything to do with her death I'd have dropped you in a heartbeat."

"Louise and I are real grateful for how you handled this case," said Mitch.

"Super. You're welcome. But there's more to this story. Vonnie's husband, Jim Owens, is a good man. I've known him for a long time, too. I've helped him out quite a bit with some business and personal issues over the years. He likes me and he trusts me. As you can imagine, he's taking this really hard. I've spent a lot of time with him over the past ten days. He's very appreciative of that."

"I really am sorry, Win. There are some real bad people at work here."

"I can imagine. Anyway, I told Jim about you and why you had come to see Vonnie. I also told him about Tommy Cleaves, and how certain you are that he wasn't the one who killed the Spencer girl. Jim actually knew Kathleen Spencer. Not very well," Win stressed, looking about, rechecking that they were alone. He continued, "He didn't grow up with her like Vonnie did. But he knew how badly Kathleen's death had affected Vonnie. What I'm leading up to is this. He gave me something just a little earlier today. He wants you to see it." Win reached into his jacket's breast pocket, brought out a large manila envelope that was folded in half, and handed it to Mitch.

"What's this?"

"Something you need to look at—some letters and mementos that Vonnie was hanging onto that had something to do with Kathleen. He'd like to have 'em back, but said that you're welcome to take the packet home with you and look through it to see if there's anything in there that could be useful to you. He thinks that if it could, in any way, help bring clarity to Kathleen's murder that it would be a fitting tribute to Vonnie."

"Thanks, Win. This could be big."

"Don't get your hopes up. You might not find anything of interest."

"Yeah, but on the other hand, there just might be something here." Mitch carefully placed the envelope into his suit coat pocket. The two men started walking toward the sidewalk where Louise and Grace were waiting.

"Oh, one other thing, Mitch." Win raised his right hand with index finger extended, and came to a slow stop. "Remember I said the locals reached out to the FBI? Well, does the name Adolf Richter mean anything to you?"

Mitch, likewise stopped, and turned to face Win. "Where in the hell did you dig that up?"

"Then you do know him?"

"Yeah, years ago. He goes by Dolf. I was still on the force in Richmond. I busted him for running a pretty big extortion ring. Lots of cops had been on the take. I also think he had a hand in a murder or two, but before I could get very far with the investigation he got deported."

"Okay, this confirms a lot of what I've heard. Deported, huh?"

"Yeah," Mitch replied, "he was a German national. Didn't have papers."

Win scrunched up his face. "Seems strange he got deported right away with an on-going investigation in place."

"I think there was a lot more to it. I could never say for sure and never really had the opportunity to follow up on it, but I'd bet my life that a detective named Ken Farmer, a real asshole, was right in the middle of the whole thing. Doesn't matter, that's all ancient history. So, why are you asking me about Richter?"

They both began walking again.

"Hang onto your hat, Mitch, maybe that history ain't so ancient anymore. Dolf Richter's handprint was lifted off the window of the front door to *Vonnie's Salon.*"

Mitch stopped in his tracks, dropped his jaw, and stared at Win. "You have got to be shitting me."

Win turned around and started to walk backward. He put his hands out to his sides with his palms forward, and just kind of shrugged his shoulders. "I shit you not. I'd say you've got some work to do. Let me know if I can help. In the meantime, let's mingle. I want to introduce you to a few people."

They rejoined Louise and Grace. The two women were engaged in a lively discussion and seemed to be enjoying each other's company.

"So, you've decided not to leave us alone after all." Louise cut a sideward glance toward Mitch.

"Sorry ladies." said Win, "My fault, I just had to clear up a couple things that I've been carrying around in my head all day."

"Well, you left us alone, and I think it's going to be a pretty pricey abandonment," chimed in Grace. "Louise and I have decided that a night out at the Kennedy Center in Washington, coupled with a dinner at The Palm Restaurant might soothe our ruffled feathers. We're going to work out the details over the next couple weeks."

"Wow, it didn't take the two of you very long to bond," said Mitch.

Louise smiled. "Men bond—women unite. Grace and I have a lot in common, and we plan to make the most of it."

Mitch and Win looked at each other, and almost simultaneously said, "This is going to be expensive."

The four of them walked into the church hall. Win and Grace worked the room with Mitch and Louise in tow, introducing them to all of the Dover somebodies who showed up for Vonnie's funeral. Mitch and Louise also shared a few words of condolence with Jim Owens and some other members of Vonnie's family.

Mitch spoke privately with Jim. "I am so deeply sorry about your loss, Jim. I can't even begin to imagine how you're able to cope with this."

"Toughest thing I've ever done." Jim's voice cracked as he struggled to control his emotions.

"If there's anything that Louise and I can do, please don't hesitate to reach out."

"No," Jim replied. "But, the two of you were among the last to see her. She didn't indicate that anything was wrong, did she?"

"Not at all." Mitch reached out and gently grasped Jim's arm. "And I can't express how deeply sorry I am that anything having to do with the Kathleen Spencer situation may have, in any way, been responsible for this."

"Don't feel guilty, Mitch. The world is full of evil people. I just hope that you'll be able to bring some of them to justice."

"I'm driven to do that. Now, more than ever. And I want to thank you for the packet of letters that Win passed on to me. I'll be very careful with it and return it as soon as possible."

"You're welcome. I hope it somehow helps. And thank you for coming today."

Mitch nodded, shook hands, and promised, once more, to return the packet.

Shortly afterward, Mitch and Louise departed and were on their way back to Maryland. It didn't take long for their conversation to turn to Mitch's chat with Winston.

"I need you to look at something," Mitch said. He reached into his breast pocket, retrieved the manila envelope, and handed it to Louise.

"What's this?"

"I don't know yet. You're about to find out for us. Win gave it to me. It belongs to Jim Owens and Jim wants it back, but he told Win that I could keep it for a little while to see if there was anything there that could help with my investigation."

Louise opened the envelope and emptied the contents onto her lap. There were five standard letter size white envelopes, all slightly yellowed with age. Each one was hand-written by the same person and addressed to Vonnie Woodall, her maiden name. Each had the same return address *K.M.S., 65 Vista Lane, Bohman's Point, Virginia.*

"Holy crap, Mitch. Do you know what these are?"

"Tell me."

"I think these are the letters from Kathleen that Vonnie told us she didn't keep."

"Keep looking. Don't keep me in suspense."

Louise shuffled through the envelopes, stopping at one that had a curious little bulge in it. She reached her fingers into the envelope and pulled out a couple sheets of folded flowery note paper. On the note paper was a hand-written letter. But Louise's eyes widened when she saw what the note paper was folded around. It was a stack of five black and white photographs.

"You're not going to believe this, Mitch."

"What?"

"Pictures."

"I gotta stop." Mitch pulled off to the side of the road, and turned on all the inside lights.

Mitch and Louise, with their heads touching, looked at each photo as Louise shuffled through them repeatedly. The photo quality hadn't suffered too much, but wasn't great to begin with. Louise tried to be extra careful because a couple of the photos were stuck together. She managed to separate them with minimal damage.

"Anything look familiar?" Louise asked.

"Yeah, that's her," said Mitch, "that's Kathleen." Then, as Louise turned over a couple more pictures—"Holy shit! Let me see them. Those two pictures, that's the car, and that's gotta be the guy. Oh, wait 'til Frankie sees this."

CHAPTER 24

Mitch pulled the car phone from its case and called Frankie. He didn't say a lot other than, "We need to talk. As soon as possible." Once again a rendezvous was set for Skipper's. Frankie would meet Mitch and Louise there in about an hour or so.

Louise pored over the letters as they drove, then read from all of them to Mitch. In the letters, Kathleen kept referring to her boyfriend as "Cap." Mitch and Louise concluded it must have been a nickname.

"She was obviously quite taken by him," Mitch said. "Nothing but praise and how much she loved him."

"I know," Louise replied. "But there really is a lot of girl code, if you will, in these letters. Vonnie was right about her being pregnant. Kathleen lets the cat out of the bag in this letter. She also says she's going to get an abortion. Then in this next letter, the last one we have, she tells her that she's changed her mind about abortion. She's going to have the baby and that she's going to drop that news on Cap and her parents real soon."

"Do any of those letters have dates on them?" Mitch was starting to pay more attention to the letters than to his driving.

"Yeah, they all do, and the envelopes are postmarked. But more importantly, keep your eyes on the road. You're drifting over."

"Don't worry about my driving. What's the date of the last letter?"

"August 20th. Why?"

"Son of a bitch. That could explain a lot."

"Like what?"

"That was the day before the murder. If that's what they were talking about on the beach that night, that could be why Cap got so pissed off. He wanted the abortion. A wife and baby at that point in time would have been a nightmare for him. He was halfway through college, and it sounds like he might have had parents who had already mapped out his future for him. Yeah, a pregnant girlfriend, he probably couldn't imagine anything worse, I'm sure."

"I agree." Louise kept flipping through the pages of that final letter. "Seems that she's really looking forward to motherhood and life with this guy. She just had to be real careful about how she said it, you know, in case Vonnie's parents got nosey and read one of these letters."

"So, she didn't come right out and say these things, but from what you're reading you're pretty sure that's what she meant."

"Not pretty sure. Positive."

"If you say so. I'm just glad I've got my interpreter with me."

Louise simply gave Mitch a smug smile of satisfaction.

Mitch and Louise were the first to arrive at Skipper's. Mitch was pleased that the same booth that he and Frankie sat in was available. They got seated, ordered some beers, and, of course, some chicken and ribs for the three of them.

Before long Frankie slid into the bench seat across from Mitch and Louise.

"Hi guys. Hope this is worth it. I gave up a poker game with a bunch of losers who just can't figure out how to win. Always makes me feel good, kickin' their asses."

"Oh, we definitely think it is," said Mitch. He told Frankie about the letters, and Louise interjected with her interpretation of the messages that Kathleen was sending. Mitch then slid the pictures across the table to Frankie. "Take a look at these."

"Son of a bitch, it's him all right. That's the guy and the car that I saw the day of the murder. Oh shit, this is real déjà vu. It's like I was there all over again. This is creepy."

After examining the pictures for a few more minutes, Frankie slid them back across the table to Mitch.

"The car looks like the one in the picture you got from Farmer's office. Too bad these are black and white. I just wish there was some way we could confirm one way or another if they are the same car."

"Here it is. You know, I recognize you two fellas, I think I waited on you before." It was Paulette, the waitress. She had a large tray with three chicken and rib dinners. Smiling at Louise, she continued, "Hi, I'm Paulette. I've seen these two in here before."

"Hi, Paulette, I'm Louise. I hope they were good tippers. I'd hate to be embarrassed."

"Oh, they were good to me. Thanks for asking."

"No problem. I'll make sure they keep up the good work."

Small talk, Natty Boh beer, and good eats took up the next thirty minutes.

"Wait a second," Frankie said as he wiped off his mouth, "let me see those pictures again."

Mitch, once again, slid them across the table to Frankie. This time Frankie gave them some real close scrutiny.

"Well, would you look at that. I'll be damned. What do you two know about continental kits, especially continental kits on a '56 T-bird?"

"Probably not much," Mitch replied. "Why?"

"I don't even know what it is," added Louise.

"It's the upright cover on the back of the car that houses the spare tire. The '56 is the only one of the T-birds that had it. You could get a couple different styles. You can see in these pictures that this one has a chrome outer band going around it. Not all of them had it. The one that Farmer was in had the chrome band."

"That's getting better, but it's not conclusive," said Mitch.

"I know, Mitch, but here's the kicker. Take a close look at the back side of the cover in this picture." Frankie pointed to a specific picture. "See that? It's a fancy monogram of the number '56."

"Okay, I see what you're talking about, but so what? It was a '56 T-bird."

"I know, but the number on the continental kit is totally unique. None of them came with it. That was added by the owner. It's nothing stock."

"So why would somebody add that?" asked Louise. "Wouldn't everybody know it was a '56 if that was the only year that Thunderbirds had the tire thingy on the back?"

"It's probably got another meaning to it," said Mitch. "I'm sure the year means more to the owner than just the year of his car. Maybe it's his high school graduation year. That night on the beach he did say he was halfway through college."

"Well, hang onto your hat, Mitch," interjected Frankie. "Here's the real kicker. The T-bird in Farmer's picture has the exact same continental kit with the exact same number '56."

"Holy shit, Frankie, this is amazing. This is no damn coincidence. We've opened up something big here. For the first time in twenty-five years, we're getting somewhere."

"This is mind-blowing," replied Frankie.

"I don't want to appear naive," said Louise, "but tell me what you guys are thinking."

Mitch looked straight at her and simply said, "The guy on the beach with Kathleen, the guy that, obviously, killed her—is Governor Parker. That's what we're thinking."

"Whaatt? That can't be."

"It was his car. It also explains a lot about Farmer. He must know that Parker is the killer," intoned Frankie.

"Yeah, but aren't you guys jumping to conclusions? Maybe he bought the car from the real killer. It's been years. Or maybe the governor has a brother and he was the one."

"Or maybe we're right," said Mitch. "You read all those letters, sweetie. What name did Kathleen keep calling her boyfriend?"

"She called him Cap. We figured it was a nickname."

"Probably was a nickname. But where did it come from? What is Governor Parker's full name?"

"I don't know," responded Louise.

"It's Conrad Allen Parker. His initials are C.A.P. I think Cap would be a pretty reasonable nickname."

Louise opened her mouth to speak, but no words could come out. Finally, "This is unbelievable. If you're right. And let me include myself now. If we're right, this is freakin' huge."

"A lot of things are, all of a sudden, making a lot more sense," replied Mitch.

The three of them kept shaking their heads collectively and muttering, "Holy shit."

They finished dinner, chatted, made plans, and discussed what the next options would be. Mitch also filled Frankie in on what he had learned about Dolf Richter being at Vonnie's. After telling Frankie that Dolf had always been deeply embedded in the Richmond underground, Frankie assured Mitch that he had contacts who could find out whatever they needed or wanted to know about Dolf.

It was finally starting to look like the following weeks were going to lead in a lot of hopefully productive directions.

"We're going to need whatever they can dig up on Dolf," said Mitch, "but I can't put some of this off any longer. I'm going to go see Farmer. There's no way in hell that the son of a bitch is not involved in all this. I've gotta look him in the eye and try to figure it out. Mainly because somebody else is telling him what to do, and I've got to find out if that somebody is the governor, or if it isn't the governor, then who is pulling Farmer's strings."

Frankie picked a little bit at the food remaining on his plate. "Be careful, Mitch. I've got a nose for this. And I can tell you that what we're dealing with is big time. Be careful."

"Oh, I'm being careful. And speaking of being careful, from now on if I call you it will be from my car phone. If you need to get hold of me and I don't answer the car phone, try the house and just let me know you need to talk. I'll get back in touch with you."

"You've lost me here, Mitch." Frankie's face had a quizzical look.

"One of my associates is a surveillance expert. I had him check out my house and he discovered that my phone has been tapped. We were going to disconnect it, then decided to let it be. It might actually come in handy sometime. You know, make them hear what we want them to hear."

"I'm guessing you suspect Farmer. Are you sure he's the one?"

"Can't imagine it being anybody else. I'll be shocked if your contacts who check out Dolf don't find that his actions are directly connected to Farmer."

"But you've already told me that Farmer's an incompetent jackass. So, he's gotta be taking orders from somebody else. If it's not the governor, then who is it? I just can't imagine that the governor, himself, would be risking the exposure, even if he is the one who needs the cover up. Somebody else has got to be running the show for him. And what's in it for that somebody else?"

Mitch leaned back and looked down at the table, then directly at Frankie. "We'll get there, Frankie. Sooner or later ... we'll get there."

Shortly afterward, the three of them walked out of Skipper's.

As Mitch and Frankie shared a quick hand shake and shoulder bump, Frankie whispered, "If I ever get my hands on Parker, I'll kill him. If he hadn't murdered that girl, I would've never been in that shed with Cleaves."

"I know," Mitch replied, "I know."

Louise slipped in between the two men and gave Frankie a goodbye hug. They got into their cars and departed.

A little more than five minutes later, Paulette, the waitress, came out of Skipper's, walked to the far end of the parking lot, and slid into the passenger side of the car waiting there. Turk had called Paulette from an outside phone booth to give her a heads up. He had been in Philadelphia following Frankie and trying to dig up some information on him when Frankie got the call from Mitch. Turk followed him to Skipper's.

"They've got something," Paulette said, "they were passing around some pictures and what looked like some hand-written letters. Seemed to have them all excited. I got a peek at one of the pictures. It was a guy in a little sports car. The picture looked pretty old. It was quick, and I didn't want to look obvious, so I really didn't see a whole lot. "

Turk looked at her from the driver's seat and nodded his head a couple times. "Good job, Paulette. You can go back in now."

Before leaving the parking lot Turk used the outside pay phone one more time.

"Don't know for sure what they've got, sir, but they're definitely onto something. I didn't see it, but it sounds like they've got a picture of a young guy in some sort of sports car. My guess is it could be the T-bird."

"Stay on it, Turk. I'll talk to Farmer." Then the Old Man hung up his phone.

CHAPTER 25

Mitch felt like a bunch more pieces to the giant jigsaw puzzle had been dropped onto the table. After he and Louise returned from Dover, Mitch called Farmer's office and made an appointment to see him. Dolf Richter's hand print could have been at Vonnie's for only one reason, and Mitch wanted to go straight to who he suspected was the source of his problems to find out why. Two days after returning from Vonnie's funeral he went to Richmond.

Mitch parked a couple blocks away from the Virginia State Capitol Building. It was 1:00 p.m. A leisure walk brought him to the massive structure which always filled him with a sense of awe.

Passing through the obligatory, but Mitch thought useless, security check, he asked where Ken Farmer's office was located and was directed to a door at the end of a first-floor hallway.

Mitch, unsure of the protocol, tapped on the door, then opened it. He stepped into the room, introduced himself, and received a friendly greeting from the receptionist. She appeared to be in her fifties and was a pleasant woman, despite the rhinestones and gaudy glasses.

"Security Chief Farmer will be with you shortly," she said.

Security Chief Farmer? He makes her call him that? What an asshole.

No magazines, no coffee, nothing to make a waiting guest comfortable. Mitch's appointment was for 1:30. Finally, at 2:15, the receptionist's phone softly rang. She picked it up, whispered a few words, then placed it back in its cradle.

"Security Chief Farmer will see you now, Mr. Armstrong."

"Thanks, I was beginning to think I came on the wrong day."

She stood, motioned to a door and said, "You can go right in."

Mitch stepped into another, smaller than expected, room, but one that was nevertheless festooned with *I love Me* plaques and mementoes from Farmer's career in law enforcement.

"Hello, Ken. How the hell are you?" Mitch didn't even attempt to mask the contempt in his voice.

"Well, well, well, Mitch Armstrong. I can hardly imagine that you would want to pay me a visit. To what do I owe this? Oh, what shall I call it—pleasure?"

"Cut the crap, Farmer. I've been waiting forty-five minutes. You've had no visitors, no incoming calls, and not a single button on any phone has been lit. What were you so busy doing, taking a nap? The only pleasure you got was making me wait."

"You don't know what goes on here. You made an appointment and you had to wait. Big deal. So, now you're here. What do you want?"

"Gee, Ken, can't we spend a couple minutes getting chummy again? We were always such good friends."

Farmer's stare was expressionless. "Truth is, Armstrong, if you hadn't called here for an appointment I was going to contact you."

"And why would that be?"

"To tell you to back off the Cleaves case. He's dead. He was a piece of shit. He deserved what he got. And your poking around is going to do nothing more than stir up coverage from certain news outlets and special interest whackos who think the governor should have stayed the execution."

"He should have."

"Bullshit! Cleaves was tried and convicted and had a bunch of appeals turned down. The system worked. He got what he deserved."

"The system sucks. And this case proves it. An innocent man died for something he didn't do."

"Let's not start this all over again, Armstrong. I know where you're coming from. But let me say this one more time. I don't know what you're after, but I did the investigation and you are way off base. So back off. Cleaves is dead. It no longer matters."

"But it does matter, Ken. More innocent people are dying. A woman in Dover, Delaware, named Vonnie Owens was recently murdered, and that's not long after Muriel Cathcart, one of the witnesses at Tommy's execution, was also murdered."

"Armstrong, this is laughable. I heard about Cathcart, probably a break-in, gone bad. But a dead woman in Delaware? How in the hell does that relate? Next thing you know, it'll be your friend in Philadelphia."

"And just what do you mean by that? What the hell do you know about him? I never mentioned him to you."

Farmer realized he had slipped up and said something he shouldn't. "I just know things," he stuttered.

"How do you know things? Are you the one who tapped my phone? What else are you doing, having me followed?"

"You're delusional, Armstrong. You've gotten so wrapped up in this, you're imagining things. A hairdresser in Delaware gets murdered and you think it has something to do with Kathleen Spencer's death in Virginia twenty-five years ago."

"To begin with, asshole, she knew the Spencer girl. And, once again, Ken, I'm not the one having mental lapses. Did you forget? I never said anything about her being a hairdresser."

"So what. Like I said, I know things."

"Well, here's something I bet you didn't know, and you're just going to love this. Your guy screwed up."

"What guy?"

"Dolf Richter."

"Richter? Like I said, Armstrong. You're delusional. First of all, Richter's not 'my guy' and secondly, that was years ago. Did you forget?"

"The only person who forgot something was you. You forgot to tell Richter not to leave any evidence behind. His handprint was found at the murder scene in Dover." Mitch couldn't help but notice a slight tightening of Farmer's jaw. "So, Ken, you're telling me to back off, and at the same time some of the people I've been in contact with are getting killed, and one of your lackeys, that S.O.B. Richter, is obviously involved."

"You're out of your mind, Armstrong." Farmer's voice started to pick up a slight shrillness. "Even if Richter is back in the states, it's got nothing to do with me. I'm telling you, back the hell off!"

The phone on Farmer's desk rang, interrupting the confrontation, and allowing Farmer to regain a little composure.

"Okay, tell them I'll be right over." Farmer dropped the receiver into its cradle. "We're going to have to cut this short. The first lady is giving a tour of the governor's mansion and they're starting early. They need me over there now." Then, as a taunt, he added, "Want to go see the governor's house?"

"What I want to see is your skinny little face telling me why Richter is back in town. I thought he was deported."

"None of my business, none of your business, Armstrong. That's an INS problem. You're nosing around too much. You need to butt out." Farmer stood and started walking toward the office door. Then with a cocky smirk and tilted head, Farmer said, "You can follow me over or you can leave."

Mitch couldn't restrain himself. He grabbed Farmer by the throat and slammed him against the wall. "Quit dickin' with me you son-of-a-bitch. Who are you really working for? I know who you're hiding, but I know he's not calling the shots. This has been going on for so long it's gotta be somebody else. Who is it?"

"What are you talking about?" His words were more of a gurgle as he fought for a gasp of breath. The fear in Farmer's eyes was palpable.

"You know damn well what I'm talking about, and you know damn well I'm going to find out."

Mitch released Farmer and backed up a step or two.

"I should have you arrested, Armstrong."

"But you won't, will you? I think I scare you just a little too much. And let me give you one more little tidbit of information. Sure, you did the investigation. But guess what, Kenny Boy? The charm bracelet was a plant. It was a plant and I can prove it."

Farmer couldn't respond, verbally or facially. He remained expressionless.

"I'm leaving, Farmer. But I'm not finished with you, not by a long shot."

Mitch turned and walked out of the office.

Farmer leaned against his desk and took a few deep breaths. After regaining his composure, he straightened his shirt and tie, combed his hair, and looked at the full length mirror behind his door, just to make sure he was presentable.

"You don't know, Armstrong," he whispered to himself, "you don't know how finished you really are."

CHAPTER 26

As soon as Farmer returned to his office, after helping the first lady with the governor's mansion tour, he settled into his desk chair, picked up the phone, and dialed the Old Man's number.

"Yes?"

"Hello. It's me, Ken."

"I know who it is, go ahead, Ken."

"Armstrong was just here. He's getting in deeper. He knows that Richter's involved. I think it's time we take the son of a bitch out."

"Not so fast, Ken. If you start ... *taking people out* ... as you call it, without giving it a lot of thought, you run the risk of creating consequences you weren't expecting. I'm not real happy about either the Cathcart woman or that Owens woman in Dover. You need to keep Dolf on a shorter leash. So far, what happened to them has not caused a major problem for us. But as we've discovered, Armstrong's obviously got connections of some sort here in Virginia as well as Pennsylvania and Delaware. I don't know yet how deep or widespread those roots are. So I don't want to do something that will create an even bigger problem for us. What we need to do is simply get Armstrong's attention in a big way. We need to make him realize that pursuing this thing just isn't worth the possible consequences. Talk to Dolf. He's got somebody that I think could help. But make sure he understands what the limitations are."

"Will do. I'll get right on it." Farmer kicked the pitch of his voice and the speed of his words into high gear. "I know how you feel, and even though I want Armstrong out of the picture, I know we need to proceed cautiously. In fact, what I'll do is ..."

Dial tone.

&

The Kegler is a rundown bar that once had a bowling alley motif. Now it's just a piece of junk that is dark, smells of cigarette smoke, and has noisy wooden floors. It is located on Chamberlayne Avenue in Richmond, an area most people want to avoid. Dolf Richter wasn't like most people. He felt comfortable on Chamberlayne, and especially liked hanging out at The Kegler. He didn't do it for the people, he just liked the grimy atmosphere. Dolf wasn't the type that ever felt the need to impress anybody.

Farmer didn't like The Kegler, but he'd rather meet Dolf here than have Dolf come to his office. Richter simply wasn't a nice person and was rude to everyone. Farmer wasn't going to run the risk of having Dolf show up at the capitol building and talk to someone he shouldn't talk to, or saying something to someone that shouldn't be said.

Farmer found Dolf inside the bar, sitting at a small table by himself.

"You always drink alone?"

"I drink with whoever I want to. Somedays that means it's just me."

"Good. We don't need anybody else here today."

"You have a job for me?"

"I talked to the Old Man recently. He wants Armstrong to get a wakeup call. A big one."

"We don't need to wake him up. We need to put him to sleep—permanently. I can do that."

"Well that's just great." Farmer's voice dripped with sarcasm. "I'll keep it in mind. But that's not what the Old Man's looking for."

"So, just what exactly is he looking for?"

"He wants something that gets Armstrong's attention in a big way. It has to say that this is bad but that it could have been much worse. It has to be threatening. But it can't be deadly. At least not this time."

"Tall order. It'll be costly."

"You know that's not an issue. So, have you got anything in mind?"

Dolf scanned the immediate area around them to make sure no one was watching or listening. "Yeah. I've got a guy. A number of years ago he and a few others made the world aware of how unhappy they were with our involvement in Vietnam. A couple people, as well as some buildings, paid the price. I can get him to do it again."

"Remember what I said. Nobody gets hurt."

"That's no fun. But I'll make sure. How soon do you need this?"

"Week or two, max."

"And payment?"

"You know that's not a problem. You do the job, you get paid, and you know it'll be enough." Farmer stood and turned to leave, then stopped and looked over his shoulder. "I won't have to ask you if the job's been done. I'll know, right?"

"Oh, you'll know. Trust me, you'll know."

As soon as Farmer was gone Dolf went to the payphone located on the wall next to the restrooms. He dialed a number, one of the many he had committed to memory. A squeaky voice answered, "Yeah, what do you want?"

"The first thing I want is for you to remember who you're talking to."

Recognizing the accent, the squeaky voice gulped and responded, "Sorry, Dolf. It's just that some people have been bugging me today."

"Well, quit worrying about other people. I've got a job for you."

"Good, I need something to do."

"I'm at The Kegler. How soon can you be here?"

"I don't know. I've got some other stuff going on. I need to ..."

"Chick," Dolf interrupted, "I didn't ask you about other stuff. I asked how soon can you be here?"

"I'm ten or fifteen minutes away."

"Then I'll see you in ten minutes."

"Sure thing." Apprehension, a product of previous experience, was in Chick's voice.

Ten minutes later, Chick Silva walked into The Kegler. After a brief recon he saw Dolf sitting alone. Chick walked over to the table, pulled out the chair opposite Dolf and sat down. Chick knew Dolf and didn't waste any time with small talk.

"So, what have we got?"

"Can you still build a bomb?"

Chick's eyes lit up. "Yeah, I can still build a bomb. A lot of people have called me the best. What and who are we getting rid of?"

"It'll be a house. From what I understand, it's a farmhouse on open land, and not visible by any neighbors."

"That sounds easy."

"The hard part is going to be making sure nobody is there. I'm under strict orders to make sure nobody gets hurt, at least not this time. So you're going to have to do some surveillance. Find out who's there, when they're there, when they're not. Maybe create a diversion of some sort if you have to. I don't know what to tell you, I'm just going to leave that up to you. But mark my words, if somebody gets hurt, that'll be very bad news for you."

"You're making me think twice about whether or not I want to do this."

Dolf uttered a faint chuckle. "Don't overthink it. It's no longer an option for you. You showed up here today. You're doing it. Details will follow."

Dolf stood up and walked out of the bar.

Chick sat there another five minute. He felt troubled. *What in the hell have I gotten myself into?*

CHAPTER 27

It was early evening by the time Mitch got home after stopping for a bite to eat. Louise was home from rounds at the hospital and was sitting at the kitchen table finishing a glass of wine.

"Hi, sweetie." Louise's voice was animated and her eyes lit up as Mitch walked through the back door and into the kitchen. "Too bad you weren't around today. I had a visitor at the hospital. Maggie, she's an old friend from med school. She lives down in Virginia and was returning from a conference up in Baltimore."

"Hey, that's great. Lots of catchin' up, huh?" Mitch replied as he settled into the chair across from her.

"Yeah, we did. But have I got a juicy tidbit for you."

"I'm all ears."

"Well, Maggie and I talked about a lot of stuff. Of course, we got around to discussing the Spencer girl's murder. She was familiar with it because of Tommy's execution being on the news and everything. I mentioned that you've been very interested in it for a while. I didn't tell her anything about how or why you're involved, just that it's been kind of a pet project of yours for a long time."

"Good, I'm glad that's all you said."

"Well, here's the interesting part. As it turns out, Maggie works at the pathology lab at VCU Medical Center in Richmond. They are in the process of relocating a bunch of offices in the building and moving lots of stuff around. So they've been categorizing, cataloguing, trying to figure out what's usable, what's worth keeping, and what's not."

"Okay, but I'm not really following this."

"She called me this afternoon after she got back to Richmond. They still have the tissue samples from the Spencer girl's autopsy. Including fetal tissue."

"This is getting kind of gross, and we already know, from what Vonnie told us, that Kathleen was pregnant."

"Well, this confirms it," said Louise. "Also, Kathleen's parents were never told. Seems that the coroner let his conscience override his sense of duty and withheld the information."

"Well, I can tell you this. There's no way I'd want to be the one that had to tell Bill Spencer about it now."

"You might not have any choice in the matter. But Mitch, that's not the important part. You're still not getting it."

"Getting what?"

"Dammit, Mitch, someday, you'll listen to me when I talk about my work-related stuff. A couple months ago I told you all about an article I read about a researcher in England, Doctor Miles Syme. He set up a lab to study something called DNA and genetic fingerprinting. He has proven that genetic markers can be taken from people and used to prove, among other things, paternity."

"Sorry. Guess I wasn't listening when you told me. Keep going."

"We have fetal tissue. If we can get a DNA sample from a suspect we can prove whether or not he was the father."

"Okay, I get it. Given what we think we know about our prime suspect, that his professional aspirations were high, it seems pretty obvious that an out-of-wedlock baby could have really mucked up the works. Hence, if he found out his girlfriend was pregnant he'd have motive."

"Here's another tidbit for you. Tommy Cleaves was autopsied before his body was turned over to the family. They have tissue samples that we can get DNA from. If nothing else, it can prove he wasn't the father."

"That doesn't exonerate him of the murder, but it would help clear the picture up a little bit. However, the issue that I'm toying with in my head right now is how do I get a DNA sample from our suspect? You're going to have to help me with that. I don't even know what you need from somebody to get some DNA."

"Blood would be best," Louise said, "but there are lots of other ways of getting it." Then, with an impish scowl, she added, "Besides, I know you, Mr. Armstrong, and I'm not so sure I'd want you in charge of collecting blood from someone. Especially, someone you don't like."

"Yeah, I get that. But I'm really not as impulsive as you think. Let me ponder this a bit."

"The other problem, Mitch, which I'm sure you've already recognized, is that I don't know how admissible any of this would be in court if it ever got that far. This is new science. I know they're making some use of it overseas. I just don't know if you could do anything with it here."

"Oh, I think we know an attorney who could do something with it. I'm just imagining the courtroom scene right now."

"Maybe there are other ways, not just in the courtroom, that the DNA link could be used," Louise said. "How about this? What if Tommy's sister smelled a possible lawsuit here. You know, some kind of wrongful death action. I don't know if that's possible, but if she thinks there's some money to be made she'd be all over it."

"If nothing else, all of this would bring a suspect into the picture and raise questions that he would somehow have to explain. Maybe, I can get the Commonwealth's Attorney looking deeper into this thing."

"There's one other problem, Mitch, we'd have to get the samples to Doctor Syme for analysis. Then we'd probably have to get somebody to come over here to the states to testify, and …"

"Whoa, whoa, whoa. One step at a time, Weezie, let's do this a step at a time."

Louise looked at Mitch with mock indignation. "I've come up with all of this for you," she said, "and you're back to calling me Weezie?"

"It's a term of endearment."

"I won't even respond to that."

"Okay, I'll never, ever say it again."

"Yeah, right."

"In the meantime, better make sure your passport is current. I might need to send you on a trip to England."

CHAPTER 28

hick Silva slowed his construction van to forty-five miles per hour and eased a little bit toward the right hand shoulder. The van was white, stolen, had Maryland tags, and the name of a non-existent plumbing company stenciled on both doors. A car, approaching from the opposite direction, passed by without so much as a slightly discernible glance from the driver. Chick continued to slow down while watching in the driver's side mirror as the car went around a bend in the road behind him and out of sight. He checked again and when he was certain there was nobody other than his accomplice in sight he turned into Mitch's driveway.

It's been fourteen years since Chick's done anything like this. Few people, especially none of the authorities, ever knew that there was a fifth member of the New Year's Gang. In 1970, along with four other disgruntled Vietnam War protestors, Chick helped set the bomb that blew up Sterling Hall at the University of Wisconsin-Madison, killing a physics professor and injuring three others. The blast was so enormous that pieces of the van that carried the bomb landed on the rooftop of an eight-story building three blocks away. More than two dozen other buildings in the proximate area were damaged.

Three of the bombers were eventually captured and sent to jail. A fourth member of the gang was never found. He fled to Canada along with Chick Silva, the here-to-fore unknown fifth member. Now, with Dolf Richter following close behind in a dark blue Dodge Dart, also stolen, Chick was about to re-enter the world of domestic terrorism. Once again, he was driving a Ford van; once again, it was loaded with ammonium nitrate and fuel oil. This time the bomb was smaller and the blast wouldn't be on the same scale. But it would undoubtedly be devastating, would be seen and heard for a long distance. And the blast would be capable of scattering parts of the van and house deep into the surrounding woods and fields. But this time there was another big difference. This time he was getting paid for it. And, he didn't care what was getting blown up, or why.

The gravel driveway twisted and turned through several hundred yards of hardwood trees before opening onto twenty-five cleared acres and the Armstrong farmhouse. Prior to today, Chick devoted several days to watching the comings and goings of Louise Armstrong. He found out when she had office hours and when she was doing hospital rounds. He also knew that Mitch was going to be in Richmond today. Dolf Richter had assured him of that.

Chick was certain he had plenty of time to park the truck, prepare the explosives, set the timer, and exit the scene. The bomb would explode long before anyone came home. Like a little school boy, Chick smirked and giggled when he thought about the surprise that would greet Mitch and Louise when they got to the end of their driveway.

I'd love to see the look on their faces when they see what used to be their house, Chick mused to himself as he finished the task and climbed into the Dart with Dolf.

"It won't be home sweet home anymore," Chick said.

Dolf didn't respond.

There was an old out-of-business gas station at an intersection not far from Mitch's driveway. Chick and Dolf planned to stop there and wait until they heard the blast and saw the smoke. It wouldn't take long. Right after that, Dolf was supposed to hand Chick a satchel full of money, and depart in a different car that he had waiting for himself. At least that's the way Chick thought it was going to work. What Chick didn't know was that he'd also be introduced to Turk.

Chick and Dolf pulled into the gas station and parked behind the boarded-up cinder block service bay with peeling white paint. Shortly after they stopped someone tapped on the passenger side window. Chick looked up at the mountain of flesh standing there, then swung his head toward Dolf.

"What's this?"

"His name is Turk, and he wants you to get out of the car."

"The hell I will!"

Dolf pulled out a small caliber pistol that had been tucked into his waistband and covered by his shirt, pointed it at Chick, and said, "Don't be stupid, Chick. Just get out of the car and let Turk introduce himself."

Huge beads of sweat began to form on Chick's forehead. He was scared and confused, but figured it was best to do as he was told. He got out of the car and reached forward as if to shake hands with Turk. Turk grasped his hand and the force of his grip caused Chick's knees to buckle. Turk pulled him to his feet and, with his other hand firmly gripping the back of Chick's neck, marched him into a dense thicket of bamboo and briars.

CHAPTER 29

It was mid-afternoon and Louise Armstrong didn't feel well. She rested her hand on her stomach. It was no longer just a twinge, but had turned into full-blown nausea. Despite the discomfort, she managed a little smile and whispered to no one in particular, "I'm not surprised." There was no afternoon clinic and she had no patients on the ward. *Paperwork can wait, I'm outta here.*

"I'm leaving, Ruth. Call me if you need me."

Ruth Yarnell, the charge nurse, nodded and replied, "Okay, Dr. Armstrong, see you tomorrow." Ruth looked up from the chart she was reviewing and added, "Hey, Dr. Armstrong, you telling him tonight?"

"Yeah. Mitch is coming home from Virginia, later today."

"Congrats, you two."

"Thanks, Ruth. It's been a long time coming. Seems like we've been trying forever."

Louise drove straight home. It took less than thirty minutes from the hospital to their little farmhouse in Newburg. Turning into her driveway, she let out a sigh of relief. *Home at last. I'm going to fix a warm bath, get a cup of herbal tea, and just stretch out in that tub.* When she got closer to the house, she saw the white van. It was backed up against the far side of the house, almost out of view, and right next to the big bay window that Mitch had recently added to their country kitchen.

"What the hell is this?" A frown tugged at the corners of her mouth.

She parked near the back door and looked around for Mitch's car, but didn't see it. She did notice the door to Mitch's workshop in the old barn standing open. *Maybe his car is on the other side of the barn. I guess he could have come home from Richmond early and is having some work done at the house that I don't know about.* Even so, it didn't feel right. She couldn't put her finger on it, but something else about this scenario made her very uncomfortable.

Louise sat in her car for a couple minutes, looking and listening. She neither heard an unfamiliar sound nor saw any movement. Finally, she turned off the ignition, got out of the car, and walked toward the white van to see if anyone was in it. She kept a safe distance, not wanting to surprise anyone, or get any surprises, herself. But there was nothing, nobody.

Louise was reluctant to go into the house. So, she turned around and headed, instead, toward Mitch's workshop. As she got closer to the barn, her pace quickened. It almost seemed involuntary. She began to walk faster, then broke into a run, but really didn't know why. Her skin started to prickle. Something inside her kept saying *this is bad, this is very bad.*

The explosion was deafening.

Dolf watched Turk and Chick until the two were out of sight. He then got out of the car and lit a cigarette. As he exhaled his first lungful of smoke he heard the blast. He walked to the edge of the parking lot and looked in the direction of Mitch's property. A large black cloud was beginning to rise above the trees.

This time it was Frankie who cursed as he reached for the phone in the middle of the night. "Who is it?" he barked.

"I need your help." The words were few, but the tone and timbre of Mitch's voice spoke volumes.

"I'm on my way." Frankie swung his feet onto the floor and hung up the phone. It had already gone to dial tone.

"This is surreal," said Frankie.

"Big word for you, isn't it Frankie?"

"Mitch, I can't believe you still have anything that even comes close to being a sense of humor."

"I'm still in a daze, Frankie, I'm still in a daze."

The two men were surveying the remains of what used to be Mitch's house. The grounds were charred; the remaining pieces of framework and siding of the house were wet from the fire department's futile attempt to save anything; the entire area smelled like an old campfire; bits and pieces of house and furniture were scattered as far as the eye could see.

Mitch picked up a fireplace brick with his left hand, then dropped it and made an expressive wave with his right arm. "Look at all this shit, Frankie. But I can fix it. All these pieces I can repair or replace, and put back together. It's the other pieces that bug the shit out of me. The ones I don't understand. The why of it all."

"Somebody, Mitch, somebody is real afraid of something you are doing or something you are finding out. This was a big time warning. They didn't expect anybody to be home. They just wanted to let you know what would happen if you had been."

"Well, that somebody has made one big stupid-ass mistake."

"What do we do next?"

"We're going to line up all the possibles and start eliminating."

"I've got some guys that can help. Don't ask any questions, just trust me."

"Right now, Frankie, I'll take all the help I can get."

Several days later in the hospital, Louise told Mitch, "It's not the noise I'll always remember. It's the total loss of control. It's like being lifted up and thrown away. There's only one other time I ever felt so helpless. It was at Ocean City, when I was a little girl, probably five years old. My dad and I were walking in the water and I let go of his hand. A big wave crashed down on us, and it swept me away. I tried to scream, but got a mouthful of saltwater and sand. I thought I was going to die. I was terrified. Then my daddy grabbed me and picked me up. I wrapped my arms and legs around him and clung on like a leach."

Mitch was sitting in a chair next to her bed as he listened. The first two days after the explosion he spent hours in that chair, sometimes doing nothing more than looking at his wife as she slept. "Your dad wasn't there this time. I'm sorry I wasn't either."

"I'm glad you weren't there. What would we do if we were both like this?" Louise glanced down at the cast on her left arm. There were also bandages on both legs, her right arm, and one covering a bad laceration on her forehead. Both eyes were slightly blackened, and her head throbbed. "I finally got up enough nerve to ask for a mirror this morning. After I looked at myself, I thought I should say something like, 'It was one hell of a fight, but you should see the other guy.' I just couldn't muster up the humor."

"The only thing you need to do is get better," Mitch replied.

"Any ideas yet? Who could've done such a thing?"

"I'm looking at Farmer. And, if I find that bastard's hands in this, I'll …" Mitch gritted his teeth and turned away.

"What about our house," Louise asked. "I know it's probably beyond repair. What'll we do?"

"I've been looking around the property. Bits and pieces of our life are laying all over the place. We'll just start over. It'll be okay. We can build a new house. What's most important, right now, is you."

Louise became silent. She gazed out the window for a short while and then lightly bit her lower lip. "Mitch, there's something else. I told everybody here that I had to be the one."

"The one what?"

"The one to tell you." Louise's eyes glazed over and a tear ran down her left cheek. Her voice faltered a little, but she managed to continue. "Mitch, we lost a baby. I was pregnant."

"What?" Louise's words didn't just fall onto Mitch's ears, they pummeled his entire being.

He and Louise wanted a child, more than either one of them could begin to express. They had tried, unsuccessfully, for several years. Just recently, they started talking about adoption.

Mitch reached out and embraced Louise.

"I'm so sorry," she whispered between the tears.

"You're sorry? No, no, no. You have nothing to be sorry about. I'm the one who got us into this."

"It's neither one of our faults. But the pain belongs to both of us. We can do it again. It'll happen."

Mitch laid beside her on the hospital bed. He stayed until she started to fall asleep. It was getting late and Louise needed the rest.

Mitch kissed her on the forehead and whispered, "Get some rest. I'll be back tomorrow."

Mitch was doing his best to tame the fire burning inside him. *I'll find the son of a bitch, and I'll kill him.* But Louise didn't need to hear that now.

CHAPTER 30

itch needed to see Fred Larkin. Fred owned the closed-up gas station just two miles from Mitch's house. He called Mitch earlier and said he wanted to talk. He said he saw some things the day of the explosion. He couldn't say for sure, but he had that strange feeling in his gut that they might be connected.

Mitch parked in front of the old service bay at Larkin's gas station. He knew that even though the station had been closed for several years that Fred Larkin still did a lot of personal and side jobs in the old service bay. Mitch knocked loud on the side entrance door and stepped in. Fred was inside and working on one of his own custom rods.

"Hey Fred, how you doing?"

"Mitch, glad you stopped by. Hey, I'm really sorry about what happened to your house. That really pisses me off."

"I'm still in shock, Fred, I'm still in shock. So tell me, what is it you saw that day?"

"Well, I was in here working. Nobody would have known 'cause I had my car in the service bay here. I think it was a little before three o'clock when I heard a car pull onto the gravel area out back. As you know, I keep all the windows in here boarded up, but I've got kind of a peephole at each one that I can open up if I need to. I was able to look out back and saw this old gray Dodge. When the guy driving it got out I about fell over. I swear he was the size of at least two of us."

"You've never seen him before?"

"No. He just kind of looked around a bit. Then he wandered off into the thickets. I figured he must have needed to take a dump or something. Then, shortly after he came back out, another car showed up with two people in it."

"Did they get out or did you get a good look at them?"

"Only one got out and I couldn't see him very well. That's because, and this is the creepy part, as soon as he got out of the car, the big guy, who was already here, grabs him by the arm and the neck and marched him off into the bamboo thicket. I waited and watched and finally only the big guy comes out. He walked over and said something to the driver of the second car, then got back into the car he came in. Then they left."

"And they didn't come back?"

"No. I waited a good while to make sure. Of course, by then the bomb had gone off and police and fire and rescue were all over the place."

"Did you get to talk to anybody?"

"Yeah, there was some state police out here shutting off the entrance to the road that goes down by your place. I talked to one of those guys and told him what I had seen. He said he'd call for a search team and asked me to wait. So, I waited and the search team finally got here, asked me a few questions, then went off into the bamboo thicket."

"And?"

"It didn't take long, Mitch, they found a body. The guy's neck had been broken. He was deader than a doornail."

"Fred, this is crazy. What the hell is going on?"

"I don't know what else to tell you. Maybe you should go talk to the state police. But it just seems to me like it all has to be related somehow. The bombing of your house, this guy getting killed right here at about the same time. I don't believe it's just a coincidence. I don't know, Mitch, maybe I'm just paranoid or something. But it seems to me like they all go together somehow."

"I agree with you, Fred, one hundred percent. So, you never saw or heard the guy in the other car."

"Never saw him, but I actually did hear him. This is really creepy, too. When the big guy was leading the other guy away, the driver of the second car rolled down his window and shouted something to him about making it fast. I could hear him, and I swear he had a German accent. He said a couple words that sounded just like one of my relatives, an uncle from Germany. I may be wrong, but that's what it sounded like. Anyway, Mitch, I don't know if any of this will help you at all. I just hope you find the people responsible for this."

"Fred, I think you've been more help than you can imagine."

As Mitch drove away from Fred's, the main thought going through his head was, *Dolf Richter, you son of a bitch, who are you working for?*

CHAPTER 31

Mitch was growing frustrated. Time passed and he didn't feel any closer to finding out who was really calling the shots. On one hand, he wanted to get more aggressive, on the other hand, he didn't want to put Louise in any more danger. He felt he was staring at dead ends no matter where he looked. Then Frankie called.

"Mitch we gotta talk, face to face, not on the phone."

"Skipper's? Late lunch?"

"I'll see you at 1:00," Frankie replied.

Mitch arrived first. He walked into Skipper's and was happy, once again, to get the same booth he and Frankie and Louise have used in their previous meetings there. Something about it made him feel comfortable. He was, likewise, pleased that Paulette, the same waitress they've had each time before would be waiting on them again.

"Déjà vu," Mitch whispered as he sat down.

He ordered two Natty Bohs and waited. About five minutes later Frankie slid into the booth on the opposite side of the table, took off his jacket, and set it beside him on the wooden seat.

"Same booth, same seats, same beer," Frankie said, "something's at work here."

"Same waitress, too. Seems like everything is falling into place to-day. Hope I'm just as happy to hear what you've got."

"I don't know if happy is the right word. But I'm definitely gonna get your attention. Let's order first. Here comes Pauleen."

"It's Paulette, dumbass, but I won't tell her you forgot."

"Hi, boys. You two are getting to be regulars."

"You've got a good memory, Paulette," Mitch replied.

After ordering their chicken and ribs and two more beers, Mitch leaned back, folded his arms and simply said, "Go for it."

"I finally figured it out," Frankie said. "Something about this has been bothering me and I couldn't shake it, but it finally dawned on me, and now I know. I know who Farmer is working for. And why."

Mitch quickly unfolded his arms and leaned into the table.

"Okay, you've got my attention."

"As you already know, and I'm not going to play with words or beat around the bush, my family is well connected in New Jersey, especially on my mother's side."

"I'm listening."

"My mother's brother is a guy named Jim DeLuca, I called him Uncle Jimmy, still do. All his friends, at least I thought they were just simply friends, call him Jimmy D. As I eventually learned, Uncle Jimmy is a pretty high ranking guy in the organization. He can get things done. You know what I mean?"

"Oh, I know what you mean. Beyond any shadow of a doubt."

"Uncle Jimmy had two sons. Eddie, who was my age, and Tony, a few years older. My cousin, Eddie and I got along real good. We played together well whenever we visited them. A couple years before the Spencer girl was killed, Eddie and I must have been about nine or ten, and Tony was around twelve, maybe thirteen, something happened."

"I'm guessing something bad," Mitch interrupted. "I think I see our order on its way. Let's continue after she brings it."

Paulette put the chicken and rib combos on the table as well as two more beers.

"Can I get you guys anything else?"

"No thanks, Paulette. We're just going to take our time and enjoy," said Mitch.

"Okay, but let me know if you need anything."

Mitch and Frankie picked at their food a little. Then Mitch looked at Frankie and said, "So something bad happened."

"Yeah, my Aunt, Eddie's mom, had taken his brother, Tony, to go shopping for something. They stopped at a little Italian café for lunch. While they were there, some guys came in and started having a big beef with the owner of the place. As best my aunt could make out, it had to do with some payments that the owner didn't think he owed. Before it was over guns came out, some shots were fired, and somehow or other my cousin Tony got in the way and was shot and killed."

"Aw, shit. I'm sorry, man."

"Yeah, we all were, Mitch. But it's been a long time now. I never said anything to you before, because we kids were told to keep it to ourselves. We all heard what had happened. We just weren't allowed to talk about it."

"Family secrets. I understand. But where does Farmer fit into this."

"It's not Farmer, it's who he's working for. Nowadays they call him the Old Man. It turns out that the Old Man was likewise well connected, but with a criminal element in the Richmond, Virginia, area. I don't know why, or what the motivation was, or if anybody else was pushing the issue, but the Old Man decided he wanted to start expanding into other states. So, he put his eye on New Jersey."

"The guys that started the ruckus in the café where your aunt and cousin were, they were working for the Old Man?"

"Exactly. At least, as I got older, that's what I discovered. Nobody could prove it for sure, but everyone strongly believes it."

"Well, you've certainly got my attention. But how much of it is hearsay?"

"Don't know. But here's the biggy. Here's what I do know. The day of Tony's funeral, there was a gathering of family and friends back at Uncle Jimmy's house. And guess who showed up?"

"The Old Man? Are you kidding me?"

"No, I'm not kidding. But listen to this. There was a bunch of kids there, cousins and friends. And we started playing. We were kids, the real impact of a funeral hadn't hit us, and now we were back at the house where everybody was eating and drinking. So we started playing. We were playing a game of hide-and-seek, and I was hiding in the coat closet in the hallway."

"And I'll bet you overheard something," Mitch said with a sly grin.

"Yeah, I did. Uncle Jimmy and the Old Man had a little encounter right next to the closet door. I didn't hear it all, and I didn't understand a lot of what they were saying. But I did hear the Old Man say that he was real sorry about what happened, and that no matter what anybody else said, he didn't have anything to do with it."

"And your Uncle Jimmy said ..."

"He told the Old Man that he had reason to believe otherwise. And this is what I'll never forget. He said to the Old Man, 'If I ever confirm my suspicions, I'm going to make you pay in a way worse than you could ever imagine. You just better hope you die first.' "

"Wow, so what makes you think this guy, this Old Man, is somehow related to our investigation?"

"Get ready, Mitch. It was one of those things that just kind of comes to you, like some sort of revelation. Just recently, like out of nowhere, I started thinking about it and then it hit me, my Uncle Jimmy kept calling this guy—Parker. The more I thought about it, the more it fit. The Old Man is Conrad Parker Sr., the father of Governor Parker."

"Holy shit." Mitch took a sip of beer. "Anyway to verify any of this? Like, was it really the Old Man, and was he or is he running some sort of organization in Richmond?"

"Already done. I did quite a bit of background work before contacting you. It's definitely the Old Man. He's also made it no secret among his closest acquaintances that he sees a campaign for president in Governor Parker's future."

"Damn," said Mitch, "no wonder he'd go to extremes to keep his son's name clean."

The main thing is I talked to Uncle Jimmy about this. I told him about the Spencer girl and your involvement. Uncle Jimmy verified everything you question. Then, he said, 'It's time.' " Frankie drew quiet.

Finally, Mitch broke the silence. "I've got a feeling I'm about to hear something big."

Frankie reached under his jacket, pulled out a white legal size envelope, and handed it across the table to Mitch. "Take a look. Here's how you're gonna stop the Old Man."

Mitch emptied the envelope. There were photographs of seven different people, five of whom were fairly young. There was also a folded piece of typewritten paper.

"Who are these people?"

"You'll find out when you read what's on the paper. Trust me, they mean a lot to the Old Man," said Frankie. "Two of them have been targeted. We just don't know which two. But that's the way it's done. They'll give me a heads up when it's about two weeks out. And it'll happen, unless you call it off. There's a phone number on the paper. They expect you to memorize it and get rid of the paper. If for any reason you need to call it off, use that number and just tell whoever answers that you're one of the Corn Bandits. That's all you need to say and that's all they need to hear."

Mitch read everything on the paper as he looked at each of the pictures.

"Do you think the Old Man will believe this will happen?" Mitch asked.

"If you need to, just mention Jimmy D. Once the Old Man finds out he's involved, he'll believe you."

"I'd still like to lean on Farmer, and get as much detail from him as we can. He's obviously taking marching orders from somebody and now it looks like it's probably the Old Man. And it's gotta be the Old Man's son, the governor, that they're protecting. He's got to be the killer."

"I agree. If you want me to, Mitch, I'm pretty sure I can get some friends to have a little chat with Farmer. They'll present a pretty strong case, and I'm confident they'll be able to get any worthwhile information that he has."

"I'd like that, but Farmer can't disappear and he can't go spilling the beans to anyone afterward."

"They'll make that clear to him. Farmer's a chicken-shit. He'll do whatever he has to do to protect his own hide."

"Then let's go for it, Frankie."

The rest of their meal was eaten in silence. Finally, Paulette brought the check. Mitch paid the bill. They left the diner together. But this time there was no joking or shoulder punching as they walked across the parking lot. They stopped next to Mitch's car and he looked at the pictures that Frankie had given him one more time.

"I've got it," Mitch said. He opened the door to his car and tossed the envelope with the pictures in it onto his front seat. "Keep me posted," he said.

"I'll let you know what happens with Farmer. It shouldn't be long. Then you'll be free to contact the Old Man."

"Take care, Frankie."

"You too, Mitch."

Paulette was looking out through the window next to the main entrance as she whispered into the phone, "They're leaving now. But the one named Frankie gave the other guy an envelope that seemed to be important. I didn't get a chance to overhear anything, but from the way they acted, they're up to something."

Ken Farmer, still at work, shuffled a few things around on the top of his desk as he talked.

"Thanks, Paulette. It's nice having a niece like you that I can count on at times when I need some assistance."

"Anytime, Uncle Ken, I think it's kind of cool being able to help the police like this."

"Thanks again, talk to you soon."

Farmer hung up the phone, then muttered to himself, "Dumb bitch. She's stupid, just like her mother."

CHAPTER 32

Ken Farmer had only been home for a few minutes when there was a loud rap at his front door.

"What the hell is this," he muttered, "this has already been a long day."

He opened the door to find a man, probably in his thirties, dark hair, olive skin, standing there holding a notebook of some sort.

"What can I do for you?" Farmer asked as he stepped out of the doorway and onto the small front porch.

"Hello, are you Ken Farmer?"

"I am, now what do you want?"

"My name's Anton. I need to ask you a few questions for a survey I'm taking."

"Get lost. I'm not interested."

"Oh, I think you will be ..."

Farmer interrupted, "I said leave. Get off my property."

"Oh, let's not be so rude, Mr. Farmer." These words came from a second, more gruff sounding voice that was right now standing directly behind Farmer.

"What the ..." Farmer quickly turned. A sharp jab to the stomach caused him to look down and see the barrel of a .45 automatic pointed directly at his mid-section.

"That's my friend, Manny," Anton said. "Now get inside Farmer, and take a seat."

Farmer did as he was told. The three men were soon sitting in his living room. Beads of sweat were popping up on Farmer's forehead.

"What's going on here?" he asked.

"Like I first told you, Mr. Farmer, I'm here to take a survey," Anton replied. "I've got some questions that I need to ask you."

"I still don't understand."

"You don't have to. All you have to do is answer me. But before we begin I need to make a few things perfectly clear. You're going to answer every question I ask, completely and truthfully. You will leave nothing out. You will hide nothing. Furthermore, after we're done here today, my friend and I will leave, and you will return to your normal daily routine. You will go back to work, and to whatever else you do. You will say absolutely nothing of this encounter to anyone. If you follow these instructions, you will never hear from us or see us again. If you do not follow these instructions, and, trust me, we will find out if you don't, you will one day be sitting at a stoplight, or standing in line at the movie theater, or dining in your favorite restaurant, and a complete stranger will approach you and blow your brains out with a gun just like the one my friend here is pointing at your chest."

Farmer glanced at Manny, the second man, who was sitting in a chair across the room from him. Manny had his legs crossed and his right hand was resting on his raised knee with the gun pointed directly at Farmer.

"Do you understand what I just said, Mr. Farmer?" Anton asked. "Complete answers. And not a word of this to anyone."

"I understand."

"Good, let's begin. First of all, who do you work for?"

"Uh, I work for the state, and report directly to the governor."

Anton began shaking his head. "Ken, you disappoint me. I really thought you were going to catch on to this a little better and a little quicker than you have."

Anton then gave a quick glance and head nod toward Manny who picked up a small pillow that was in an adjacent chair. He covered the gun with the pillow and pulled the trigger. The blast was still fairly loud and the bullet struck the couch only inches from where Farmer was sitting. Farmer lurched to his feet and was immediately shoved back down by Anton.

"Any more evasion, today, Ken and the next bullet is going to find you."

"All right, all right. Maybe I didn't understand the question, I'm not trying to pull anything." Farmer was now gasping for breath.

"I'll try again," said Anton, "you work for somebody, an ultimate authority, he may not sign your government paycheck, but he's the one who calls all the shots for you. Who is it?"

"He's called the Old Man."

"What's his real name?"

Farmer stole a quick look at Manny, who was still pointing the gun at him. "His name is Parker. Conrad Parker Sr."

"Conrad Parker Sr. So that would make him Governor Parker's father. Am I correct?"

"Yes, you are."

"Good. Now tell me how you met him. What was your first encounter? What did you talk about? Did he ask you for anything? Did you agree to help him in any way? What has been your relationship since then? And remember, don't leave anything out."

Farmer then went into a long dissertation about how he first met the Old Man at the Montague Mill restaurant while investigating Kathleen Spencer's murder at Bohman's Point. He explained how the Old Man wanted his son kept out of the investigation and that Farmer needed to find someone other than his son to pin the murder on. Farmer also made it clear that despite whatever suspicions he had, nobody ever told him for sure or in any way confirmed that Conrad Parker Jr. was either the murderer or was in any way involved in the murder. He also went on to detail how he was given a tip about Tommy Cleaves, how he followed up on the tip, met Cleaves, and eventually arrested him and charged him with Kathleen's murder.

"Do you still think that Conrad Parker Jr., that is Governor Parker, is the person who killed the Spencer girl?" asked Anton.

"As I said, nobody ever told me anything one way or another. Cleaves really did look guilty, and we did find the girl's charm bracelet in Cleaves's car. But I'll have to admit I've always had some doubts about Cleaves and some suspicions about Parker."

"But you never followed up on any of it. Why?"

Farmer dropped his head a little, took a long pause and a few very deep breaths, then finally looked up. "I don't know, I guess I just didn't think it was worth looking into."

Anton looked at Manny. "We're not getting anywhere, kill the son of a bitch."

"No, no, no, wait, please," Farmer screeched. "Okay, it was because I got put on the Old Man's payroll."

"Keep going," said Anton.

"He kept me busy," Farmer continued. "I was on the police force and was able to help him with a lot of his, can I say, underground endeavors. He also made sure I was keeping an eye on his son, and doing whatever I could, from my perspective, to keep him out of trouble to help advance his political career."

"Okay, enough of the Old Man," Anton interjected, "who is Dolf Richter and who does he get his marching orders from."

"Why do you want to know about Richter?"

"Doesn't matter. All you need to know is that I want some answers."

"He's German. He was big into Richmond criminal activity. He got deported. The Old Man somehow, I guess with fake IDs and passport, got him back into the states. He's very loyal to the Old Man. He currently takes assignments from me, but only because the Old Man told him he had to."

"Is he the one who planted the bomb at Mitch Armstrong's house? And if so, was that an assignment that you gave him?"

Ken Farmer felt like the walls were closing in on him. He cleared his throat a couple times then said, "Nobody was supposed to get hurt. The Old Man was real upset that Armstrong wasn't giving up on the Spencer murder, especially after Cleaves was executed. The Old man said we had to send a real loud message that told Armstrong it was time to back off if he knew what was good for him."

"So you had Richter do it."

"He arranged it, and he was there. He also made sure there was no other witness or participant left over."

After a long silence, Anton said, "Okay, I've heard enough. Manny, you satisfied?"

"Yeah," was the extent of Manny's response.

Anton turned his attention back to Farmer. "We have reasons for keeping you alive. But as I said earlier, that will only work as long as you keep one hundred percent silent about anything that happened here today."

Farmer kept rubbing his hands together and his voice quivered. "I will. Please believe me, I will."

Anton continued, "If at anytime in the future something comes to your attention that might in any way involve or impact Mitch Armstrong, I'll expect you to tell me. What you'll do is go to The Kegler, I know you're familiar with it, tell the bartender that you have a message for Anton. Then you go straight home and wait for my call. The consequences for not doing this will be fatal. Do I make myself perfectly clear?"

"Yes, perfectly clear." Beads of sweat fell off Farmer's forehead like raindrops.

"All right, we're out of here."

Anton and Manny stood up, and without so much as a final glance over their shoulders, walked out of the house.

Farmer spent the next thirty minutes sitting motionless on the couch wondering what he had just done, and who he should be more afraid of, the Old Man or these two.

CHAPTER 33

It's been more than a month since the bombing and Mitch felt like things were slowly getting back to normal. Louise was recovering well and able to spend a few hours each day with a couple patients. The rebuilding of their house had begun and they were, for the present, living in a rental house on the outskirts of La Plata. Mitch had arrived home before Louise, grabbed a beer, and was sitting on the front step when she pulled into the driveway.

"Hey there, buddy," Louise said as she walked up the cement walkway from the driveway to the front steps. "You look like you're deep in thought."

"I am, could you possibly guess about what?"

"So what's troubling you now? Anything new?" Louise was about to burst with what she wanted to tell Mitch, but decided to hold back until she found out what was running through Mitch's head.

"I was actually thinking about everything you've told me about this DNA stuff, and thought if we could just link Parker to Kathleen with that information it might be enough to persuade the Commonwealth's Attorney to look into it. But I know we need some kind of blood or tissue sample from Parker and I was just running a bunch of scenarios through my head. You know, different kinds of ways it could be done, some of which aren't real pleasant."

"Mitch, this is so amazing. We are so in tune with each other's thought waves. This is exactly what I wanted to talk to you about. I mean exactly. I mean about getting a blood sample. Let's go inside. Not that anybody could hear us, I just don't want to take that chance. I've got some juicy stuff to tell you."

Once they were inside and sitting at the kitchen table, Mitch smiled at Louise and said, "Okay, Dr. Armstrong, you've got my attention."

"What if I told you, you're not going to have to worry about how to get the governor's blood sample? What if I told you he's actually going to give it to us?"

"Give it to us?"

"Well, in a manner of speaking—yes."

"As I said just a moment ago, you've got my attention. I mean, really got my attention."

"I was talking to my friend, Maggie, today. She's the one who works at VCU Medical Center."

"Yeah, I remember you telling me about her."

"You need to understand, she's real political, she can't stand Governor Parker or any of his policies, to the point she's willing to do some things that are—oh, let's just call a spade a spade—illegal."

"Now, I'm not following you."

"Okay, just listen. In two weeks the governor is hosting a kickoff event for the statewide Blood Donation Month. A bloodmobile is going to visit the capitol building, and the governor, along with a number of other government officials and legislators, are each going to donate a pint of blood. Of course, we know they're just doing it all for show and publicity, but here's the good part. The blood will be transported to Virginia Blood Services headquarters where it will be analyzed, classified, catalogued, and stored. Maggie has a friend who works there and the friend asked if Maggie could possibly come over that day and help. Evidently they're a little short-staffed right now."

"Okay, now I'm intrigued."

"Mitch, Maggie called me and could barely contain herself. She's aware of what's going on. I've pretty much kept her up to speed. She's thinking she might be able to get a sample of Governor Parker's blood."

"This is incredible."

"Oh, it just keeps getting better and better. She already has the tissue samples from the fetus and from Tommy Cleaves. Once she gets the governor's blood, she'll give them all to me, and I'll just have to figure out how to ship them to Doctor Syme in England. She's taking a big risk here, Mitch."

"I know. Tell her to be careful and we will do everything we can to keep her totally in the shadows." Mitch paused and scrunched his eyes a little, then said, "On second thought, find out exactly when, and as much as you can about the bloodmobile being at the capitol building. I'd like to see if I can keep Maggie as distant from this as possible. I'd hate to see her stick her neck out and get caught up in this thing. If we need her to try to get the blood sample I'll let you know, but first, let me check on some things."

"Gee, am I sensing a phone call to Frankie or one of his *contacts?* That is what you call them isn't it, *contacts?*"

"Frankie's my friend. Sometimes you just have to look the other way."

"Oh, I am. I not only don't want to see anything, I don't even want to think about what's probably going to happen."

"It'll be okay."

"Sure," said Louise, feigning a little exasperation. She stood up and started walking toward the refrigerator, then stopped. "Oh, I almost forgot. Maggie told me something else. You'll know more about what to do with this information than I do. Maggie has a romantic interest, a boyfriend, who works in the hospital morgue. She was very discriminate about it, but Maggie filled him in on a lot of what we are doing with regard to this case. He got access to the report from Kathleen's autopsy. Kathleen had bruises on her neck consistent with strangulation by a right-handed attacker. Didn't you tell me that Tommy Cleaves had a cast or big bandage on one of his hands at that time?"

"Yes, his right hand. I've also read all the trial documents over and over. There was never any mention of strangulation, just that she was probably held under the water until she drowned. But if she was bruised by a right hand and he couldn't use his right hand, this would definitely be something worth looking into."

Louise opened the refrigerator and retrieved a few fresh strawberries. As she began to nibble on the berries and exit the kitchen she watched Mitch take the power cord from the carry bag of his car phone, which he always brought into the house, and plug it into an AC adapter.

"Somebody's making a super-secret call," said Louise.

"Yes, I'm calling Frankie. This is one time I'm not taking any chances at all. This is too big and too close to actually proving something."

Louise walked through the open doorway and into the dining room. She leaned her back against the wall adjacent to the doorway and listened. She had a pretty good idea of what she was going to hear. *I know this is going to be better for Maggie,* she thought. *I just hope it doesn't blow up in Mitch and Frankie's faces.*

"You're lucky I'm still here," Frankie said as he picked up his phone. "I was about to head out for an early dinner and a movie."

By yourself?"

"No, of course not. Don't you think I'm capable of having a date once in a while?"

"Sure. I think you're capable. I just didn't think anybody would want to go out with you."

"Knock off the crap. I'm actually serious now. What do you want?"

"I'm looking for somebody who might know how to hijack a bloodmobile. Any ideas?"

"Whaaat? Who are you working for now, Dracula, or some other ghoul?"

"Sometimes I think I should be. But forget that. Do you remember us telling you about that DNA stuff?"

"Yeah, pretty much."

"Well I might have been given an opportunity to get a sample from our prime suspect. But I'll need some help."

"Vehicle hijacking, huh?"

"There's going to be a bloodmobile at the capitol in a couple weeks and when they leave they're going to have a pint of our boy's blood with them."

"And all you want me to do is get my hands on it."

"It's gonna be tough, and if you don't want to get any of your people involved, I've got another way. But it would involve someone that's not used to these kinds of things, and I just don't want to put her in that kind of jeopardy."

"So, I'm the one you jeopardize."

"Gimme a break, Frankie, you know what I'm saying."

"Yeah, I'm just bustin' your balls."

"Okay, okay. So, any thoughts?"

"Tell me again, how much time do I have to get ready?"

"Couple weeks."

"It sounds doable, but I'll need a lot of information."

"Which I'm still in the process of gathering," said Mitch.

"Okay. Once you've got all you can get, let me know and we'll meet somewhere. At that time I should be able to tell you straight up whether or not we can make it happen."

"Sounds good, I'll be in touch."

"Okay, later."

CHAPTER 34

M itch's next phone call to Frankie was shorter and sweeter than he expected.

"Frankie, I've got some information for our project."

"Great, fill me in."

"Okay, it's next Wednesday at 10:00 a.m. A bloodmobile from VBS, Virginia Blood Services, is going to show up at the Capitol. The governor, Farmer, and a few of the state legislators are going to parade down from the governor's office to the bloodmobile. They'll each donate a pint of blood, and be fawned over like visiting royalty. They'll rest inside the bus for several minutes, then go speak to news reporters, and let everyone know that if more people could be as brave and compassionate as they are, humanity would be saved from whatever ills it is facing."

"Sounds much like what I figured."

"Yeah, and then after everybody is done bleeding and talking, the bloodmobile departs and heads back to Virginia Blood Services headquarters to do whatever they do with it there."

"Like I said, Mitch, it sounds right on track with what I learned."

"Good, so how about we meet at Skipper's tomorrow and hash out all the details."

"I'm going to do you one better. We don't have to meet at all."

"What?"

"I brought some guys into this who got real excited about doing it. They know enough about the whole story to know that it'll possibly put them in good graces with my Uncle Jimmy. Plus, we already did some research and found out pretty much everything you just told me. They assure me that they know what it is we want them to get and they know, or will figure out, how to get it. You're gonna have to trust me, Mitch, but these guys are good. I can vouch for them. One of them, in particular, has done a lot of driving for us. If it was meant to be on the road, he can drive it."

"I do trust you, Frankie. You know that."

"I know, Mitch, I do. Listen, the only thing we want to keep under wraps right now is the drop off point for the package. That's where it'll be left for you to pick up. Right now they're pretty sure where that's going to be, but it's always subject to change. I'll contact you about that early Wednesday morning."

"Something else, Frankie, we also gotta plan on how to let everyone know in case we need to abort."

"Right. I'll give you the name he's using and contact information for my lead guy by Wednesday morning."

"Okay, Frankie, it's looking good. Call me if you need anything before then, and let me know if you get anything from Farmer that doesn't sound right or makes you think we need to change anything."

"Will do."

The following Wednesday was a beautiful day. The bloodmobile arrived exactly on time. As promised, the governor, plus a few sycophants and state legislators were at the Capitol to make blood donations. After a couple hours, as things were wrapping up, three men dressed in

Virginia Blood Services uniforms walked casually through the crowd and up to the bloodmobile. Everyone assumed that Butch Krause and his two henchmen, Mikey and Tim, were all part of the bloodmobile team. They looked professional and interacted in a pleasant and helpful manner with the crowd, and the last of the blood donors who were leaving the vehicle.

"Is everything okay, you don't feel light-headed do you? Can I get you anything?" Butch asked a staffer who was one of the donors, just stepping down from the bloodmobile.

The staffer smiled and said, "No, thanks."

Finally, Ken Farmer, with his right sleeve rolled up to expose the bandage around his forearm, grabbed a bullhorn and stood in front of the bloodmobile. "Attention, please," he announced to the group. "We are finished here today, and the bloodmobile will soon depart to take our donations to VBS Headquarters in Henrico County."

Most of the onlookers had experienced Ken Farmer before, and had already turned their backs and started to walk away.

Farmer continued, "The governor and I would both like to ensure you that this is a simple and relatively painless way that you, too, can make a difference in someone's life."

Most of Farmer's comments to the onlookers did nothing more than echo remarks already made by the governor.

Farmer walked away and the crowd continued to disperse as Butch, Mikey, and Tim boarded the bloodmobile which looked like a big white bus with only two small, tinted windows on either side. Outsiders cannot see in.

Butch immediately went to the driver's location and activated the switch that closed the entrance door to the vehicle.

"Who in the hell are you?" screeched the driver.

"Your new boss, now shut up," Butch replied.

Butch, Mikey, and Tim all pulled short barreled .38 revolvers from inside their jackets.

"Everybody back here," Mikey shouted. The two blood collection specialists, as well as a public relations guy who travels with the team, all quickly complied. Tim forced one of the collection specialist and the PR guy to sit on the floor, back to back. He gagged them both and tied them together.

He turned to the other technician and said, "We're going to need you for a bit."

"Be quiet, be still, and be helpful," growled Butch. "Do that and nobody gets hurt. Don't do that and you'll all get dumped by the side of the road."

Butch then turned to the driver. "Get out of the seat and get in the back with the rest of them."

"What's going on here?" said the driver.

Butch immediately smacked him on the back of his head with the gun barrel. "Didn't you hear the part about keep quiet? Now get in the back!"

The driver did as asked with no further questions.

Butch moved into the driver's seat, put the bloodmobile in gear and drove away.

To the dispersing crowd nothing looked amiss. Several waved at the bloodmobile, and Butch smiled and waved back at them. Twenty minutes later Butch was parking the bloodmobile on Bethlehem Road, not far from VBS headquarters and main collection facility. A dark sedan, engine running, was waiting for them.

Mikey had forced the untethered specialist to gather all the blood donations, ensure that each was clearly identified with the donor's name, and place them in a transport container. The specialist was then tied and gagged back to back with the driver.

Neither Butch, Mikey nor Tim gave any hint of being interested in the blood of any one particular donor. The incident was made to look like a heist of all the blood.

"Y'all take care now," Butch said to the four captives as he was departing the bloodmobile. "Sooner or later somebody will find you."

Butch and the other two ran to the waiting car, climbed in, and were gone in seconds.

Shortly afterward, Mitch picked up his car phone and listened to Frankie ask, "How close are you to The Kegler?"

"Ten minutes maybe. Been waiting to hear from you."

"There's a guy behind the bar, about the size of King Kong. Just tell him you're looking for something that Butch left for you, and he'll hand you a package. He has no idea what's in it."

"He says nothing. I say little. That's how I like it."

"Talk to you later."

"Thanks, Frankie, I owe you one."

Mitch walked into The Kegler and straight to the bar. Not only was the bartender as big as Frankie said, he was wearing a wife-beater T-shirt and looked to be as hairy as King Kong.

"Hi, I'm looking for a package that Butch left for me."

King Kong didn't say a word, change his expression or even look Mitch in the eye. He simply reached below the bar, picked up the blood transport container and handed it over the bar to Mitch.

Mitch turned and walked out without saying another word.

CHAPTER 35

Maggie did as promised. She drove up from Richmond to La Plata, met with Louise and gave her the tissue samples from the fetus and from Tommy Cleaves. All were properly packaged in preservative containers as small as possible for easy transport.

Louise then managed to conduct a trans-Atlantic phone call and spoke to one of Dr. Syme's assistants. She told him about the blood sample and the types of tissue samples she had. She said she would like to personally deliver them and perhaps even talk to Doctor Syme. She didn't go into detail about who or what the particulars were, just that the samples would all have unique identifiers and that this information would be used to help bolster a criminal investigation. The person to whom she spoke seemed very cordial and more than willing to help.

Exasperation finally caught up with Louise as she looked through the side window at the cars they were passing. "Dammit, I wish this was a vacation trip. I can't believe I'm getting ready to board a plane for Europe—by myself—and carrying some blood and body tissue, hoping to hang a murder charge on someone."

"If you don't want to do it, I'll understand," Mitch replied.

"Oh, sweetie, it's not that. I know it would attract too much attention with the wrong people if you went. It's just that there are so many things over there that I would like us to have the chance to see and enjoy together. I'm going to be there, you're not. And even if you were, we couldn't go sightseeing anyhow."

"I promise you. Once this is all over, we'll go on a European vacation. We've earned it. You, especially. I'm still a little concerned about whether or not you should be taking this trip."

"I'm fine, Mitch. I wouldn't be doing it if I thought there were any health risks. Everyone at the hospital agrees my recovery has been great."

The rest of the trip to Baltimore Washington International Airport was free of worrisome dialogue about the way things were going in the investigation. Mitch was full of hope that Louise's meeting with Doctor Syme would result in something that could be used to add some conclusiveness to his suspicions. And, if they were lucky, it could lead to getting DNA evidence introduced in a trial.

Mitch kissed Louise goodbye at the gate and watched her depart from view as she walked through the boarding tunnel. He waited until the aircraft pushed away from the gate, then began his walk to the airport exit. He hadn't said anything to Louise, but the sixth sense he's developed over the years had kicked in and was sending him a message that was nagging at him stronger and stronger with every step that he took. Just before he got to the terminal exit he suddenly stopped.

"Richter," Mitch said aloud. "That son-of-a-bitch. That's who it was."

Mitch recalled that, for some strange reason, the man walking a few people behind Louise, as she went down the boarding ramp, had gotten his attention. It's been years since Mitch has seen Richter, but he was certain that's who it was. The man was tall, skinny, and wearing a familiar looking, checkered, fedora-style hat. He also had the same shuffling gait as Richter. It was a pronounced manner of walking attributable to a knee injury. Mitch was well aware of Dolf's knee injury since he is the one who gave it to him.

Mitch turned and raced back to the boarding gate, bumping into other passengers and well-wishers along the way. At the departure gate ticket desk, he shoved his way to the front of the line.

"Flight 63. Is it still on the ground?"

"Sir, please, you'll have to wait your turn," said the uniformed attendant with a feigned smile.

Mitch slapped his investigator's badge on the desk, hoping it would help.

"I'm not a passenger. I need to know if Flight 63 is still on the ground."

"No sir, it's not. Is there a problem? Do I need to call security?" she asked.

Mitch ran both hands through his hair and grabbed the back of his neck. "No, it's okay, I need to get a message to somebody on that flight. Is there any way I can contact them?"

"You can't contact a passenger in flight, but if you go to our main office here in the airport, someone might be able to help you. Maybe send a telegram to the arrival destination gate that can be passed on to the person."

"Thank you. Now, how do I get to that office."

The gate attendant gave Mitch directions to the airline office. As he made his way down the concourse, Mitch started thinking about how he could send a message that would give Louise a warning, but still appear innocuous to anyone else.

The airline office was off the beaten track and not very welcoming. Usually, when passengers or family members showed up here it wasn't for anything pleasant.

"Hi," said Mitch to the young executive wannabe sitting behind the desk. "I need to talk to someone about sending a telegram to a destination arrival gate."

"Where would that be?"

"London. My wife is on Flight 63. It just departed."

"So, you didn't get to the terminal in time to say goodbye. Sorry, can't help you."

"It's not that at all. My wife, Doctor Louise Armstrong, is going to attend an international physicians' conference in London. She's a speaker. I just found out that someone who she is not expecting is actually going to be there. That person is very interested in a paper my wife wrote that my wife wasn't planning to talk about. I'm just trying to give her a heads up. It's really important to her, and could land her a great position in a hospital she's been looking at." Mitch tried to look and come across as truthful and desperate as possible.

Evidently, his made up story was working. "Let me check on this," the young man said. He then picked up a phone, turned his head away from Mitch, and placed a phone call to what Mitch assumed was a supervisor. After a short muffled conversation he hung up the phone, looked at Mitch and said, "We can do it, but it has to be a real brief message. You understand, the airline doesn't like being in the practice of providing messenger service. We're a transportation company."

"I get it," replied Mitch. "I'll keep it short and sweet. It's for Doctor Louise Armstrong. Just say, 'Call me. Dolf Richter is going to meet you at the airport,' and say that it's from Mitch."

The young man wrote down the message, confirmed it with Mitch, and promised that it would be there by the time the flight arrived.

Mitch was in a rage as he drove home. He had already toyed with the idea of going home, grabbing his passport, and heading back to the airport to catch a flight to England. He quickly dismissed the idea, given the amount of time it would take.

He stopped at a gas station and called Frankie. *Who knows?* Mitch thought. *Maybe Frankie has some contacts in England.*

Frankie did not answer.

Mitch arrived home, walked into the living room and began pacing in circles on the hardwood floor. Everywhere he looked he could see Louise—the curtains, the paintings, the Hummel knickknacks sitting on a wall shelf. "What in the hell have I gotten her into?"

Then Mitch got an idea and immediately went to the antique secretary-type desk in the corner of the living room. Mitch lowered the foldup writing surface and grabbed the small spiral notepad from inside the desk. Louise would use that notepad to scratch messages to herself whenever she was talking on the phone or just as a reminder of some task needing done.

"Please be here," Mitch murmured over and over again to himself as he flipped through the notebook.

"Yes!!!!!!!" he yelled loud enough that the neighbors probably heard him.

Louise had written down some notes from her previous phone call with Doctor Syme's laboratory. She also included all the contact information necessary in order to reach them through British Telecom.

After a couple false starts, a call to an overseas operator, and forgetting that he was dealing with a five hour time difference, Mitch finally found himself listening to the voice he hoped to hear.

"Yes, this is the office of Doctor Miles Syme. How can I help you?"

"Am I speaking to Doctor Syme?"

"No, this is Andrew, I'm the senior research assistant."

"Andrew, this is an emergency. My wife, Doctor Louise Armstrong, is onboard a flight to London that is going to land at 9:30 this morning, your time. She has been in contact with you folks and is bringing a blood sample to you. After her plane departed I learned that somebody is going to try to stop her from getting the sample to your lab. She doesn't know that this person is going to try to interfere with her. I need to speak with Doctor Syme to see if there's anything he can do."

"He's not here right now, but I'm aware of Doctor Armstrong's visit. In fact, the matter has been turned over to me. I know this relates to a criminal investigation, and we are very anxious to assist in any way that we can. Would it help if we could get somebody to meet your wife at the airport?"

"Absolutely. She is going to call me immediately after she lands. How soon can you put something together so I can call you back and know what to tell her?"

"We've only got a little less than two hours to work with, but I'm sure we can do something. Call me back by nine o'clock."

"Thank you so much. I'll speak to you then."

Coffee and pacing occupied the next hour or so of Mitch's life. Finally, shortly before 9:00 a.m., London time, Mitch started working on another call to Doctor Syme.

At 9:02, he heard Andrew's voice.

"Doctor Syme's office, Andrew speaking."

"Andrew, it's Mitch Armstrong."

"Yes, Mr. Armstrong. I have delightful news."

Delightful? Mitch thought to himself. *Only the Brits.*

"Yes, please tell me, what did you work out?"

"One of our assistants, her name is Catherine, will meet Doctor Armstrong at the airport. Hoping to make it clandestine, we would like you to tell your wife, when she calls you, to go into the women's loo, the one that is on the main concourse and directly across from Murphy's Bistro Lounge. A woman wearing a white scarf and red shoes will be there. She'll arrive at approximately noon. All your wife has to do is walk in, look around, and say she is looking for her friend. Catherine will identify herself, and your wife will give her the samples and any message she may have for us. I then suggest that your wife attempt to procure an immediate return flight."

"You're a life-saver, Andrew. It sounds like this will work."

CHAPTER 36

The airplane was still taxiing in. "Everyone please remain seated until we have come to a full stop and the seat belt light is turned off," announced one of the flight attendants. At almost the same time, another attendant tapped Louise on the shoulder.

"Doctor Armstrong?"

"Yes, that's me."

"After you process through customs, you need to proceed immediately to the passenger desk at our arrival gate. A transatlantic cable has been sent to your attention and we have a copy for you at the passenger desk."

"Well, uhh, thank you. I had no idea that someone was sending me a cable or telegram or whatever. Do you have any idea what this is about?"

"No, I'm sorry Doctor Armstrong. All I know is that the message is waiting for you."

"Okay, thank you again."

Louise was having a tough time wrapping her head around whatever this could possibly be. *Did something happen to Mitch? Has something happened at Doctor Syme's lab, or did they change their minds?* As soon as she got inside the concourse, Louise went straight to the check-in desk at her gate.

"I'm Doctor Armstrong," said Louise while simultaneously displaying her passport, "I understand you have a message for me."

"Yes, if you would simply sign here." The desk attendant handed Louise a logbook which she signed and the attendant annotated as *receipt of telegram*. The attendant then gave her an envelope with her name handwritten on it.

Louise stepped away from the desk, opened the envelope, and removed the message. She immediately saw that the sender was Mitch. It didn't surprise her since only a couple people knew she was taking this trip.

Next, she read the message and felt a wave of panic sweep over her. *Call me. Dolf Richter is going to meet you at the airport.*

"Dolf Richter? Meet me? What in the hell could this possibly mean?" she thought aloud. Louise knew, all too well, who Dolf Richter was. Her mind raced. *He's probably the one who killed Vonnie and almost killed me. Now what?*

Louise turned back to the gate desk attendant. "Can you please help me? How can I go about making an overseas phone call from here at the airport?"

The attendant directed her to a bank of public telephones. He told her that inside each booth, posted next to the phone, she would find written instructions on how to place an overseas call through British Telecom.

After a few awkward moments of dealing with a foreign operator and learning what was expected in order to place a collect call, Louise finally heard the phone ringing.

"Hello."

"Mitch?"

"Thank God, it's you. I've been praying you got my message. Are you okay?"

"Yes, I'm fine. What's going on?"

"I didn't see his face, but I'm ninety-nine percent certain that Richter was on the flight with you. In fact, and I don't mean to frighten you, but he's probably watching you right now."

"Watching me? Help me out here, sweetie. Explain what's happening."

"All I can imagine is that he somehow knows or suspects that you're on a mission regarding our case. But I've been in touch with someone at Doctor Syme's lab and we're going to work it out."

"Mitch, I'm frightened."

"I know you are. Just listen to me. First of all, Richter is tall and skinny. He was wearing a coat and tie, and a checkered fedora. I know how he operates. He isn't the type to try anything with too many other people around. I'm guessing he's more interested in where you're going and who you're meeting. Don't try looking for him, you'll appear too obvious."

"I don't have to look. I think he's already found me. There's a guy fitting that description across from me at the newsstand. He's doing a crappy job of hiding the fact that he's watching me."

"Yeah, that would be Richter."

"What am I supposed to do?"

"The main thing is don't go anywhere alone. Make sure you're with other people. I need you to go to the main concourse and find a place called Murphy's Bistro Lounge. There's a ladies' room right across the corridor from it. It's 10:05 your time right now; at noon go into that ladies' room and look for a woman wearing red shoes and a white scarf.

Tell her you're looking for your friend. She will introduce herself as Catherine. Give her the samples and any notes or instructions you have for them. If nobody else is in there, I want you to leave before she does. I know this is a lot, but are you following me?"

"Main concourse, Murphy's Lounge, restroom at noon, pass off the stuff to Catherine, make sure I'm never alone," Louise rattled off the instructions.

"You got it. Between now and then you have to stay wherever there's a lot of people. That's really important. Don't give Dolf any opportunities. Then, after you and Catherine part company I want you to go straight to the ticket counter and get booked on the first available return flight. I don't care what airport it goes into—Washington, Baltimore, Philadelphia, Richmond, whatever. I'll be there. Just call me as soon as you get your ticket."

"Won't Richter know something is wrong?"

"Yeah, but he's going to be confused and won't, at least shouldn't, be able to find out what flight you're on or where you're going."

"Okay. I'm on my way. Love you."

"Love you, too. Oh, one other thing, I don't want you to go to baggage claim. Just leave it there. We'll worry about your bag later."

"Okay. Love you. Bye."

"Bye."

Mitch could only feel a slight bit of the tension easing up. He had been hesitant about letting her do this alone and now was kicking himself for not trusting his gut. He wouldn't relax until Louise was safely home.

Everything went according to plan. Louise met with Catherine and gave her the blood and tissue samples as well as a handwritten note for

Doctor Syme thanking him for all he was doing. Catherine was carrying a purse big enough to put the samples in and not look suspicious. Louise thanked Catherine profusely and urged her to be careful.

Louise exited the ladies' room first and headed toward the ticket counter. After waiting several minutes, Catherine departed. Louise did an admirable job of trying to look nonchalant, and trying not to look for Dolf, even though she knew he must have been watching.

The concourse wasn't very crowded and Louise was distracted by a squealing baby in a carriage. She didn't notice Dolf coming up behind her. The pain in her left tricep was excruciating as Dolf grabbed her and whispered in her ear with a gruff voice, "Make a scene and you're dead. Now head over to that sitting area."

He pushed her into the direction he wanted to go. Louise and Dolf sat down on adjacent chairs. He still had a tight grip on her arm, but had positioned himself to shield from view the fact that they were anything other than friends.

"What do you want?" Louise stammered.

"Who are you planning to see?" Dolf opened his jacket and revealed the gun that had been dropped at the airport for him. "Give me any shit or start acting crazy and I'll kill you. You already know I have no qualms about doing that."

Louise was shaking and starting to gasp for breath.

"Give me a second, here," she pleaded.

"Start talking." Dolf gripped her tighter.

Louise was scared. She was in trouble. She knew that anything she said could put everyone at Doctor Syme's lab in danger too. Her head was spinning as she tried to figure out what to say. She took a deep breath and got ready to talk when she heard a familiar voice.

"Well, look at you two." It was Frankie. He had walked up behind the chair Dolf was sitting in, reached around Dolf's head with both arms, grabbed the gun from Dolf's waistband, and jammed the short barrel into Dolf's crotch. "Move, or so much as twitch, and you'll spend the rest of your life sitting down to pee."

Louise's eyes bugged wide. Like a rush of adrenaline, she could feel the relief envelope her body. "Frankie?"

"What a coincidence, huh? Introduce me to your friend since we're getting so chummy." Frankie's face was pressed up against Dolf's and they were both looking at Louise. "Which one of us is best looking?"

Louise was stunned. She looked at Frankie, then Dolf, then back at Frankie. "His name is Dolf," she stammered.

"Yeah, I kind of figured that. He's got the wise-ass look, I was expecting."

Louise's mouth was agape. She tried to speak, but couldn't.

"You gotta get out of here," said Frankie. "Go get a ticket to get home. Don't look back, just go. Write down your flight details on a piece of paper and give it to the bartender at Murphy's. Tell him it's for me. Just go. I'll keep our asshole friend here occupied."

Louise got up and started walking away, then stopped and turned as if to say something.

"Just go, Louise. Get a ticket. I'll make sure Mitch gets the information and is waiting for you. Go, get a drink on the plane and try to relax."

By 2:45 p.m., London time, Louise was on her way back to Washington. She had managed to get the last available seat on a flight going into Dulles Airport.

Frankie and Dolf walked almost every foot of the airport, visiting every baggage claim area, every gate, every ticket counter. Finally, Frankie and Dolf stopped at Murphy's and retrieved the message, Louise had left for Frankie. She was flying into Dulles, arriving at 5:30 p.m. on Pan Am Flight 498. Frankie would call Mitch. In the meantime he took Dolf down to the area where motor vehicles picked up passengers. A limo with two people in it was waiting.

Frankie shoved Dolf inside and said to the driver, "You know where to take him." Frankie then turned around and went back into the airport.

Mitch met Louise at the Dulles arrival gate. She practically collapsed into his arms.

"I've never been so scared. What happened? How did Frankie get involved? How did he get there?"

"He only told me a little bit when he called with your flight information. I didn't know he was going to be there. But I'm sure glad he was. He was ready."

Louise then told Mitch how and where Frankie showed up, and that she had no idea what happened to Frankie and Dolf after she left them.

The drive home was largely uneventful. They were both exhausted. Mitch and Louise spent the rest of their evening wrapped in each other's arms.

The phone rang at 11:00 a.m. the following morning. Mitch grunted something into the receiver.

"I figured I'd catch you still at home. I'm back in Philly." It was Frankie.

"Talk to me Frankie. I'm dumbfounded."

"As I told you a little while ago, some of my contacts have put a little pressure on Farmer and explained to him that it would be very dumb not to keep us informed of anything that might involve you. So, we got a call from Farmer telling us that Dolf was going to England because the Old Man's network had learned that Louise was taking a trip. They weren't sure why she was going, but figured even if it didn't have anything to do with your investigation, it would be an opportunity to put some pressure on her and maybe find something out."

"Those bastards," growled Mitch.

"Yeah. I didn't find out until the morning she was leaving. I tried calling you, but couldn't get through. You must have been on the way to the airport. So, I figured what the hell. I need a trip. Uncle Jimmy hooked me up with a private jet to make sure I got there first. Had some people waiting for me. Then everything just kind of fell into place."

"And Dolf?"

"Oh, he's still kickin', and, if I was him, I wouldn't come back. But he probably will. It's just that now he's got a better idea of what he's dealing with."

"Frankie, I can't begin to tell you how much …"

"Don't say another thing," Frankie interrupted, "after all, what are friends for?"

"Yeah, but you really stepped out this time. I owe you."

"I'll remember that," Frankie chuckled.

CHAPTER 37

Once Dolf returned from Europe, it didn't take Anton and Manny long to locate him. They had lots of contacts in Richmond, most of whom didn't like Dolf at all and would like to see him off the streets. It's just that most of the local two-bit gangsters were very wary of the man that Dolf ultimately reported to, and they weren't referring to Farmer, it was the Old Man who got everyone's attention.

When Anton and Manny walked into The Kegler it was mid-afternoon, and the place was coming alive and starting to get real noisy. When asked, the bartender was quick to point out the table where Dolf was sitting. The bartender had heard of Anton, but had never met him, so he didn't know who these two were. He had no idea why Anton and Manny wanted to meet with Dolf, but like so many other people, the bartender did not like Dolf Richter either.

"So you're Dolf Richter," Anton said as he sat down on the chair, opposite from Dolf.

Dolf looked up from the Playboy magazine that had been occupying his attention. "Who in the hell are you?"

"Somebody you're going to wish you never met."

"Get the hell away from my table."

"I wouldn't talk that way if I was you," whispered Manny as he sat down in the chair next to Dolf. Under the table Manny tapped Dolf's leg with his gun. "That's a .45 with a silencer. You're either polite to us or I'll put two slugs in your gut. And not a soul in this place will know anything ever happened, 'till closing time."

"So, what do you guys want?" Dolf put some muscle in his voice, but Anton could see that his eyes were darting around the bar looking for a familiar face or anybody who could help.

Anton just smiled. "I know you're scared, Richter, and you have every reason to be scared because this is not going to end well for you. Just how badly it ends is going to be totally up to how well you satisfy us with the answers to some questions."

"Who are you and what do you really want?"

"Okay," Anton replied, "I'm going to lay all my cards on the table. Who do you work for, that is, who gives you your marching orders? Did you kill or do you know who killed Muriel Cathcart? Did you kill or do you know who killed Vonnie Owens? Did you order or have anything to do with the bombing of Mitch Armstrong's house? Who ordered you to fly to London to intercept Mitch Armstrong's wife? Who has it in for Mitch Armstrong and why?"

Dolf sat motionless and speechless, staring at Anton.

"I've got a better idea." There was a hint of impatience in Anton's tone. "Let's go out back and discuss it. That way you won't feel like you're on center stage, and won't have to worry about what other people here are thinking of you or what they might be hearing."

The three men stood and Manny motioned, with a head nod, toward the rear of the bar. "We've already checked it out," he said, "there's an exit door next to the restrooms. It leads to an alley where the dumpster is at."

Manny led the way. Dolf and Anton followed. Anton draped his arm over Dolf's shoulder as if they were good friends sharing a couple laughs. Once they were outside the mood shifted dramatically.

Manny spun around, punched Dolf in the chest and threw him up against the dumpster. He pulled out his .45 auto with the silencer and fired one shot into Dolf's left foot. Dolf started to scream and Manny shoved a wad of cloth napkins that he had picked up inside the bar into Dolf's mouth. "The more quiet you are, the better things will be.

"Let's try it again," said Anton, "who do you work for?"

Dolf pulled the wad of napkins from his mouth. He was wheezing heavily. "Ken Farmer. He gives me the jobs. He pays me."

"Who does he report to?"

"He's never said, but I always knew it was the Old Man."

"And who is the Old Man?"

"Parker, the governor's father."

"Okay, let's try this again. Who do you work for?"

Manny stomped on Dolf's left foot and Dolf's scream was again muzzled with a mouthful of napkins.

"The Old Man. He's everybody's boss." Dolf was gasping, crying, and crumbling downward all at the same time. "I work for him, but Farmer's the intermediary. He passes on the orders. The Old Man told me to do whatever Farmer says."

"Did Farmer and the Old Man order the killing of the two women, Cathcart and Owens?"

"Nobody ever said kill, they just said get all the information you can and make sure they don't come back to haunt us."

"But there's an understanding."

"I guess you could say that."

"What about the bombing of Mitch Armstrong's house?"

Dolf hesitated before answering. "They kind of left that up to me. They said it had to be a big and unmistakable message. But they didn't want Armstrong to be killed. They just wanted to make sure it would give him reason to back off and stop looking into the case. And they didn't want anybody else picking up the slack on his behalf."

"Why are they so concerned about Armstrong investigating the case?"

"Nobody ever told me directly. But talk has it that the Old Man's son, Governor Parker, was involved in the murder that Tommy Cleaves was executed for. They seemed to feel that Armstrong is somehow getting close to proving it."

Anton stood there for a while, hands in his pockets and staring at the ground. Finally, he raised his head and looked at Dolf then at Manny.

"Well what do you think, Manny, I do believe that Mr. Richter has done an admirable job answering our questions."

"Yeah, you're right. He did even better than I thought he would. I guess we should go easy on him."

Manny and Anton both turned and looked at Dolf.

"We were planning, Dolf, to put a couple rounds in your gut and then throw you into the dumpster. Let you die a very slow and painful death. But you've been a bit more cooperative than we expected you to be. Soooo …"

Dolf looked at the two men with an expression of hopeful expectation.

"We'll simply make it quick and easy."

Anton nodded at Manny. Manny fired a round into Dolf's head. The two men then walked leisurely out of the alley.

Two weeks passed and Mitch was working on a case for a new client when he got a call on his car phone. This rarely happens, so when it rang he immediately pulled over to the side of the road to answer it. It was Louise, and she was breathless.

"What's up, sweetie?" Mitch asked, "You sound like something's wrong."

"Actually, nothing's wrong, but a whole lot of things are right. I'm at the hospital and just had a telegram delivered to me. It's from Andrew in England. Remember? He's the one at Doctor Syme's lab you spoke to. It says, Sample 1 tests positive for paternity. Sample 2 does not. He will forward a full written report. Mitch, Sample 1 is Parker, Sample 2 is Cleaves."

"Have I ever told you that I love you? This is great. We've got something now. I've got to get hold of Frankie. See you at the house."

"See you later. Love you too. Bye."

Mitch immediately called Frankie and gave him the news. Frankie said he had people around and didn't want to talk, but would call Mitch later. He said that he had some news.

Mitch was home and answered his phone on the second ring. Because of the tap that had been discovered on his farmhouse, Mitch had his surveillance friends install a device on the phone at the house he was renting that could detect a wiretap. He felt free to have open conversations once again. The caller was Frankie.

"Mitch, as you know, my boys have been in touch with Farmer. No need to rehash that. Now, I've also got confirmation about Richter. He works for the Old Man but gets his instructions from Farmer. He's dangerous, Mitch, and for that reason I thought you should know that he won't be a problem anymore. My boys have taken care of that. Just don't ask me anything else."

"Frankie, I knew I could count on you. I'm going to concentrate on the Old Man and Governor Parker. Somehow I'm going to bring that son of a bitch to justice."

"Just be careful Mitch and call me if you need something."

"Will do."

CHAPTER 38

S ome homeowners have given names to their mansions in the Ginter Park section of Richmond. *Everly* is the home of the Old Man, Conrad A. Parker Sr.

Everly has been in his family for over one hundred years, and, one day, ownership will pass on to Governor Parker, the Old Man's son. *Everly* isn't a quintessential mansion on a hill. It isn't beautiful. Some people might call it grand. Most, however, would call the huge Gothic home, with its granite block construction—intimidating. After passing through the security gate, and reaching the top of the curved driveway, a person rarely feels comfortable walking up the steps that eventually lead to the front door. Gargoyles project menacingly from the rooflines at either side of the entrance portico. They seem to dare you to step inside.

Mitch paid little attention to them as he scaled the steps and approached the main door. He reached for the huge brass knocker, but before he could lift it, the door opened from within. An impeccably dressed man who looked more like a Secret Service agent than a member of the domestic staff greeted Mitch.

"Mr. Armstrong?"

"Yes, I am."

"Please, follow me."

Mitch stepped inside and the man-servant closed the door. Without another word the—*porter—doorman—butler*—Mitch couldn't think of what to call him, began walking down a long hallway. Mitch fell in behind, assuming he was being led to the Old Man. They stopped next to a large, dark, oaken door. The man opened it, and with only a hand gesture, no spoken words, motioned for Mitch to enter the room. Mitch stepped in, and the door closed behind him.

The room was cavernous, more of a library than just a room. The walls were lined with dark mahogany bookshelves, filled with expensively-bound books, most of which have never been in the hands of a reader. Small tables and chairs were discriminately placed around the room, allowing for private conversations. The room had an aroma, not unpleasant, but the result of 100 years of cigar and pipe smoke, as well as the essence of rich brandy, that had wafted permanently into the walls.

Mitch had learned a lot about the Old Man's family—its politics, its power and influence, its money, its supposed crimes, and, of course, its women. This was, obviously, the room where so many deals were brokered over the years—power grabs, political payoffs, personal retribution, financial sleight-of-hand, and the list goes on.

The Old Man was seated at a large mahogany desk in the middle of the room. He had a full head of white hair, large bushy eyebrows, and a golf course tan. He looked amazingly fit for a man of eighty-eight years.

"Mr. Armstrong."

Mitch nodded.

"Please, have a seat," the Old Man made a friendly hand gesture in the direction of the plush leather chair, sitting in front of his desk.

"No thanks. I don't plan to stay long."

The Old Man cocked his head off to the side. "Okay, Mr. Armstrong, you're obviously a man who likes to get right to business." His words came slow, but strong. "Let's cut the B.S. and get to business. What do you want?"

"I want you to stop doing this to me," Mitch said.

"Doing what?" the Old Man asked with a quizzical smirk.

"Don't patronize me. You're the one who just said to cut the B.S. I'm being followed, my phone has been tapped, two people who were trying to help me have been murdered, my house was blown up, my wife nearly died, and my unborn child was killed. That's what you're doing."

The Old Man took a deep breath. Mitch could see his chest rise. He looked directly at Mitch. "So, you're visit here today is, what—a request—a demand—or, God forbid—a warning?" There was an obvious hint of mockery in his tone.

"Maybe a little of each, but I'd focus on *warning* if I were you," Mitch shot back.

The Old Man removed his glasses with one hand and took on a look of deep concern.

"I would advise you, Mr. Armstrong, to not use that tone with me again, and to be very, very careful with your words." His voice had changed. It was no longer cordial, but now carried an obvious menace that tainted everything he said. "First, let me offer my condolences. I am extremely regretful that you have had such a run of bad luck. But I can assure you, I've had nothing to do with it, and I have no idea why you would think that."

Mitch was pissed. "First you patronize me, now you lie to me. I know you're behind this because you're protecting your son. I know that he's a spineless piece of shit who killed a beautiful young girl, twenty-five years ago, and let somebody else pay the price for it. And you know that I'm getting close to providing rock solid evidence."

"That's ridiculous," the Old Man retorted. "There's no way you could ever prove such an outlandish claim." He forced a chuckle as he spoke.

"That's where you're wrong. You've taken care of your son for his entire life. Without daddy to lean on, he's a big zero. He's relied on you for all that he has, all that he is. But I'll get to your son, and I've learned enough that I'm sure I'll be able to make him talk."

The Old Man's eyes narrowed. "There's a button under my desk, Mr. Armstrong. It lets me summon, for lack of a better term, the staff. I could press that button and you would not leave here alive."

"But you won't press it," Mitch scoffed.

The Old Man's lips curled into a sneer, "And why won't I?"

Mitch opened his coat, exposing a white, legal sized envelope, tucked into the breast pocket. It was the envelope Frankie had given him.

"May I?" asked Mitch.

The Old Man nodded.

Mitch pulled out the envelope and tossed it onto the desk. "Go ahead, take a look."

The Old Man slowly shook out the contents. Seven wallet-sized photographs, very recent and very candid, spilled onto his desk. Spreading them out, he studied the faces of his two daughters and five of his grandchildren.

"One of your daughters lives in Cambridge, Massachusetts," Mitch said. "The other lives in Atlanta, Georgia. Saint Bernard's in Cambridge and Portsmouth Hope in Atlanta are the private schools your grand-children attend. Your daughters are stay-at-home moms. But as you know, neither they nor their kids spend much time at home. They're out and about a lot. They like to mingle with all sorts of people. They go to soccer practice, little league, church choir, shopping. All in all, both families appear to be close, active, happy. So, let me make this perfectly clear. If you ever push any button, call any of, as you say, your staff, or do anything, from this moment on, to again interfere with me or my family, you will be signing the death warrant for at least two members of yours."

Mitch picked up one of the pictures, glanced at it and said, "Nice looking." He threw it back down on the desk. "The money's been paid. The plan has already been put into motion. I don't know which ones have been targeted. But I do know this. There's only one person in the world who can call it off, and that one person is me."

The Old Man glanced down at the pictures then slowly redirected his stare toward Mitch. He couldn't, nor did he want to, conceal the anger that was starting to well up inside of him. In a stern, but mea-sured tone he said, "Most people would be a bit frightened to see and hear something like this. But I'm not most people, Mr. Armstrong. I've been around the block a few times. I know what it takes to, as you say, put a plan like this into motion. I also know what it takes to put a stop to it. Let's not mince words. I simply don't believe you. You don't have the personal stature required to order something like this against someone like me nor do you have the access to the kinds of resources that would be necessary to carry it out. Finally, Mr. Armstrong, and listen carefully to what I'm about to say. You are actually the one who should, right now, be quite frightened."

Mitch stared at the Old Man for a few moments, then said, "I was told you'd take some convincing. And I was told the way to convince you was to simply say that, uh ..." Mitch paused for a moment, then continued, "Jimmy D. sends his regards."

Immediately upon hearing the name, Jimmy D., the Old Man dropped his head slightly and looked, once more, at the seven pictures lying on his desk. Mitch watched as much of the color drained from the Old Man's face. The Old Man leaned back and allowed his shoulders to slump down a little. Looking again at Mitch, he spoke with a barely discernable voice, "*Touché*, Mr. Armstrong. *Touché*."

"I'm not the heartless bastard you may think I am," Mitch replied, "but make no mistake about it, when it comes to protecting my family, I, not unlike you, will stop at nothing—absolutely—nothing." Mitch peered, long and hard, into the Old Man's eyes. "I think we're finished here. Don't bother calling anyone for me. I can find my way out."

Mitch turned and walked out of the room. The Old Man stared blankly at Mitch's back as it disappeared into the shadowy hallway.

Mitch motored slowly down the driveway and departed *Everly* through the gated entrance which opened as he approached it. Shortly after turning onto the street outside of *Everly* he spotted a familiar car parked on the side of the street and less than a hundred yards away. It was Frankie.

Mitch pulled up so the two cars were nose to nose, got out of his car, walked up to Frankie's car, and slid into the front passenger's seat.

"Frankie, what are you doing here?"

"I knew what you were doing. I just wanted to make sure you were okay."

"I'm pretty sure Jimmy D. did the trick. I don't think the Old Man is going to continue being a problem."

"So, now what? Where do we go from here?"

"Straight to the Commonwealth's Attorney's office. I think we've got enough to at least get his attention. He's never been a fan of Governor Parker, and almost ran against him in the last gubernatorial primary election. I've got a contact there and, hopefully, we can set up a meeting with the Commonwealth's Attorney, himself."

"You think we've really got enough for that? You gotta take into account that, despite what they've been doing with that DNA stuff in other countries, it isn't going to be admissible in court."

"I've already talked to Win about that. His take on it is that if this ever got to court, the DNA is just icing on the cake. The DNA proves motive, and even after it's thrown out, a jury will have already heard it. In addition to that, we've got pictures, we've got eyewitness accounts, we've got Kathleen's letters to Vonnie that, despite the girl code, can be shown to prove that she was pregnant. We've got Farmer's original meeting with the Old Man."

"You think Farmer would testify? You'd have to put him into some kind of protection. The Old Man would do whatever he could to keep Farmer off the stand. As a minimum he'd let Farmer know that if he said the wrong thing it would cost him his life. That's the kind of people they are."

"I'm well aware of that. We'll take care of Farmer. The real plus would be getting the governor on the stand, I really don't think that he would be a very good witness in his own defense."

"You're always the positive one, Mitch. I hope you're right."

"I'm feeling good about it, Frankie. I really am."

CHAPTER 39

The telephone interrupted the early evening stillness. It's been a while since Mitch and Louise had some quiet time alone. Louise had already picked up the phone just as Mitch was about to say, "Let it ring."

"It's for you, sweetie. Some lady who says she's calling from Governor Parker's office."

Mitch stood up, walked over to where Louise was standing, and took the phone from her hand. "Hello. Yes, this is Mitch Armstrong. Okay. You said tomorrow? Yes, I should be able to do that. Okay, I'll see you then."

"What was that all about?" asked Louise.

"That really was, in fact, the governor's office. Evidently, he's been told some things. He wants to meet with me tomorrow afternoon. Two o'clock."

"Are you going to do it?"

"Of course I am. He wouldn't want to see me if this was all a big nothing. I can't wait."

"Do you think you should take Frankie or Win or somebody else with you?"

"No, I'll be fine. I can tell when I need backup. I won't let it get to that point. But I will call Frankie and let him know what's going on."

Two o'clock the following day found Mitch sitting in a comfortable chair in the waiting area inside the governor's office suite.

"Governor Parker is ready for you, Mr. Armstrong." One of the governor's attractive administrative assistants led Mitch to the doorway of Governor Parker's private office.

"Governor Parker, Mr. Armstrong is here."

"Thank you, Jennifer, please show him in.

With that, the assistant, Jennifer, ushered Mitch into the governor's office and closed the door behind him.

"Have a seat, Mr. Armstrong." Governor Parker motioned toward a sitting area next to a window. There was a small table and two chairs. Mitch sat down and casually crossed his right leg over his left knee. Governor Parker sat in the opposite chair. "Well, it seems like you've been a busy man," the governor continued. "What's this all about?"

"What's what all about?" Mitch feigned ignorance.

"Don't pretend you don't know what I'm talking about, Mr. Armstrong. You've got some kind of vendetta against me. I don't know if it's political or what, or if somebody else is behind it. But I don't appreciate the way you've been digging into my past. I don't like you snooping around and making insinuations about me, my administration, my personal life, or my political career. I'm on the short track for some big things, and if you keep sticking your nose into places where it doesn't belong, it could wind up costing me. And believe me when I say this—if it costs me, it's going to cost you too—very much so."

"Cost me? Oh, I don't think so. Maybe I should mention something—your father and I have already had that conversation."

"You've spoken to him?" That revelation caught Parker by surprise. "What are you doing? Playing games with my family?"

"Let me make something perfectly clear. I'm not playing games. Tommy Cleaves was executed this year for a crime he did not commit. You could have stayed the execution. But you let it proceed, and I know why, and you know perfectly well what I'm talking about. You're the one who did it. You killed Kathleen Spencer on a summer night, twenty-five years ago. And you allowed Tommy Cleaves to pay the price for what you did."

Parker forced a laugh. "You're out of your mind, Armstrong." Parker's eyebrows were drawn upward causing short lines to form across his forehead. He began to involuntarily scratch his nose as a rush of adrenaline to the capillaries in his nose caused it to itch. Mitch smiled. Those were telltale signs of someone who was lying.

"The only person out of his mind, Governor, is you for denying it. I was on the beach that night when you did it. I was watching you. I know it was you. I know what kind of car you were driving, a '56 Thunderbird, which you still have. I have documented evidence that Kathleen was pregnant. I have scientific evidence that proves you were the father of the baby. I know that your family had big plans for you, and that this unwanted pregnancy would have gotten in the way. I know that Kathleen wanted to keep the baby. I know that your father leaned on the investigating police detective in a way that caused him to pin this murder on someone else. One way or another, Parker, I'll get you into a courtroom."

Governor Parker stood up and began an aimless wander around his office. He stopped next to a bookshelf and adjusted a couple of framed pictures. He had a scowl on his face. Some people would find it a little intimidating. He hoped it was an expression that conveyed a combination of anger, disgust, disdain, self-assurance—anything to make

Mitch feel uncomfortable. Finally, he looked at Mitch and spoke, "You are getting in way over your head, Mr. Armstrong. You have no idea who you are confronting or the resources I have at my disposal. Especially for dealing with someone who is presenting threats to the governor, threats that are sourced by nothing but lies and assumptions."

"Lies and assumptions? Weren't you listening to anything that I said. You can huff and puff all you want, Governor. You're not scaring me. Few things do. Plus, you know I'm right on target. And did I mention this? When I drop this bombshell onto Peggy Brittman, Tommy's sister, she's gonna smell money and most likely try to take some sort of legal action against you and the state of Virginia. Even if it wasn't true, it could be a political career-ender for you. But the fact is, we both know it is true. Once again, I might have only been a kid, but I have proof I was there. You're going to have to accept that."

"All right, Armstrong, I'll spot you a couple of things. Kathleen and I were boyfriend and girlfriend, at least for that summer. And, yes we, more than once, spent some time on a blanket on the beach at night. I vaguely recall having an argument with her one night. Maybe that was the night you were there if, in fact, you really were. But to say that I killed her, that's ridiculous. I mean, who would ever think that a teenager like me would have done such a thing?"

"We saw you do more than argue."

"We? Somebody was with you?"

"What's the matter? Having more than one witness concern you?"

"No. Why should it?" Parker stuttered. "You didn't see what you're claiming. The very last time I ever saw Kathleen she was standing at the water's edge yelling at me. I don't even remember what it was about. Yes, I pushed her and she fell. I turned my back on her and left. As far as I knew she was okay. She was still yelling at me. She was alive, she wasn't dead. I didn't strangle the bitch. So, what do you want?"

"What do I want? I'm here at your invitation. I didn't set up this meeting, you did. I think the real question is 'What do you want?' "

"I want you to drop this whole witch hunt. You have no idea what or who you're dealing with, Armstrong. Things are only going to get worse for you."

Mitch stood and walked toward the door, then stopped and turned around. "It's almost sad, Governor Parker. You've been protected by so many people for so long that you literally don't have a clue how bad things are for you right now. Ask your father. He'll tell you that you're the one who doesn't know who he's dealing with."

Mitch walked out of the private office, then smiled and nodded at Jennifer as he walked past her and out of the main suite area. Mitch shook his head in disbelief as he walked down the hallway toward the exit. *I can't believe that moron actually said that Kathleen was strangled. That fact never came up in trial.*

Mitch reached into his breast pocket, removed, and turned off the Pearlcorder L400 miniature tape recorder that had captured every word.

Mitch took one little detour before leaving the building. He went to Farmer's office. He was, again, greeted by the same secretary who asked if he had an appointment with Security Chief Farmer.

"Is he in?" Mitch asked.

"Well, yes, but you do need an appointment to see him."

"I don't need shit," Mitch responded.

Mitch walked straight to Farmer's adjoining office, pushed the door open, walked in, then slammed the door shut.

Farmer looked up from his desk. The shock and fear in his face was palpable.

"What are you doing, Armstrong?"

Mitch walked straight to Farmer's desk, reached across, grabbed him by the shirt, and pulled him out of his chair.

"I know some of my friends have already talked to you, Kenny boy. But I just had to add my two cents. Cross me and you're dead meat. Count your blessings that you're not already six feet under, asshole."

Mitch let go of Farmer, turned and left without another word. Once he was out of the office and back in the hallway, he couldn't help but say aloud, "That felt good."

Mitch called Frankie on the way home. "Parker's dumber than we thought, Frankie. I've got him on tape admitting that he was on the beach with her that night, that they had a fight, and that he pushed her. Not exactly what we saw and heard but it's very incriminating when we add to it the information he doesn't know about, or isn't completely aware of."

"I'm not sure of the legal technicalities here, Mitch. We'll definitely have to get Win involved, but I think we've got our man."

"We need to get together and review some things. Can you come down sometime tomorrow or the next day or two?"

"Tomorrow works. Your house at noon?"

"See you then."

CHAPTER 40

M itch, Frankie, and Louise sat around the kitchen table listening to the recording of Mitch's visit with the governor.

Frankie was shaking his head. "I still find it crazy that you got through security with that thing."

"Oh, I forgot to tell you, Frankie. I should thank you and the boys who visited Farmer for this. I played one of our trump cards. I called Farmer and had him send somebody to meet me at the main entrance. I never had to go through security."

"Good job, Mitch."

They had been discussing options for about an hour when a loud knock echoed through the house and all three heads turned toward the front door.

"Just another surprise I've got for you guys," said Mitch as he stood up and went to answer the door.

"Hey, Mitch, how've you been?"

"Great, Win, and you?"

"I never complain."

"Win, how the hell you doing?" Frankie was on his feet and moving around the table where he gave Win a warm embrace.

Louise, likewise, stood and greeted Win Winston.

Never one to waste time, Win climbed into the previously unoccupied chair and said, "Okay, bring me up to speed."

Mitch laid out everything for Win, taking it from the very beginning. He wanted to make sure Win had as good a grip on the whole scenario as possible. This consumed the better part of the next two hours.

Mitch began with the night of Kathleen's murder and took it all the way through Farmer's investigation, Tommy's trial and execution, Mitch's visit with Muriel and her death, his visit with Bill Spencer, Vonnie, the bombing, Dolf Richter, the '56 T-bird, DNA research in England, Louise's trip to England and how Dolf tried to interfere, the DNA results, the Old Man's involvement, and, finally, Mitch's visit to the governor's office.

Neither Frankie nor Louise ever hesitated to interject and add their take or perspective to a particular element of the story. All the while Win scribbled notes on a legal pad.

Finally, Mitch said, "That about wraps it up. So, Win, what do you think?"

"You got yourself quite a thriller going here," quipped Win.

"We're at a point, as you can see," Mitch replied, "where there's no doubt that Governor Parker is the one who killed Kathleen Spencer. I want to see charges brought against him. I know the DNA stuff hasn't been used in court yet, but can't it still be admitted?"

"Mitch, I'd figure out a way to bring your grandmother's dreams into evidence if I had to. And trust me, if I was the prosecutor and had the governor on the witness stand, I'd break him. You've got more than enough to work with. The problem is going to be the pushback from the governor's office and from the Commonwealth's Attorney.

The governor is very popular, his party is in control of the state legislature, and as much as everyone in politics wants you to believe they
are civic-minded and looking out for your interests, that really ain't the
case. They love power and being in control. There's going to be more
resistance, probably obstruction, than you could ever imagine."

"I figured there'd be some resistance, but like I've mentioned to
others, the Commonwealth's Attorney isn't a big fan of the governor
and almost ran against him in the last primary election."

Win pushed back from the table causing his chair to rest on just the
two rear legs. He tilted his head way back, as if looking at the ceiling,
and took a deep breath. Then, he gently lowered himself back into
position. "It's going to be tough, no matter what," said Win. "Our job
is to convince the Commonwealth's Attorney. We can't leave even the
tiniest reasonable doubt. If this guy has political aspirations, like you
implied he does, he doesn't want to risk even the slightest chance of
bringing charges against the sitting governor and then not being able
to prove them in court. It would be political and professional suicide.
Hell, what am I saying, that's the kind of stuff that winds up leading to
personal suicide."

"This isn't sounding so good," interjected Louise.

"Don't get discouraged," replied Win. "I'm just trying to show you
that we need to look at something like this from all angles. The upside
is that if we do play our hand right with the Commonwealth's Attorney, and do as good a job of convincing him, just as we've convinced
ourselves, he'll buy into it. And if he has the political aspirations you
suspect he does, he will realize that he'd be showing the public how the
governor had been dishonest, how he had lied to the public and be-
trayed their trust. More importantly he would show the public that the

governor had allowed an innocent man to pay the ultimate sacrifice for something that the governor, himself, had in fact done. The Commonwealth's Attorney would then be a hero and well on his way to calling the governor's mansion home after the next election."

"That's why you're here, Win. What do you propose we do?" asked Mitch.

"We begin with getting people to like us. Didn't you tell Frankie you had a contact in the Commonwealth's Attorney's office?"

"Yeah, I do."

"What kind of contact? What can he or she do for us?"

"I became good friends with a guy that was on the police force with me in Richmond. Ray Taylor is his name. We called him Cuz. He was real friendly, a country boy from West Virginia. He started going to law school at night, and last I knew, he was working as an Assistant Commonwealth's Attorney for Middlesex County and was doing a really good job. The real plus is that Middlesex County is where the murder took place. I haven't spoken with him in quite a while, but I feel pretty confident that he'll be receptive to talking to us."

"Great, we need to get to him as soon as possible. As soon as you can arrange a meeting, I'll make myself available."

"I'll do that," said Mitch. "Now, there's one other thing I want to bring up to you folks."

"Us folks?" said Louise, with one eyebrow very arched. "Oh, please do."

Mitch simply cut a quick sideward glance in Louise's direction.

Win poked Frankie on the shoulder. "Momma ain't happy."

Louise smiled at Win. "I love him to death. He just surprises me on occasion."

"Okay, I could have started this better, but here's the deal. I want to talk to Bill Spencer about this."

"What do you mean by talk to him?" asked Frankie.

"I want to let him know where we are on this."

"Do you really think that's a good idea?" asked Louise with obvious concern.

"I owe it to him. I've brought him nothing but upsetting news over the past several months. I don't know how much longer that guy has. He recently lost his wife. As close as they were, I wouldn't be surprised to hear that he's one of those kinds of people that dies of a broken heart. Ever since I first visited him, and because I visited him, there's been a huge question mark placed over his daughter's murder. Now he doesn't know if justice has been served. I just want to tell him what we've got and that we're going to see that the real S.O.B. who killed his daughter is going to be held accountable for it."

"I think we can do it," said Win, "but you never really know how these things are going to pan out. I hope you're not jumping the gun with this guy."

"I don't know, I just feel like I've gotta do it. I wouldn't want anything to happen to him while he's wondering if we're getting anywhere with this."

"You have to do whatever you think is right," said Frankie.

Mitch looked at Louise. She smiled a little, nodded her head up and down ever so slightly, and gently spoke. "I love you, Mitch. I'll support whatever you do."

CHAPTER 41

Mitch found himself, once again, sitting on the uncomfortable oak bench outside of Bill Spencer's office. Bill's secretary, Mrs. Penny, had already assured Mitch that Dr. Spencer would be with him shortly. Mitch did not feel quite as apprehensive about this meeting with Bill Spencer as he did last time. However, there was still an element of uncertainty nibbling away at him.

Finally, there was a short ring on Mrs. Penny's phone. After she hung up she told Mitch that Dr. Spencer was ready for him and to just go ahead into his office. Mitch got up, walked over to the door to Spencer's office, tapped once, then opened it and walked in.

"Well, Mr. Armstrong, to what do I owe the pleasure of your visit this time?" Sarcasm dripped all over Spencer's words. He remained seated behind his desk.

"Let me begin by offering my condolences. I recently learned that your wife, Margaret, had passed."

"Thank you Mr. Armstrong, I do miss her dearly. But of course, I'm quite sure that offering your sympathy is not the reason you came here today."

"I have some news to share with you, Dr. Spencer. May I sit down?"

"I was hoping your visit was going to be short enough not to require sitting, but go ahead, take a seat. Let me just say, this better be worth it."

"I'll get right to the point," Mitch said. "We have, with almost one hundred percent certainty, identified the man who murdered Kathleen."

Bill Spencer rested his forearms on his desk and leaned forward. "I'm listening. I'm not real comfortable with your statement of almost one hundred percent. But go ahead, continue."

"In my mind, really, there's actually no question about it at all. We've linked him to the red Thunderbird that I told you about last time I was here. We have a statement about a very incriminating meeting that the lead detective in the case had with our suspect's father during the investigation of the murder. And, I had a personal encounter with the suspect in which he all but admitted doing it."

"I'm sorry, Mr. Armstrong, but I'm still not getting a strong sense that you have proven your point. You seem to be leaving something out."

"You're very perceptive, Dr. Spencer. However, what I need to tell you may be a little shocking."

"Go ahead. Little can ever shock me, anymore."

Mitch cleared his throat and briefly hesitated, then started speaking. "At the time of her death, your daughter, Kathleen, was pregnant." Mitch paused to allow the words to sink in.

Mitch braced himself for the emotionally charged response that he anticipated. But surprisingly, after a brief staring contest, Bill Spencer said, "Now it's my turn to shock you a little, Mr. Armstrong. I'm not at all caught off guard by what you said. Margaret had suspected it.

Private things that only women know or can sense had pointed her in that direction. She shared it with me when she was all but certain, even though she hadn't yet approached Kathleen about it. We really didn't know this boy that Kathleen was seeing that summer at Bohman's Point. And, quite frankly, we were hoping that the pregnancy scare was all in Margaret's mind. But nevertheless, I don't see where that factors into this equation."

"My wife is a doctor," Mitch began, "and several months ago she enlightened me about something very new that is happening in the field of medical science. It so happens that a doctor in England has done a lot of work and research into something called DNA. I'm far from well-versed in this, but this DNA involves some sort of genetic markers that each of one of us has and that are totally unique to each of us."

"I've heard a little about this. This is a college campus, after all, and I do interact with other professors."

"Well it turns out that one of the things that this DNA allows us to do is somehow determine paternity and maternity status with regard to a child," Mitch had to stop and clear his throat a little, "or even a fetus."

Bill Spencer was silent, but his eyes said a lot.

Mitch drew a deep breath and continued, "Tissue that has been preserved from Kathleen's autopsy included some fetal tissue. A sample of the fetal tissue, along with a blood sample from our suspect, were sent to the doctor in England. Please know, I'm not at liberty to tell you how we got that blood sample. The important thing is that the analysis confirmed that our suspect is the father."

Mitch stopped for a minute to gage how this was settling with Spencer.

"And you're sure, Mr. Armstrong, that this person would in fact be the murderer?"

"Quite sure, Dr. Spencer. It fits perfectly well with what my friend and I saw and heard the night of Kathleen's murder as well as what we learned from our conversations with the lead detective."

Bill Spencer dropped his gaze and stared at his desk top for a few moments, then looked up at Mitch. "Okay, Mr. Armstrong, just who is this mystery man."

"This may be hard to believe, Dr. Spencer, but rest assured there is more corroborating evidence than what I have already shared with you. The man in question is Conrad Parker, the governor of Virginia."

Bill Spencer seemed to melt backward into his chair.

"Governor Parker, are you sure of this? I just can't imagine that a governor would be, or could be, involved in this. It doesn't make sense."

"Sir, I know it sounds crazy, but twenty-five years ago he was still a college kid. And, please don't take this wrong, but I'm kind of surprised that, in recent years, you didn't connect or at least see that Virginia's governor and Kathleen's boyfriend had the same name."

"Margaret and I never really considered him a boyfriend. Just a summer fling. In fact, I never even met him, and Margaret only spoke to him once or twice in passing. We didn't even know his name. Kathleen just referred to him by some nickname."

"Cap?"

"Yes, that was it."

"Someone else told us the same thing. We believe it simply stands for his initials, C.A.P., Conrad A. Parker."

"Mr. Armstrong, you really feel certain about this?"

"I did not see him actually commit the murder. But I know, with 100 percent certainty, that he was the person with Kathleen that night on the beach, that he and Kathleen argued, and that he assaulted Kathleen. Tommy Cleaves did not kill Kathleen. Conrad Parker did."

"Not that you will, but if you had to testify in court about these things, are you certain that you could, under penalty of perjury, say that Governor Parker is the one who killed my daughter?"

"Yes I could, and yes I would. In about a week or so, I and a lawyer friend of mine will meet with the Commonwealth's Attorney that has jurisdiction. We will present our findings and pursue any possibility of bringing charges against the governor. Given that the DNA evidence might not yet be admissible in court is going to be an issue, but we're going to give it our best shot. Of course, there's also the fact that Tommy Cleaves' sister, if and when she gets wind of this, will do her best to make headline news out of it, and that could actually help us."

"Anything else?"

"I think I've told you all that I intended to."

"I need to let this sink in. Like last time, you've given me a lot to ponder."

"I promised to keep you informed. I will continue to do so as things progress, that is, if you want me to."

"I would appreciate that. As for now—goodbye Mr. Armstrong."

Bill Spencer did not stand. He simply gestured toward the door.

"I'll be in touch, Dr. Spencer." Mitch stood up and walked out of the office. He said goodbye to Mrs. Penny and breathed a huge sigh of relief after he got into the hallway. He couldn't remember a time when he looked so forward to going home.

CHAPTER 42

Two days later, Mitch and Win drove to Saluda, Virginia, to meet with Cuz Taylor. It was a nice day and Mitch felt like walking so they parked several blocks away and walked to Cuz's office on Bowden Street.

"You seem to know you're way around here," quipped Win as the two men meandered down the street.

"I've been here a few times over the years," answered Mitch. "When I was a kid we'd come here once in a while from our place at Bohman's Point. Sometimes my mom wanted to shop. Sometimes we'd come just to look around. Lot of history here."

"Yeah, I know this is an old city."

"There are lots of old historic buildings in this town. The Christ Church is one. It's where that famous Marine hero, Chesty Puller, is buried. He was raised here in Saluda. This is also where Tommy's trial took place. Because of that, I've spent some time here just trying to get a feel of things. That probably sounds kind of spooky-like to you, but I think it got me a little better grounded."

"I get what you're saying. Whatever it takes, Mitch. We're all a little different, and no one can say who's right."

"Well, here we are."

Mitch and Win stepped into building and soon found the office of the Assistant Commonwealth's Attorneys. They entered the office. Mitch immediately saw Cuz. He was wearing a white shirt and tie, had just snatched a handful of papers from the copy machine when he looked up and saw Mitch and Win come into the room.

"Mitch Armstrong! Good to see you. Wow, how long has it been?"

The two men shook hands and gave each other a shoulder to shoulder pat on the back.

"It's been a few years, Cuz. How are you?"

"Doing great, thanks."

Mitch turned to face Win, then back to Cuz. "Cuz, this is my friend, Win Winston. Win this is Cuz Taylor."

The two shook hands.

"Follow me," said Cuz, "can I get you guys some coffee or something?"

Both Mitch and Win declined.

"So what have you been up to since you left the Force?" asked Cuz.

"Kind of what I told you on the phone the other day. I've been doing a lot of work as a private investigator. It keeps me busy."

The three men chatted a little while. Mitch and Cuz shared some police stories with Win. They also got caught up on family matters, personal lives, and professional activities since leaving the Force.

"So what brings you two here today?" asked Cuz.

"Not really sure how to start this," said Mitch. "Win is an attorney and has been helping me with an investigation I've been working on."

"Win, didn't you say you're from Delaware? And, Mitch, you live in Maryland, and here we are in Virginia. I'll have to admit I'm intrigued as well as a little confused."

"There's a lot to the story," said Mitch, "and it'll make more sense as we move along. But I want to cut right to the chase. It's a murder case. The murder was committed in Virginia, and the evidence points right at a very high-ranking Virginia state government official."

"Whoa, Nellie," Cuz blurted out as he pushed his chair away from the desk. "I sure wasn't expecting this."

"If we gave you enough evidence, such as eyewitness testimony, voice recordings of admission, third party testimony of cover-up payments, and some DNA evidence, would that be enough to convince the Commonwealth's Attorney to empanel a grand jury and present charges?" asked Win.

"Win, you know as well as I do that, first of all, a lot depends on the quality of the evidence. Secondly, you mentioned DNA evidence. That's fairly new science and it hasn't yet been used in a case in the United States. They may have already used it in the U.K., or, if not, are planning to. But, so far, not here. I know some of the district court judges. They might give it a shot, might allow it. They're like anybody else. If they see something they really think has a lot of promise, they might go for it, just so they could say they were among the first on board. That is, if it turns out to be as accurate and valuable as it claims to be."

"Yeah, I get it," said Mitch. "They want the credit but not necessarily the risk."

"You could put it that way."

The room settled into silence as Cuz rested his chin on his chest and seemed to be staring a hole into the top of his desk.

Finally, he looked up and said, "Okay, let's have it. Who are we talking about?"

Mitch cocked his head a little to the side and looked at Win.

Win smiled, shook his head up and down, and said, "You've been waiting for this moment."

Mitch turned and looked straight at Cuz.

"It's Governor Parker."

Cuz, who had been leaning forward with anticipation, collapsed backward into his chair. "You guys have got to be shitting me," he said. "C'mon, Mitch, is this some kind of prank? I remember we used to do this kind of stuff all the time at the station."

"I wish it was a prank," replied Mitch. "Sorry, Cuz, this is the real deal. It has to do with something that happened a long time ago. But as you know, there's no statute of limitations on murder. Especially when somebody else was held accountable for it."

"You know I have to talk to the CA about this, and I'm going to need something to convince him that it's worth looking into. I mean he'd like nothing more than to hang something on Parker. They're definitely not friends. But he's not going to do anything like that unless he's one hundred percent sure that there's enough evidence, good evidence, to get a conviction. So, tell me, what can you guys give me that I can take to him?"

"We really need to be the ones," said Mitch, "the ones to lay out our case in front of him. I'm just hoping that you can arrange a meeting."

"Let me add something." Win interjected. "Check me out. It's easy enough to do. I've been practicing law for a long time. First in New Jersey, now in Delaware. I do a lot of criminal cases. I'm good. I don't lose. I know when a prosecutor's evidence stinks and when it doesn't. Knowing everything that I know now, there's no way in the world I'd want to be the governor's defense counsel."

Cuz took several deep breaths, opened and closed a file folder several times that was lying on his desk, rearranged two pens and a pencil, then started a drum roll type of finger tapping on the edge of his desk. Finally, he gave a five second silent stare to Mitch, then the same to Win. "All right," Cuz said, "let me see what I can do. I'm not promising anything, but I will talk to the CA and see if I can convince him to meet with you."

"Great," said Mitch.

"But you do realize that there's going to be a lot of deep thought going into this. You just don't go and accuse the governor of something. And of all things, murder, without feeling like you've got an iron clad case."

"We're well aware of that," answered Win, "and I promise you that when we sit down with the CA it will not be a waste of his time."

The three men looked at each other, shook their heads slightly, and stood up.

"Mitch, I'll be in touch."

"Thanks, Cuz. You won't regret it."

After exchanging some pleasantries with Cuz and, once more shaking hands, Mitch and Win exited the office.

Walking down the hall, Mitch heard a familiar voice. Someone was berating a young staffer for some minuscule infraction.

"Well, Ken Farmer, imagine seeing you here," said Mitch with a big fake smile. "What a coincidence. It's almost like you've been following me. So, what are you doing here?"

"My work needs me all over the state, not that it's any of your business. I think the more appropriate question is—what are you doing here?"

Taking advantage of the interruption, the staffer, who was at the receiving end of Farmer's recent tirade, slipped away.

"Sightseeing with my friend," Mitch replied. He turned toward Win. "Win, this is the infamous Ken Farmer I've been telling you about. Ken, this is attorney Win Winston."

Farmer looked at Win, then directed the scowl already etched onto his face toward Mitch.

"Attorney? You in trouble?" Farmer tilted his head to the side and stared once more at Win. "If so, you should've hired a different lawyer. Looks like you got the short end of the stick." Farmer added a little snicker to go along with his emphasis on the word, short.

Mitch looked up and down the hall to see if it was clear. He grabbed Farmer's coat lapel and with his forearm pressed across Farmer's chest, slammed Ken against the wall.

"You're still too stupid to know when to keep your mouth shut. I don't think you want word to get back to Anton that you've been a bad boy."

Farmer's eyes bugged wide open and as he was about to speak Mitch interrupted.

"Don't say a word, Ken. It'll only hurt you." Mitch released Farmer. He and Win continued to walk down the hall toward the exit.

Farmer could hear Mitch saying to Win, "See, I told you he was an asshole."

CHAPTER 43

Despite the fact that only three years ago, John Hinckley, standing in a sidewalk crowd, came close to killing President Reagan, many high-level politicians in 1984, still have a penchant for rope lines and pressing the flesh. That was the case for Governor Parker. It was also the case for his Chief of Security, Ken Farmer, on this crisp, fall morning.

On days like this, when the governor's schedule indicated a motorcade to somewhere, it was not unusual for forty or fifty people to show up outside of the mansion, trying to catch a glimpse of, or get a handshake from, the immensely popular governor.

"Nice day, Governor," said Ken. "Looks like we've got a good crowd. I think I see a few news people too. There's *The Times, Channel 3*, and that dimwit from *Channel 10*."

"Keep them entertained, Ken. I'd rather do some hand-shaking."

"Yes sir, can do."

"Tell them I'll do a news conference after the ceremony."

Ken Farmer and Governor Parker walked shoulder-to-shoulder from the executive mansion toward the waiting limo. Farmer jealously guarded his space and access to the governor. Governor Parker's close staff hated Farmer. He offered nothing of intellectual substance, did not seem to have a grip on the nuances of political life, and knew nothing of most current issues facing the governor or the legislature. But for some unexplained reason, he always had the governor's ear, and never seemed to be more than an arm's reach away.

Governor Parker was on his way to the dedication of a new middle school in Richmond. The school, specifically for academically gifted students, was to be called Conrad A. Parker Middle School. It was being named in honor of the governor who, as a state senator, introduced the funding legislation for this project, and then, as governor, signed it into law.

As they approached the waiting crowd, Governor Parker veered off in one direction to visit with the throng that was pushing at the rope barrier, hoping for a chance to shake hands with and possibly say something to the governor. Farmer turned in a different direction toward the microphones and notepads of the news reporters. Governor Parker liked the people, Ken Farmer liked being in the limelight.

Other members of Governor Parker's security team felt that Farmer hindered rather than helped their operations. That meant, much to their chagrin, that they were not always allowed the physical proximity to either Farmer or Governor Parker that they felt was necessary to do their job properly. But Farmer was the boss, so they did things his way.

Governor Parker made his way down the rope line shaking hands and exchanging friendly quips. "Hey, nice to see you. Thanks for coming out. I appreciate your support."

He eventually came face to face with an elderly gentleman in a gray overcoat. The gentleman raised his hand and waved at the governor as if he knew him.

"Remember me?" Bill Spencer shouted over the crowd of noisy onlookers.

"Sorry, I don't seem to recall," Parker replied. However, he put a big, friendly smile on his face, and extended his hand toward Bill, even though Bill had placed both hands back into the pockets of his overcoat.

"Well, maybe you remember my daughter!" Bill's icy stare seemed to fill the space between the two men.

"Your daughter?" Parker's smile retreated from friendly to confused. He stopped reaching and started to withdraw his hand.

"Yeah—you killed her."

Parker's feet felt as if they were suddenly encased in concrete. His expression turned blank and his eyes locked onto Bill. Every muscle in his body froze. He was absolutely motionless.

POW—POW, POW—POW.

Something like this can happen more quickly than most people realize. The screaming and panic didn't even begin until after all four shots were fired.

Bill fired the first bullet while the gun, a short barrel .38 special, was still in the pocket of his overcoat. It caught Governor Parker in the middle of his chest right below the sternum. Bill fired the next two shots after he withdrew the gun from his pocket. The second bullet ripped through Parker's heart, the third entered Parker's head just above the left eye. With the fourth and final shot, Bill did to himself what he had, twenty-five years ago, said he wanted to do to Tommy Cleaves. He brought the gun barrel up to his own right temple, and pulled the trigger one last time.

Farmer instinctively knew what the sound was. But even so, by the time his reflexes allowed him to turn, the shooting had stopped. His jaw agape, Farmer watched as Governor Parker collapsed to the ground. He didn't even notice the other body, not more than three feet from the governor, crumble in a likewise manner.

"Oh shit! Oh no! Oh no!" Farmer ran toward the governor.

Another member of the security team had already reached the governor. He dropped to his knees into the pool of blood that quickly formed around Parker's head and upper torso. He searched for the carotid artery and looked for other signs of life.

When Farmer got there, he almost puked at the sight of the blood on the ground and the fragments of skull protruding from the back of the governor's head. The other team member looked up at Farmer. Then he slowly lowered his eyes. Farmer knew what the man suspected.

The screaming had already started, but only now did it reach Farmer's ears. People were running in all directions. The news reporters crouched for cover. Nobody knew exactly what happened and all feared there was more to come. The rest of the security detail formed a phalanx to surround the two bodies. Police disembarked from the escort cruisers. They had already called for an ambulance. It was only a matter of a minute or so before the wail of a siren could be heard in the distance.

Mitch was with Win Winston and they were on their way to Saluda. They had an appointment with Guy Pittman, the Commonwealth's Attorney. Cuz Taylor had come through, laid the groundwork, and set up this meeting. Mitch and Win felt confident that they would be able to convince the Commonwealth's Attorney that charges should be brought against Governor Parker. They were listening to some music on the radio when an announcer interrupted …

"Breaking news. We have just learned that there has been a shooting outside the governor's mansion in Richmond. First reports are that the gov-

ernor has possibly been injured. Nothing else can be confirmed at this time. Stay tuned for updates as more information becomes available."

And the music started to play again.

"You have got to be shittin' me!" Mitch swerved onto the shoulder and slid to a stop. Some words that Frankie spoke shortly after they became certain that Governor Parker was Kathleen's killer came back to haunt Mitch. Frankie blamed the abuse he suffered from Tommy Cleaves on Parker and swore that he'd kill Parker if he ever had the chance. Mitch blew it off as Frankie just venting a bit. But now, he started worrying, "Win, you don't think Frankie could have done this do you?"

Win was in total disbelief. The shock had muted him and he could do no more than just shrug his shoulders.

"Oh, please Frankie," Mitch said aloud, "don't let this be you." He pulled his car phone out of its case.

As he was about to dial, the newscaster came back on. *"We've just gotten an update. We can now confirm that Virginia Governor Conrad Parker has been wounded in a shooting outside of the executive mansion in Richmond. He has been transported to VCU Medical Center. Reports are that the, still unidentified, shooter is also injured. Stay tuned for more information as it becomes available."*

Mitch turned down the volume and dialed Frankie's number. "Please answer, Frankie, please answer."

"Hello."

"Thank God you're there."

"Mitch. I didn't know you cared so much. Are we sweethearts now?"

"Shut up, Frankie. This isn't a joke. Turn on the radio and find a news station. Parker's been shot."

"Whaatt?"

"I'm not kidding. I gotta go. Just listen to the news. I'll be back in touch." Mitch hung up the phone, glanced at Win, shook his head, and turned the radio volume back up.

Not much later the music stopped once more, and the commentator reported, *"With great sadness, we can now confirm that Virginia Governor Conrad A. Parker has died from a gunshot wound that he sustained outside of the executive mansion just less than an hour ago. Police have also reported that the shooter has been identified as sixty-six year old William Spencer of Media, Pennsylvania. Spencer is also deceased, apparently, the result of a self-inflicted wound. Police have not speculated on a motive for the shooting, but are reporting that ... "*

Mitch snapped off the radio and stomped on the accelerator. He had already turned around and was heading home. He needed Louise more than ever.

"Bill, what have you done, what have you done?" Mitch kept repeating aloud. Win remained silent. He was uncharacteristically lost for words. He, as well as Frankie and Louise, thought that telling Spencer about Governor Parker before there was an indictment was a bad idea. Mitch, however, was anxious to close the gap he felt he had reopened in Spencer's life.

Louise heard the twin pipes of his '57 Chevy as Mitch pulled into the driveway of their rental home. She was standing in an open doorway as he came to a stop. Despite the chill in the air, she walked, without a jacket, halfway to the car and met him with a hug.

"Are you okay?"

Mitch didn't reply.

"Don't go beating yourself up Mr. Armstrong. You didn't do anything wrong."

"You and Frankie, and Win all warned me."

"It wasn't a warning, Mitch, it was our opinion," said Win, who was walking close behind. "And who knows what would have happened if Spencer didn't know until after Parker was indicted. Things could have even been worse."

"I don't know how things could have been worse," Mitch replied. "But now what? Has justice been served? Do we back off? Do we let Parker be honored as a dead hero? Do we let Bill Spencer be forever remembered with scorn. Do we forget that Tommy Cleaves died for what Parker did? What do we do?"

"I don't know, Mitch. We'll talk about it." said Louise, "We'll figure it out. Frankie called. He's on his way here."

⤿

Later that evening the four of them were sitting at the kitchen table. Win was leading the conversation.

"I called down to Virginia and talked to your friend, Cuz Taylor," said Win. "He's had a talk with the CA and said the CA would like you to keep a lid on it for right now. Until they sort things out, he'd really like to be as compassionate as possible with the governor's immediate family, his close associates, and, for that matter, the people of Virginia."

"I can understand that," said Mitch. "I guess in some respects, although it seems hard to say, I did get what I was looking for. The real killer got the penalty he deserved, and Bill Spencer got the retribution he sorely wanted. And now Bill's joined his wife. I don't know what kind of person this makes me, but that's just something I'll have to deal with."

"Things led us where they led us," said Louise, "it's as simple as that."

"She's right," said Frankie. "The governor had to be held accountable for his actions. As did Dolf. And as far as Bill Spencer is concerned, I'd bet on the fact that he would have done this no matter when he found out that the governor was the one. We all read the transcripts. We know what he said and how he acted at Tommy's trial. He wanted his daughter's killer dead, and he was more than willing to be the one to do it."

"What about Farmer and the Old Man?" Mitch asked. "They need to answer to somebody. Justice doesn't exist until people get what they deserve. How are we going to make that happen, or should we?"

"Give it time, Mitch," said Win. "It's like what Cuz was getting at. Those who don't know all the facts and thought highly of the governor need time to mourn. We wouldn't get anywhere if we tried to go after anybody else right now. Just give it some time. We'll still be able to do this, and we'll still all be with you."

The kitchen light remained on well into the wee hours of the morning. The conversation was therapeutic.

CHAPTER 44

Ken Farmer was at *Everly*, sitting in an overstuffed, burgundy, leather chair in the hallway adjacent to the Old Man's office. He was staring at the floor, lost in thought, probably scared, and didn't hear the approach. A well-polished black wingtip shoe tapped the side of his brown loafer.

"Mr. Parker will see you now."

With some timidity, Ken Farmer entered the Old Man's domain. The senior Parker, pen in hand, was making an entry into a large, custom-bound journal that lay open on his desk. Without looking up, he beckoned Farmer closer with a come-here motion of his left hand and said, "Sit down, Ken."

Ken eased himself into the leather chair, facing the desk. After a few moments of awkward silence, Ken spoke. "I'm really sorry, Mr. Parker. There was no way of knowing that Armstrong would have continued to push this thing like he did. And Bill Spencer—who would've guessed?"

The Old Man stopped writing, stared at the journal page for a moment, then looked up. His voice was a husky whisper and heavy with sarcasm. "You're sorry? There was no way of knowing? Oh, how very comforting that is to me, Ken." The Old Man paused and looked off into some faraway place, that world of what could have been, but now is nothing more than a hazy blur. "We were going to make a run for the White House," he said very softly.

Turning to Farmer, he continued, "Let me tell you something. Mitch Armstrong was just following his conscience, doing what he thought was right. And Bill Spencer? He was simply acting out of revenge, or remorse, or, perhaps, both. But that doesn't matter, because they're not the ones I hold responsible."

He laid his pen on the desk and hesitated briefly before returning his gaze to Farmer. "There's a concept here, Ken, that you don't seem to understand. There will always be enemies at the gate, and whenever they're able to breach the wall, the fault lies with the defenders. Your primary responsibility, for as long as you worked for me, had been to defend my son from any possible consequences of that Spencer girl's death."

Farmer felt himself sink deeper into the chair.

The Old Man, shaking his head ever so slightly, muttered, "You could not have failed any worse." He, then, picked up his pen and went back to work. After scratching a few more words into his journal, he raised his prickly white eyebrows and, without moving his head, peered over the top of his glasses. "That'll be all, Ken."

Farmer knew better than to say anything else. He rose and walked out of the room. *This was not good, this was definitely not good.* He couldn't shake the feeling of foreboding that began to envelope him.

After departing the mansion, Farmer drove aimlessly for over an hour before heading home. He finally parked in front of his house, walked up the concrete path leading to his front door, and picked up the evening newspaper from where the delivery boy had tossed it. The paper's headlines were still ablaze with stories about the fatal shooting of Governor Parker. He unlocked the door and stepped inside. He dropped his coat and the newspaper onto a chair in the entrance hall, and flicked on the wall switch for the living room light.

"Hi, Ken."

Farmer immediately recognized the voice. It caused his skin to tighten. He turned and faced the darkness of the hallway behind him. He blinked a couple times, subconsciously hoping it would make the image that was slowly taking shape and moving toward him disappear. It did not. There was terror in Farmer's voice as he finally spoke. "Turk, what are you doing here?"

A few minutes later, Turk positioned Ken Farmer's lifeless body into a recliner chair in the living room, turned on the television, and walked out of the house.

❧

Back at Everly, blue and red lights flashed in the driveway as a paramedic team wheeled the Old Man out through the main doorway and into the waiting ambulance. A sheet covered his body from head to toe. Inside the mansion, police forensic experts scoured the Old Man's office. They placed a small caliber handgun, pried loose from the Old Man's fingers, into an evidence bag. They took pictures of everything. The forensic team collected hair and body fluid from the top of the desk where the Old Man had collapsed. They also took the Old Man's journal into custody.

Sorry about your luck, Jimmy D. – looks like I beat you to the punch. were the final words entered into the Old Man's journal. The page was speckled with blood.

❧

Soon after hearing about the Old Man's death, Mitch knew he had to make a phone call. Mitch didn't know any of the Old Man's daughters or grandchildren, but he did know that if he failed to make the phone call, if he failed to call off the hit, two more senseless deaths would be added to this long-running tragedy.

He had, as instructed, committed the number to memory, and was hoping that Frankie was right, that all he had to do was identify himself in a certain way. He didn't want to run the risk of trying to explain anything. The phone rang once.

"Talk to me." The voice on the other end was abrupt and clear, but not loud.

"I'm one of The Corn Bandits," was all that Mitch said.

"I'll pass the word," the voice responded, then hung up.

CHAPTER 45

It's been a couple weeks since Governor Parker was killed and the news frenzy was still in high gear. Mitch and Frankie just finished a visit with Mitch's friend, Cuz Taylor, in Saluda. The Commonwealth's Attorney still hadn't decided which way to move with the information Mitch had provided. Cuz promised to let Mitch know as soon as any decisions were made, but asked Mitch to remain silent until then. Mitch agreed. He had no desire to stir the pot anymore right now.

After leaving Cuz's office, Mitch and Frankie drove over to Richmond. They headed down North Second Street and stopped next to one of the entrances into Shockoe Hill Cemetery. Mitch planned to visit the gravesite of Tommy Cleaves.

Roscoe Cleaves, a distant relative of Tommy Cleaves, had been buried at Shockoe Hill in the early 1900s. Roscoe had purchased two plots, thinking that one day he and his wife-to-be would be buried side by side. Roscoe was killed in a mining accident before they married. The second plot remained unused for seventy-five years.

Tommy's family, more precisely his sister, Peggy Brittman, made arrangements with Roscoe's family descendants to allow her to use the empty gravesite for Tommy. Tommy's share of the Cleaves' estate, which he had signed over to Peggy, was more than sufficient to cover the cost, and still allowed Peggy to walk away with a few extra dollars in her pocket. "Thanks for the new car, Tommy," were her parting words at his little funeral.

⤳

"You're sure you don't mind doing this?" Mitch asked.

"Nah," Frankie replied, "like everybody says, he's dead, why should I care. But I'll wait in the car anyway. If I went to look, it could still stir up some bad feelings I've got inside. Don't want to risk acting crazy and have you get pissed off at me all over again."

"You know I wouldn't get pissed at you."

"Yeah, but I'm going to stay here anyhow. Besides, it'll be cold as a witch's tit out there."

Mitch parked the car, then got out and walked up a small grassy incline to a spot about thirty or forty yards from where he left the car. He looked around for a few minutes, and eventually found the marker.

Standing over top of Tommy's grave, Mitch said, "Tommy, I came here to tell you I'm real sorry you got punished for something you didn't do. That shouldn't happen to anybody. I just wish I could've done more to stop it. But I wanted to let you know that we nailed the bastard who killed that girl. And Kathleen's dad, well, he got his restitution too."

Then, Mitch unzipped his pants.

"Here's another reason I'm paying you a visit today."

Mitch watched a small cloud of vapor rise into the cold air from the warm yellow puddle he was depositing on top of Tommy's grave marker. When he was finished, he pulled his zipper back up and said, "That—you worthless son-of-a-bitch—was for Frankie."

Mitch walked back to the car. Frankie had gotten out to smoke a cigarette and was finishing up as Mitch approached.

"Ready to go?" asked Frankie.

Mitch nodded and they both got back inside.

"I'm done with him," Mitch said. "I'm finally done with him. I also sent him your regards. I think you'd have liked it."

"This has been quite a ride, Mitch. Parker gets killed. Then, next thing you know, the Old Man and Ken Farmer are both done for. I guess now you'll be on the road to getting your life back to normal."

"As normal as can be. But I'm gonna make sure that we stay in touch. In fact, Louise is already lining up some of her single girlfriends to meet you."

"Oh, that's all I need."

"No worries. She knows what she's doing."

"Really? Then why did she pick you?"

Mitch cut a sideward glance toward Frankie. "Real funny."

The two men sat in silence as they motored away from the cemetery. Once they made the turn from North Second onto East Charity, Frankie looked over at Mitch and said, "We were the Corn Bandits, Mitch. We used to be like brothers."

"We still are, Frankie. We still are."

Neither one was aware that inside a car, parked on the side of the street, Turk watched them drive away. "I'm not done with you, Armstrong," he whispered.

The End